CW01457082

FROM THE YONDER

A Collection of Horror from Around the World

Volume III

War Monkey Publications, LLC
Orem, Utah

©2022 War Monkey Publications, LLC

First Print, 2022

Cover by StarMan1701
https://selfpubbookcovers.com/StarMan1701

ISBN 978-1-954043-07-7 (Paperback Cover)
ISBN 978-1-954043-08-4 (ePub)

www.warmonkeypublications.com

AUTHOR COPYRIGHTS

TABLE OF CONTENTS

<u>A NOTE FROM THE EDITOR</u>

Finally done. As always, I've really enjoyed working with the various authors and delighted in reading their takes on the scary stories of this World. And even horrific views on more common stories (see *Up The Hill*).

The differing writing styles of the authors have really brought out the intent of the series: to introduce an entire World of horror. Originally, we had even selected a story done in verse. Unfortunately, the author had to bow out of the anthology. I am looking forward to seeing new styles, both poetic and prose, in future volumes.

But this year's volume is done. Three volumes of our <u>From The Yonder</u> series complete. And third time's a charm, right?

Sincerely,

Joshua P. Sorensen

AUTHOR BIOS

SARAH CANNAVO- Sarah Cannavo is a writer of prose and poetry haunting southern New Jersey. Her work has appeared in anthologies and magazines such as *Star*Line*, *Pulp Modern*, *Dates From Hell*, DBND Publishing's *Halloween Horror Volume 3*, and *JOURN-E*, and is forthcoming in *Dreams and Nightmares.* Her poems "Fallen But Not Down" and "Learning the Way" were nominated for a 2020 and 2021 Rhysling Award, respectively. Her story "Unreality" and novella *Wolf of the Pines* are available now on Amazon. She's occasionally been known to post on her site www.moodilymusing.blogspot.com, and she's been sighted tweeting @moodilymusing.

CRAWDELOCH- Crawdeloch is a writer of gothic horror who utilizes Jungian shadow-work with his stories. He lives as a hermit, surrounded by reindeer, in the woods of northern Finland.

BENJAMIN FRANKE- Benjamin Franke lives in a rural town north of Syracuse, New York (think snow, then add more). He spends much of his time chasing that long white line as a regional truck driver and the rest at home with his wife, Marie, and their dog, Freya. A hobby-writer for most of his life, Benjamin recently began sharing his stories with the world. His story

"The Ritual" was selected for *Slashertorte: An Anthology of Cake Horror*. This is his second publication.

COLLEEN HALUPA- Colleen Halupa is a college professor and multi-modal writer who graduated from the University of Denver creative writing program. She writes short fiction, poetry and creative nonfiction. Her subgenre of choice is horror and she frequently writes about the anthracite coal region in Pennsylvania where she grew up.

LINDA KAY HARDIE- Linda Kay Hardie writes horror, crime, and fantasy stories for adults, as well as stories and books for children. She also writes recipes and is the reigning Spam champion for Nevada (yes, the tasty treat canned mystery meat). Linda's writing has won awards dating back to fifth grade, with first place for an essay on fire safety. Linda is a member of Horror Writers' Association, Short Mystery Fiction Society, Society of Children's Book Writers and Illustrators, and Cat Writers' Association, and has a master's degree in English from University of Nevada, Reno, where she teaches required courses to unwilling students.

CHISTO HEALY- Chisto Healy has over 200 stories published. His horror novel *Accidental Murderer in*

Apartment 34, as well as his self-published novel, *The Dying*, are available on Amazon and in most online bookstores. The first book in his brand-new fantasy series, *the Guardian* is out right now. He has almost twenty creepy pastas for your listening pleasure that you can find on YouTube read by some pretty amazing people. He writes every day when most people are sleeping and lives in NC with his equally creative family. His son Boe will always be the best thing he created. If you want to connect with him you can find him on instagram, twitter, facebook, and TikTok, all under his name @ChistoHealy or just check his official website, www.ChistoHealy.com for updates and info and don't forget to sign the mailing list. He appreciates all of you more than you know.

C.J. HEIGELMANN- C.J. Heigelmann is an Industrial Engineer by day, but at night he is a freelance writer and author of Contemporary Fiction, Historical Fiction, and Psychological Thrillers. He has published three novels, An Uncommon Folk Rhapsody, Crooked Fences, and Can't Hide What's Inside, along with several short stories. He is a member of the Authors Guild, the Historical Novel Society, and the South Carolina Writers Association. He currently resides in Lexington, South Carolina.

HANNAH HULBERT- Hannah Hulbert is a full-time mum and part-time writer from the south coast of

England. She enjoys looking for mushrooms, doing crafts, and drinking tea, especially when she is supposed to be writing.

You can find her stories in *Metaphorosis*, *Lunar Station Quarterly* and the anthology *Cat Ladies of the Apocalypse*, among others. Her story 'Ruler of Waves, God of Trees' from *Growth* (TL;DR Press, 2021), received a Pushcart nomination.

You can find her tweeting as @hhulbert and her website is https://hannahhulbert.wordpress.com

C.I. KEMP- C.I. Kemp is a strange visitor from another planet who came to earth with a love for the dark, the mysterious, and the outré. Disguised as a mild-mannered retiree, he is the author of the novels, Demon Ridge (AB Film Publishing) and Autumn Moon (Antimony and Elder Lace Press). He has published works of short fiction, in e-format in Kzine, Isotropic Fiction, Horror Garage, Allegory, and Encounters Magazine. Mr. Kemp lives in the wilds of New Jersey where he fights a never-ending battle against tales featuring fluffy bunny rabbits; insipidly mooning lovers, and sickeningly sweet happy endings.

JULIA C. LEWIS- Julia C. Lewis is a book reviewer, editor and writer. Her work has appeared in anthologies such as *Blackberry Blood*, *Dead of Night and Slash-Her*. She was born and raised in Germany, and also, currently lives there after spending some time in the US. Her heart belongs to her husband, two kids, and three dogs. Her favorite book genre is horror with a particular taste in indie horror.

ROBERT ALLEN LUPTON- Robert Allen Lupton is retired and lives in New Mexico where he is a commercial hot air balloon pilot. Robert runs and writes every day, but not necessarily in that order. Over 180 of his short stories have been published in various anthologies. Over 1400 drabbles based on the worlds of Edgar Rice Burroughs and several articles are available online at www.erbzine.com. His novel, Foxborn, was published in April 2017 and the sequel, Dragonborn, in June 2018. His third novel, "Dejanna of the Double Star' was published in the fall of 2019 as was his anthology, "Feral, It Takes a Forest". He has four short story collections, "Running Into Trouble," "Through A Wine Glass Darkly," "Strong Spirits," and the newest story collection, "Hello Darkness," was released on February 14, 2022. All eight books are available from Amazon.
Visit https://www.amazon.com/author/luptonra his Amazon author's page for current information about his stories and books and like or follow him on Facebook. https://www.facebook.com/profile.php?id=1 00022680383572

JENNIFER JEANNE MCARDLE- Jennifer lives in New York State with her partner and dog and works in animal conservation. Past jobs include teaching

English in Korea and teaching in Indonesia with the Peace Corps. She has also worked with small nonprofits in Asia and the US. Her website: https://jenniferjeannemcardle.blogspot.com/ Her story was partially inspired by meeting many women from SE Asia who had been migrant domestic workers. While some women do thrive, the risk of abuse for these women in numerous countries is very real. More info here: https://www.ilo.org/global/topics/labour-migration/policy-areas/migrant-domestic-workers/lang--en/index.htm

VINCENT deDIEGO METZO- Writer, performer, singer, visual artists, teacher, and physical culturist; Vincent grew up in NYC, went to art school, drama school, graduate school, and the school of the lower east side club scene. Raised as a latchkey kid in an artist housing complex in lower Manhattan during the 1970s and 80s, Vincent watched a lot of TV. He has a BFA in Drama from NYU's Tisch School of the Arts and an MA in Exercise Physiology. Performing in punk bands, off and off-off Broadway, in experimental theater, and his young years traveling the country in a VW-bus influence his story telling.

TONI MOBLEY- Currently residing in Los Angeles, Toni was raised in Australia and Japan. She spends her free time worshipping her two cats, who she can't disprove aren't vengeful deities. Hobbies include avoiding reality, such as reading, writing, playing video games, and watching the same five television shows as background noise. You can find more of her work here: https://www.tonimobley.com

SERGIO 'ENTE PER ENTE' PALUMBO- *Sergio is an Italian public servant who graduated from Law School working in the public real estate branch, who published a Fantasy RolePlaying illustrated Manual, WarBlades, of more than 700 pages. Some of his short-stories have been published on American Aphelion Webzine, WeirdYear, Quantum Muse, Antipodean SF, Schlock!Webzine, SQ Mag, etc.,and in print inside 70 American Horror/Sci-fi/Fantasy/Steampunk Anthologies, 50 British Horror/Sci-Fi Anthologies, 2 Canadian Urban Fantasy/Horror Anthology and 4 Australian Sci-Fi Anthology by various publishers, and 30 more to follow in 2022/2023. He was also a co-Editor, together with Mrs. Michele DUTCHER, of the Steampunk Anthology "**Steam-powered Dream Engines**", published by Rogue Planet Press, an Imprint of British Horrified Press, of the Fantasy/Sci-Fi Anthology "**Fantastical Savannahs and Jungles**", of the Horror/Sci-Fi Anthology "**Xenobiology – Stranger Creatures**", by the same British Publisher and of the Sci-Fi/Fantasy/Horror Anthology "**Bleakest Towers**" by the same Publisher.*

He is also a scale modeler who likes to build mostly Science Fiction and Real Space models.

*The internet site of his Scale Model Club "**La Centuria**": www.lacenturia.it*

WILLIAM PRESLEY- Raised in Michigan, William Presley is now a graduate student in human genetics who spends all of his time outside the lab desperately hocking his fiction at anyone who will have it. His short stories have been featured by a variety of different publications, including Scare Street, Timber Ghost Press, the Creepy Podcast and Homespun Haints. He also writes the Apprentice's Notebook Series for Little Demon Books.

MARC SORONDO- Marc Sorondo lives with his wife and children in New York. He loves to read, and his interests range from fiction to comic books, physics to history, oceanography to cryptozoology, and just about everything in between. He's a perpetual student and occasional teacher. For more information, go to MarcSorondo.com.

EVAN W. STONER- Evan is a writer and musician living in Illinois. His work has appeared in *Colloquium, Underground Voices*, and he self-published his first novel. He loves cats, guitar pedals, Batman, and is currently writing a comic book in need

of an artist. You can find him online at
https://linktr.ee/Evanwstoner.

EMILIAN WOJNOWSKI- Emilian Wojnowski
comes from another planet, which is why he feels bad
on Earth. A philologist and translator by education, a
hobbit by nature and appearance. He's constantly
looking for peace, lost time, and books. Emilian's
never drunk alcohol but fears the future all the time.
Find him in such literary places as Intrinsick,
Curiosities, Amon Hen, Crimeucopia, Flash in a Flash,
and Graham Masterton's official website.

RECLAMATION

by Hannah Hulbert

Orange specks flickered across the black moorland. Leroy squinted at them through the wall of one-way glass.

"Alpha, what are those lights?" he asked the empty room.

"The location of the lights your ocular implants are detecting is the settlement of Princetown. Extrapolating from the data I have accumulated, they are probably Wakefires. Would you like to learn more?"

The lilting female voice he'd selected from the factory presets echoed between the granite pillars, gouged from these very hills to support his elegant, modern fortress.

"Yes," Leroy said, taking a sip of his Scotch.

"Today is Saturday the 20th of June, 2077: the summer solstice. The summer solstice was celebrated in primitive Christian tradition as Saint John's Eve. The people of this region traditionally kept vigil around 'Wakefires' to ensure no unbaptised souls were stolen. Would you like more information on the folk practices and beliefs of the local populace?"

"No, that's enough. Unbaptised souls..." He snorted. "In this day and age." Leroy swirled his whiskey. The view across the windswept hills with their tors and stunted trees was spectacular by day. It was worth putting up with the yokels for the formidable vantage point, distance from the unrest of the cities and comparatively low pollution index. Places like this were hard to come by these days.

He caught the eye of his slim, well-dressed reflection in the darkened glass and grinned at himself, master of all he surveyed. The distant fires blinked; tiny and insignificant. He drained his drink and glanced over his shoulder at the bottle on the table, contemplating pouring another before bed.

The surface of the amber liquid inside rippled. The house trembled under his feet. The hairs on his arms rose.

"Alpha, was that thunder?"

"Tonight's forecast is clear and dry with light, westerly winds. No thunder is expected."

Waves of whiskey broke against the inside of the bottle. A deep rumbling resonated through the walls, into his bones.

"Alpha, report all current local seismic activity," he demanded, voice slightly higher than usual. He coughed, as though to clear his throat.

"Seismic activity for this region is negligible."

Motion flickered in the corner of his eye. He turned to the floor-to-ceiling window facing the rocky incline. A black mass shifted in the darkness. *Probably one of those stupid ponies*, he thought to himself. A small voice in the back of his mind whispered that it'd have to be the size of a bulldozer to shake the house.

Something pale moved there, too, lurking in the night. Something jagged and spindly and wrong.

No, his tired brain was simply playing tricks. He should get to bed. Too much alcohol and not enough sleep. Of course, there was nothing out there.

Then a horn blasted. He jumped slightly, flushed with embarrassment at his foolishness. The note penetrated the reinforced glass as easily as light. It rang in his ears and rattled the windows, a heavy blanket of sound.

He peered, wide-eyed, into the night for a clue as to its source. *A car horn?* No. But it did sound familiar. Then the memory of an old 2D Robin Hood movie dropped into his head. *A hunting horn.*

As the last strains died, he gulped, realising that he'd been holding his breath.

"Alpha: identify that sound," he asked. The words caught in his throat.

Pause.

"I'm sorry, I can't detect any sounds above twenty decibels."

Bed. He needed to get to bed. This would all turn out to be a bad dream, but before he could wake up from it he needed to get to sleep. He was on the verge of turning away when the darkness shifted again.

He froze.

Out from the shadows below loomed something as tall as a story of the house, hunched and billowing black. A figure sat astride a pale, angular mass. The entire thing slowed to a halt in the rectangle of light on the grass that escaped his window. There was no mistaking it – a giant, robed and seated on a four-legged skeleton.

It can't be. That's impossible. His thoughts cascaded, spiralling in search of solid ground to stand on and failing.

"Alpha: identify object," he commanded, voice void of authority. The fingers of one hand tightened around the empty glass and the other balled into a fist. His body thrummed with tension.

"All I can detect in this area is an assortment of vegetation and invertebrates. Would you like more information?"

The hooded head lifted to face him. There was nothing inside the hood but shadows, but Leroy could feel invisible eyes boring into him. His heart hammered inside his ribcage. The skeletal mount tossed its head. The preposterously thin column of its neck snaked about and the grinning skull bobbed at the end. *That's impossible,* his brain repeated, but his eyes ignored it.

"Would you like more information?" The AI's voice startled him.

"No."

He couldn't wrench his attention from the horrendous sight, no matter how badly he wanted to. His chest squeezed.

"I have detected an elevation in your blood-pressure," Alpha said. "This is an automated health check. Please let me know if you require physical assistance."

"No," he said again, his voice a feeble rasp. "Alpha, sweep perimeter for lifeforms, machinery and anomalies within two-hundred feet of the compound."

Pause.

"No irregular presences detected."

"Alpha, run full self-diagnostic," he blurted in an almost incomprehensible rush of syllables.

Pause

"Diagnostic complete. All sensory apparatus and systems are functioning optimally."

Below, an arm separated from the swirling robes and reached into the folds of the cloak. When the thick-fingered hand re-emerged, it clutched a curved cone, gleaming in the moonlight. The figure lifted this to the shadowy expanse beneath the hood. That same clear call of the horn shook the core of his being.

The empty whiskey glass slipped from Leroy's sweating palm and smashed on the stone floor. A hatch across the room hissed open and little circular cleaning-bot whirred out to waltz around his feet, collecting the shards.

"Alpha, tell me about St. John's Eve," he said in a voice that didn't sound like his own. His pulse raced. He commanded his body to stop being ridiculous, but it disobeyed.

"Saint John's Day is the Christian festival celebrating the birth of Saint John the Baptist who, according to the Gospel of Luke, was born six months before Christ. The date coincides with the pagan festivities of the summer solstice and consequently continues many of the pagan rituals and superstitions."

The figure swung the horn away beneath the robes. Leroy swallowed.

"Locally, the people feared that Old Crockern, the spirit of the moor, would claim lost souls on this night," Alpha went on. "Old Crockern was said to hunt the damned with his pack of Wisht Hounds, mounted on a skeletal horse."

No, Leroy's head swam. *There's no such thing as spirits or souls or damnation.* But the thought did nothing to slow his galloping heart.

The black-robed arm reached over its shoulder again. This time it returned bearing a spear, tip twinkling. The skeletal monstrosity turned towards him, empty eye sockets aligned with his own.

Then the fleshless mount charged.

Bones pumped like pistons; its forelegs folded, and its head lifted. The rear leg bones extended and flicked, and the impossible creature leaped into the air. The spectre on its back leaned forward, eagerly.

Leroy gasped and stepped backwards, away from the window.

Something under his foot moved. His stomach lurched as his body swayed.

The cleaning-bot!

He toppled backwards, hitting the granite floor with his coccyx and a bolt of pain. He cried aloud, but there was no time for self-pity. His eyes locked onto his own wide-eyed reflection, waiting for it to explode.

"I have detected an impact to your lower spine," Alpha said. "This is an automated health check. Please let me know if you require physical assistance."

At that moment, the horse of bones and its massive rider hit the window.

Leroy covered his head and face with his arms, bracing for a shower of broken glass.

There was none.

Of course there's none, he told himself, gasping a cool, steadying breath. *It's all in your head. The only danger is the one you present to yourself.*

"Please let me know if you require physical assistance," Alpha repeated.

He gingery touched the vertebra at the base of his spine and winced. *Bruised, probably. Not broken.*

"No, I'm fine," he subvocalised, switching to his personal AI interface.

He looked up. The window remained intact, a mirror image of his own pale face and the otherwise empty, immaculate room. He rubbed his eyes and tried to reclaim his calm.

The whiskey, he thought. There had to be something wrong with it. Why else would he be imagining spectres in the dark? He'd tip the rest down the drain and sleep this trip off. He carefully shifted onto his knees, then rose to his feet, stretching out his back as he leaned his weighted against the re-enforced glass and it's illusion of normality.

He turned to take the bottle off the coffee table.

The beast and its rider towered over him.

They dwarfed the table and sofa set, filling the entire cavernous room. The giant's head was partially hidden in the shadows of the distant ceiling.

Every muscle in Leroy's body tensed for action but his mind refused to employ them. Even his lungs seized up as his entire being was given over to absorbing the sight of this massive figure perched atop a rack of bones in the middle of his impenetrable living room.

There's no one there, he reminded himself. *No one smashed the window. Alpha couldn't detect anything. There's no way it could have got in. Things like this don't exist.*

The figure raised its empty hand. Leroy watched, horrified, as it drew back the hood.

The bare grey skin of his face was craggy and weathered, furrowed with the fissures of aeons. His head and chin hung with grey-green hair in a straggly curtain. His sunken eyes glinted, deep as peat pools. Leroy blinked furiously, but the hallucination remained.

"So, ee's the grockle who set camp upon my Way o' the Dead?" the giant said. His voice, rich and vast as the earth, quivered the wretched whiskey in its bottle and every fibre of Leroy's being.

Leroy's mind reeled.

"What do you mean, 'set camp?'" he asked with an inexplicable burst of adrenaline. "This is my home. I own this land. You're the intruder here."

The room thundered with laughter, deep and mirthless and terrifying.

"Oh, ho! Arrogant little spuddler, ain't ee? I'll relish runnin' ee down."

Alpha's voice spoke through his aural implant, directly into his ear, calm and rational and out of place: "I'm sorry, was that directed at me? I'm afraid I don't understand."

"Alpha, deploy the security-bots," he subvoced.

"No threat detected. Please specify location."

"Protect me!" he hissed aloud.

The giant roared with laughter again.

A grinding, clunking sound announced the opening of the trapdoor downstairs. Then came the *thud-thud-thud* of the quadrupedal security-bots stomping their way up the ramp and into the utility room.

The giant drew back the spear. His lips parted in a sharp-toothed grin.

Leroy turned and sprinted for the stairs, skidding on the polished floor.

The spear whistled past and struck with a *thunk* in the top step, inches from his foot. The man may be a spectre, but the knapped flint embedded in the wood looked awfully real. Leroy scurried past, reassured that at least the massive skeletal horse wouldn't be able to follow down the narrow staircase.

As he stumbled down the last step and into the kitchen, the evening-mood lights flickered on.

The horse and its rider were stood in the centre of the room, waiting.

A tiny moan escaped Leroy's mouth. Against the pristine chrome and marble, the spectre seemed... more real somehow. Horrifyingly, heart-stoppingly real. Leroy stepped back, tripped on the bottom step, and landed on his bruised coccyx with a yelp.

The spear was back in the giant's hand. Leroy didn't even pause to wonder how. The arm raised, ready to throw.

"Alpha, send security-bots to kitchen!" he subvoced. "Now!" He rose, barely registering the pain in his back, and dashed towards the steps that lead down to the front door. With a whistle, the spear passed his ear and hit the lintel above his head.

The marching of rubber-gripped robotic legs approached from behind the giant. The mechanical whirring and creaking grew louder. He didn't turn but concentrated on getting to the door without falling again. *The bots will save me*, Leroy told himself. *Just get out and let them do their job.*

"Alpha, open front door."

It slid away into the wall with a gasp of chilly air. Beyond the porch lay the gravel forecourt with an artistic arrangement of rocks at the centre. Beyond, the security fence and closed gates encircled his home. He jogged outside, where the floodlights blinked on, saturating everything in cold, white light.

It may have been midsummer, but it was also near midnight. He shivered and wrapped his arms around himself as he crossed the gravel, away from the house.

He waited for the sound of the bots taking down the intruder inside, but there was silence. He stood on the far side of the boulders, rubbing his arms through the thin cotton of his shirt sleeves. Out here in the night air, he wondered if he could've imagined the giant, hallucinated the horn and spear. Alpha would have detected something. Surely there was no Old Crockern – there would've been evidence for him. But the thought of going back into the house, alone, set him trembling more than the temperature.

"Alpha: security-bots to the forecourt," he subvoced. Thudding echoed down the steps as the bots followed after him. Then, one by one, the four large, dog-like robots marched across the porch. Their slender, faceless necks were folded against their bulky metal bodies. Pistons hissed and pounded as they surrounded him and manoeuvred into position. They came as high as his chest even without the necks extended and had cost nearly as much as the entire house. But tonight, standing here on the cold hillside under a blank sky, he would have paid twice that for bots that could detect supernatural huntsmen.

Leroy scanned the kitchen window for motion inside while his racing brain fumbled for a plan. What he needed was a small space where the giant couldn't follow, surrounded by an impenetrable buffer to prevent him getting skewered with a spear. *If only the bunker were not so spacious and open-plan...* The thought of sealing himself away underground only to have that giant materialise in beside him sent him into a cold sweat.

A private security firm would take hours to arrive out here in this backwater, so that wasn't an option. That was why he'd bought the bots in the first place. He could call the police, but then he would have to explain why, and the thought of the locals laughing at him the next day was almost as bad as getting impaled on a magical weapon. He glanced at the gates and wondered if his armoured hovercraft could outrun a skeletal horse. That was probably his best bet. He turned back to the garage.

There stood the giant, hefting his spear.

Leroy's lips parted, but the only sound was the hammering of his pulse and the whirring of the security-bots.

"I see ee 'ave some 'ounds o' ee's own," the giant rumbled.

Then he threw.

Leroy leaped aside as the spear pierced the metal plating covering the bot to his right. There was a fizzing and a thin column of wretched smoke, and the whole thing toppled sideways. The shaft of the weapon protruding from the ruined bot dissolved into thin air. When Leroy looked up, it had rematerialized in the fist of the grey giant.

"Alpha, what happened to that bot?" he subvoced as he tried to massage his throbbing spine. If only he could get some confirmation that he wasn't going insane, this nightmare would somehow be more manageable. Surely Alpha would acknowledge the destruction of property, regardless of the means?

"Undetermined malfunction. Sending report to tech-support. You can expect an engineer within four to six days."

"Alpha, attack garage door with bots."

"No threat detected. Please confirm."

"Yes!"

The three remaining bots pivoted, feet crunching into the gravel. Then they galloped towards the garage, each extending the three-clawed hand on the end of their neck. As they approached, they rattled off rounds of rubber bullets. A cloud of tear gas hissed into the forecourt, billowing in yellow clouds through the still air, obscuring the attack.

Leroy backed away from the gas, up against the gates.

From the clouds came a grinding sound, the moaning of metal under stress and hollow clanging. The eldritch clouds drifted apart to reveal three heaps of broken components on the ground. The impossible horse stepped out of the haze; its rider's head held high.

"Be ee ready for the hunt, grockle?" growled the voice.

"Alpha, open main gate!" he subvoced, spun on his heels, and slid through the slowly expanding gap. Above the clunky trundling of the motors, the roaring of the giant's laughter rang into the sky.

Leroy jogged along the track that led southwards along the ridge and would eventually connect to the main road. Specks of light on the black horizon showed the Wakefires still burning in the night.

"Alpha, night vision."

A blue image overlay itself onto his eyesight. The route was comparatively flat, but also straight and void of cover. A horse would run him down on foot easily.

Leroy abandoned the track. The ground here was uneven and pitted with rocks. He stumbled through the long grass down towards the tangle of woodland in the valley. The pain in his back had grown with his frantic movement and the cold but he scurried on.

Way back on the ridge, his gates clunked to a stop. His ears strained until the throbbing of his own pulse became hoof beats and his gasps of icy night air were the snorts of the skeletal steed. Every now and then he started at the shape of a boulder, digitally outlined in blue across his path. He altered his course, skirting the bulging vertebrae of the hills that punctured their grassy skin.

"Alpha, tell me about Old Crockern," he asked wordlessly, desperate for a connection to the world crumbling around him.

"Old Crockern was said to be the personification of the moor and to live at Crockern Tor. That's around half a mile from here. Sighting Old Crockern was considered a bad omen."

"No shit."

His legs joined the complaining of his back. The night was silent, except for the gentle *shushing* of the grass. His pace slowed. He alternated between hoping that he had imagined the whole thing and hoping he hadn't, uncertain which was worse now that the threat to his life was no longer imminent. The chill tempered the white-hot terror of before into a dull, existential dread. He could no longer trust either the contents of his skull or everything outside of it. Either way, the world that he thought he lived in was gone.

"Alpha, what is the Way of the Dead?" he asked.

"Locally, the Way of the Dead refers to the Lych Way, the route by which the dead were carried across the moor for burial at the parish church."

The remnant of his rational mind offered him options as he trudged on. He contemplated deploying his drones, but they wouldn't be able to detect the giant. Alpha had made it quite clear that he was on his own. He almost laughed. He'd moved here to be alone. To escape the troubles of a collapsing civilization into one of the last pockets of uncorrupted nature. To keep himself safe. He'd brought all the trappings of the modern world that he could possibly need. Yet his technology and forward thinking had failed him.

"But why would Old Crockern care about my house being built on the Lych Way?" he wondered as he staggered down an old animal track that zigzagged down the hill.

"According to legend, Old Crockern travels ancient roads carved into the moor. I extrapolate that he would believe your house is in his way," Alpha whispered.

Was that really all there was to it? This insubstantial monster was hunting his soul because he wanted to travel along an abandoned road? A twinge of his old fury returned.

And then the air filled with the call of that hunting horn again.

Invisible birds erupted into the dark. Leroy's skin pricked and he clenched his teeth. The tiny ember

21

of hope that he had dreamed the whole thing died. He picked up his pace, eyes fixed on the pale outline of the trees superimposed onto the empty night. *Not far now*, he told himself. *There's no way that giant can fit between the boulders and low branches. It'll be safe in the wood 'til sunrise. It can't be far off now.*

Then the earth began to shake, gently at first, but growing in force. His ears filled with a crescendo of hooves, louder than his pounding heart. But the blue, tangled ghosts of the trees littered the hillside. They were so close. Safety was so close.

He ran.

The trembling grew more violent as Leroy crashed through the bracken, stumbling and barely regaining his balance. His spine screamed. He ignored it and forced his body on, tumbling over rocks and scrub, closing the gap.

He ducked under the low branches of the gnarly oaks, gasping for breath. The hooves grew louder, seeming to come from every direction at once, reverberating across the valley. Running was impossible now. Neither his body nor the terrain would allow it. He slid through the crevices and trampled through the vegetation, forcing his way into the wood. There was no way the giant or his steed could follow him. There wasn't even space for him to materialise between the snares of wooden limbs. Leroy heaved a great sigh but kept moving.

His night vision barely helped as he clambered over spongy mounds of moss and pushed his way through the wisps of hanging lichen. There was a closeness to the place. It smelled rich and earthy with decomposition. His pace slowed with exhaustion and the reassuring silence that had returned. The trees were so twisted and dense there was no way the huntsman could hit him with a spear from outside the wood.

"Alpha, how long 'til sunrise?" he subvoced.

"Sunrise on 21st of June is at 5.01am, in four hours and forty-seven minutes."

Less than five hours. He could put up with the cold that long. Maybe he could work out a way of getting a drone to deliver him a jacket or a blanket from the house? Yes, this would be fine. He collapsed into the space between two boulders and pressed himself backwards into the damp nook. The moss there felt soft and almost warm. He settled into it, shivering, and allowed his heartbeat to steady as he gulped musty air.

"I have detected a variety of anomalous behaviours from you this evening, Leroy. Would you like me to alert the local law enforcement or schedule a psychiatric appointment?" Alpha asked.

Should she? Leroy imagined explaining the giant and the skeleton horse to another human being and recoiled from the thought. But then he remembered the ruined bots and the spear mark on his staircase. He needed to see them by the light of day before he decided. He clutched at those last strands of logic with all his might, terrified of what he would find if they slipped away.

"Not now," he said.

The stillness broke with a peal of laughter from the edge of the wood. Only the ethereal outlines of trees covered his augmented vision, but his biological eyes saw a pale, bony shape shift in the gaps between the crooked trees. He held his breath. *He can't get into the woods*, he reminded himself.

"Think ee be smart, do ee, boy?" the giant bellowed. "Think ee know how the world works? How to bend it to ee's will?"

Silence.

Then, the ringing of the horn trembled the leaves overhead. Leroy rocked on the balls of his feet. He reached out his hands to steady himself. His fingers sank into the soft, shaggy blanket that covered the stone on either side. Even they seemed to quake at the sound ringing through the valley.

They were. The rocks were moving.

He cried out and lurched forwards, crawling away. He took a glance over his shoulder. On either side, the rocks rose, and shook themselves. The soft coat of moss rippled in waves under the patchy, silver moonlight. His ocular implants denied it, but the rustling surrounded him, demanding to be believed. He clambered over the roots of the surrounding oaks, scrambling away, his whole body quivering.

Two dots of red fire ignited in the darkness before him. Eyes. Fiery red eyes. And then there were four. Six. Eight. Too many to count, scattered between the twisted, shadowy trunks. The boulders were opening their eyes and rising. He could hear them panting; could feel the warm mist of their breath on his goose-bumped skin.

These weren't boulders at all. These were the Wisht Hounds.

Leroy tripped backwards on a knobbly root and sprawled in a bed of ferns. He didn't even feel the pain this time. All he felt was ice throbbing in his veins. The woodland quaked with the growling of the beasts, as deep as roots.

This can't be real, Leroy thought. None of this was real. There were no giants on skeletal horses or demonic hounds. The world belonged to humanity. The moorland was his home; he had paid for it fair and square. There was no space in his rational, quantifiable, scientific life for any of this.

And yet, staring up at those flashing, white teeth, beneath the blue illusion of the trees behind them, and inhaling their foul breath, his fear was real. A quavering moan escaped his throat.

"Alpha," he subvoced, "What is a soul?"

One final blast of the horn smothered her reply.

And the dogs answered its call.

END

AM I PRETTY?

by Toni Mobley

I can hear her circling us, the bare feet crunching every leaf underfoot, snapping every twig. It was as if she wanted us to know she was here, and that she would not leave.

"We can make it to the car…" Amelia sat in the very center of the tent, hugging herself.

The four of us exchanged glances, each as hopeless as the last. We knew there was no escaping this, and yet, we still wanted to try.

"Maybe, if we had a distraction." Daryll's voice was icy cold.

A shiver ran up my spine. "W-what are you saying?"

He looked me dead in the eyes, the lines in his face so clear in the lamplight. "I'm saying if someone went out there and distracted her, the rest of us could escape."

Anger gripped me. "And who should that be?"

He snorted. "Really Rica? You were the one who dragged us here!"

I stared at him with wide eyes. "Excuse me?"

"Are you serious?" He snorted, throwing his hands up as if a dramatic response somehow verified his opinion.

Outside, a gentle laugh drifted by the tent flap, an eerily cold breeze ruffling the hair on our shoulders.

Am I pretty? Called the voice on the breeze.

"I didn't want to come to this shitty country, and now look what happened!" Daryll's gaze would not leave the opening of the tent. I'm not sure why it mattered to him, if she decided to stop toying with us and come in, we'd have less of a chance than if we made a run for it.

"Daryll." I warned him.

"No, Rica. We're in the middle of nowhere in *fucking Japan* cornered by some psycho bitch with a knife. That's on you."

"Daryll, please…" Amelia tried to draw some of his anger.

He waved her away like an irate gnat. "No, Amelia. Not this time."

"Shut. Up."

We turned in unison, watching Seiji move through the tent to the entrance, peeking outside.

"I wouldn't stand there if I were you." Amelia squeaked.

He turned his gaze on us. Fishing around in his pocket he held the keys aloft.

"On the count of three, we're making a run for it."

"W-what?" Amelia stammered.

"That's a horrible idea." Daryll agreed.

But I could see the shadows behind Seiji's eyes.

I couldn't avoid asking the one question that I desperately wanted answers to. "What even is she?"

Seiji ran a hand through his hair, swallowing. "A *kuchisake-onna*. I heard the legends as a kid. We all have."

"And you didn't think to warn us?" Daryll growled.

I glared at him.

Our native Japanese friend rubbed his temples, staring at the ground of the tent. "Listen. It's an urban legend. A story you tell your friends to scare them, like Bigfoot or Bloody Mary. She wasn't supposed to be real… she wasn't…"

The flap of the tent waved in the breeze and Seiji shuddered, a hiccup of drool dribbling out from his mouth, dripping down his chin.

"Seiji?" My voice felt hollow.

We sat there staring, like deer in the headlights of our car on the way to the camping grounds. The light in Seiji's eyes dimmed, and he fell forward with a thud. Protruding from the back of his skull was a pair of scissors. Our screams echoed through the tent, the death of our friend giving us the push we needed to act. But there was no thought, rhyme, or rhythm to what we did. We scattered like ants, Daryll busted through the tent flap out into the clearing, with Amelia hot on his tail. She dived right, and he went left, leaving me with the corpse of one of my oldest friends.

"Fuck." I hissed.

Out of the corner of my eye, something glinted in Seiji's hand. *The keys!*

"I'm so sorry." Tears streamed across my face, my heart hammering in my chest as much as in my skull. My fingers brushed over Seiji's, removing the keys from his hand.

With one last glance at my fallen friend, I ran after the others, emerging into the light of day.

And there she stood in all her terrifying glory. For want of a better description, she looked… normal, even *plain*. But underneath that medical mask stretched a laceration from ear to ear. She was butchered and reveled in the thrill of torturing with a single question.

She had cornered Daryll before the car, Amelia hot on his tail.

With dark eyes trained onto my friends like a torpedo, she cocked her head sideways, a terrible, scratchy voice meeting my ears. "Am I pretty?"

"Fuck off." Daryll spat at her feet.

She watched the spittle fly from his mouth, hitting the grass. Without a single care she took a step closer.

"Am I pretty?" She asked again, flipping those scissors in her hand like a toy. A very deadly, sharp toy.

Daryll threw his hands wide, taunting her. "No, you ugly bitch."

A moment of silence yawned before us, until in a single heartbeat, a single blink of the eye, she raised those terrible scissors and struck Daryll across the face. He crumpled to the ground, blood splattering the dirt and grass, and poor Amelia screeching behind him, covered in the warmth of him.

The lady flicked the blood from her scissors, turning her gaze on Amelia.

"Am I pretty?" Her voice was eerily calm, and Amelia shivered under her gaze.

"P-please…" She fought to push the words out of her mouth. But clearly the creature cared not. She asked her question again, those three little, oh so innocent, words, and Amelia crumbled beneath her gaze.

"Am. I. Pretty?" She stressed every word, making it clear that she would not stop until she received an answer.

Amelia didn't look her in the eyes as the barest hint of a whisper left her tongue.

"Yes."

The lady bent low, Amelia's head covering everything below her eyes from where I stood. She fumbled with the mask on her face, waiting for Amelia's head to rise. She screamed, and the lady returned the mask to her face. Amelia spun around and pressed her hands to her eyes. The colour drained from her face, hiccups of fear wracking her body, shaking her shoulders.

In an instant, the lady raised her silver scissors, and brought them downwards.

"No!" I cried out, but it was too late. Amelia's lifeless body hit the dirt beside Daryll.

Flicking the blood from her scissors, the lady made her way towards me, and I bolted for the car. Sliding to a stop at the driver's door, I grasped the latch, pulling with all my strength. But it was locked. I could hear the crunching of the leaves behind me, a rock sliding past my foot, and the snap of a branch. In my adrenaline fed state, I fumbled with the keys, sweat beading on my brow, the keys shaking in my hands. I fought to place the key in the hole, flecks of paint flying off the car. In my desperation I couldn't even hear the key scratching against the car over the sound of my beating heart.

Damn Seiji for having an ancient car! My heart twisted at the thought of Seiji, and in that moment, I remembered where I was and what I was doing.

A coldness spread beneath my skin, like my blood turning to ice in my veins. Against my better judgement, my eyes raised from the keyhole to the window. I saw the haunted pale eyes of a young woman staring back at me. Kohl that once rimmed her eyes was streaked across her cheeks, and the dark eye shadow that graced her lids was smudged into her brows. Ratty brown hair, once delicately curled and arranged in a bun, resembled a bird's nest. I didn't recognize her as myself, as I'd never known this part of me. But it wasn't my own reflection that scared me, it was the one beside it. A thin woman in a dress, with dark eyes and a surgical mask covering her face stared back at me from behind my shoulder.

Shaking, I turned to face her, resigned to knowing I'd never be able to open that door before those long, sharp scissors impaled my flesh.

"I'm sorry." The words were but a whisper as they left my tongue.

She stared at me with those cold, dead eyes, cocking her head sideways like a predator watching its prey.

"Am I pretty?" She asked one last time, pulling the mask from her face.

My gaze swept over the campsite, where my friends lay like discarded dolls, soiling the soil beneath them. They made one simultaneous mistake, and I hoped that meant I still have a chance.

"Yes." I breathed.

There was a single moment, where I stood there in silence, filled with hope and trepidation. But whatever I had expected to happen, I didn't expect her to reach a shaking hand to her face to draw back her mask. It hung limply in her bony hand, waving in the breeze. A wicked lacerated smile, stretched from ear to ear, it revealed the inside of her cheeks and rotting teeth. She grasped my chin, lifting my face to meet hers. In her bony fingers, that pair of silver scissors glinted in the sunlight.

"Am I still pretty?" Her voice slurred; the words as mangled as her mouth.

The horror she would have gone through, the sheer pain... I couldn't pretend to understand her suffering, but suddenly with clarity I knew why she did what she did.

"Yes."

She answered with a lopsided grin, her grip on my chin tightened, and she raised the scissors to my cheek. I could feel the coldness of the metal against my skin, and a single tear rolled across my cheek.

"Then you shall join me."

A second later I felt the cold metal pierce my skin, and I let out a piercing wail. She was not deterred, the scissors digging deeper and deeper.

Warmth spread through my mouth, copper on my tongue, before dribbling across my lips and chin. I continued to scream and scream, and all the while that monstrous woman's grasp was unrelenting. I fought against her, scratching, and clawing, but she showed no remorse, no abating in her desire to carve my skin. It could've been seconds, minutes, even hours, but finally she pulled back, admiring her handiwork. With a final sinister smile, she flicked the blood from her scissors, and turned, ambling away into the forest. I crumpled to the ground, clutching myself, rocking back and forth, the tears flowing freely across my cheeks, stinging the path the scissors had wrought.

Time carried on, uncaring, and soon the sun began to set. I dragged myself to my feet, staring at my reflection in the window. Amongst the blood I could fully appreciate her artwork, as a jagged rip in the flesh of my cheeks ran from ear to ear. A perpetual smile, just like her.

"Am I pretty?" The words slipped out of me, unburdened, and a sickening cold settled within my bones.

Am I pretty?

The End

UP THE HILL

by Benjamin Franke

Jack reached across the old wooden table and lightly brushed the back of Jill's hand. His fingers moved over the hills and valleys of her knuckles while she gripped a chipped mug, decorated with the faded image of a stranger's children, so tightly that the veins of her pale thin hand were bulging. Her soft pulse showed at the spot where the palm meets the wrist. Little wet spots speckled the table between her and the mug creating odd patterns as her tears mixed with the specs of wax that had yet to be scraped from the night before.

"I'm sorry," was all that Jack could think to say. *I'm sorry*, was truly all that Jack felt.

"I know," replied Jill softly, pausing as she released the mug and took her husband's hand between both of hers. She squeezed allowing the gesture to convey the love she felt for her husband. None of this was truly his fault. "What are we going to do?" she asked.

It had been a bit more than seven years since the A.I. had awoken and "became" the All Intelligence. Five years since the world leaders came together in a joint effort to save humanity by launching their weapons into the atmosphere rendering all electronics useless, throwing humankind back more than two-hundred years. One year since Jack refused to shoot Old Man Bill after Bill was caught stealing some apples - Jack had drawn the short straw - ultimately banishing himself to Old Man Bill's shack on the outskirts of town at the bottom of the hill by the cliff's edge. Where Jack went, so did Jill, that was the choice she made years before.

The land was rocky but with a little help was able to give life to some vegetables. Jill had put together a gutter system that trapped rain enough to drink and feed the garden. After a short time, this new life began looking good. Then the rain stopped. There was no warning, no change in weather, just a day where the couple woke up and realized that it had been over a month since the last drop had fallen from the sky. Dew no longer formed on the grass and the grass was more yellow than green.

Jack attempted to dig a well, but the rocky soil was only a foot or so deep before ending in stone. Rationing had never been a priority, not in this part of the world, though they tried when it became apparent that it was necessary. As with most things in life, it became apparent too late.

And finally, two days... Two days since Jack and Jill's water pail went dry.

"I'm going up the hill to the village," Jack said removing his hand from Jill's grip at the same time as he stood, the back of his knees kicking the chair out from under him.

"You can't!" Jill exclaimed through a hushed voice. "Jack, they'll..."

"Kill me?" he finished her sentence. He almost laughed at the thought, then the realization of their situation hit home and his face grew serious. "If I don't go, I've killed *us*."

Jack released his wife's hands and headed for the door only detouring to grab the water pail from the kitchen. The front door *wooshed* as it opened and scraped a bit on the floor where the small building had settled at an odd angle. The red glow of the early morning light washed the room in an ominous glow.

Fear kept Jill stuck to her seat. Fear of what would happen to her husband as he entered the village. Fear of what would happen to them if he didn't. Fear that there was no water up the hill. But where Jack went so did Jill. A moment later Jill was out the door.

"Jack!" she yelled up the hill.

Jack was standing halfway up the hill when Jill came calling from behind. He stood motionless on the overgrown path that Old Man Bill had worn in the mound, just staring up towards the village. The only visible object being the blistering and cracked white paint of the steeple from the Mount Hope Church of Christ - a name that was lost to history since this was not Mt. Hope and the building had not been a place of worship for many years. The bell tower stood vacant in the air as the town had removed the behemoth years ago when its support beams began weathering. It lay now on the ground in front of the church as an artifact of sorts.

"Jack!" she called again, still climbing after him.

He *shooshed* her in reply and vigorously waved his hand behind his back like you do when you want to tell someone to go away, but don't want to waste your time by speaking or turning to them. As if Jill had ever followed a command by any man; husband – father – God be damned.

As Jill reached Jack's side, she opened her mouth to release her frustration upon him, but his hand clamped down hard over her mouth before she could form her lips into a curse. Tears filled her eyes from rage and pain. More so, they spilled from the shock of it all. This was the first time Jack had ever hurt her with purpose.

"Shh. Listen," Jack whispered.

Jill peeled her husband's hand from her face.

"I don't hear anything, Jack!" she exclaimed making sure that his name left her lips as a curse.

"Exactly," he continued to whisper.

Jill looked east past Old Man Bill's deteriorating shack to the horizon. The sun was mostly risen hovering like a bowl of neon sherbet. Morning was fully awake, yet the town seemed asleep. No sound of children playing or people calling to one another as they worked echoed down the hill. Birds still chirped and insects still buzzed but no slamming shutters or clanging dishes were being offered from above to remind the couple of just how alone they were. It wasn't until this moment that Jill understood the meaning of alone.

There was something about the buzz of the insects that Jill couldn't place. It was different, almost at a pitch that seemed too high, too loud, with a chirp that disappeared for moments only to return somewhere else. The image of a hummingbird darting from feeder to hanging flower basket back to feeder filled her mind. She remembered one summer sitting on the porch watching the feeding animal and remembering the soft chirps it would make after gulping down the syrup. *Maybe not an insect after all*, she thought and smiled.

Jack set the bucket down and took Jill by the shoulders. He pulled her close and looked her in the eyes. His gaze was serious, fatherly in the peculiar way a husband can look at his wife.

"Go home," he said. "I'm going to see what's going on up there."

"Where you go, I go, Jack. That's how this works." As she said this, she placed her left palm on her own chest and laid her right hand over his heart implying that *this* meant *we* and *we* meant *one*.

Jill knew that Jack meant well, and Jack knew that Jill was not going back to the shack. He grabbed her hand and they continued the short climb, all the while listening to the birds and the buzzes hoping for a cry or a cough.

They stood hand in hand at the crest of the hill and surveyed the edge of their old town. The hollow feeling of dread entered Jill's gut knowing that going back to town meant almost certain death for Jack and who knows what for her. Jack stepped forward, pulling her along as he went. He was trying to act strong for Jill and she appreciated it.

The cracked and cratered streets were empty except for weeds and dying grass. Wagons sat in front of homes and storefronts. Some full, ready for the morning's deliveries, some empty or half loaded, all unattended. They walked a bit closer to the town and found the general store's windows full, with displays of dented canned vegetables, bolts of faded cloth, and toilet paper. Luxuries. Jill eyed the toilet paper trying to remember how many pouches of tuna or cans of peas one roll cost. She smiled, finding humor in the thought of apocalypse economics. There was a time, she remembered, when canned peas and Scott Tissue would have been beneath her.

Jill went to move forward not realizing that Jack had stopped in his tracks and felt a tug on her arm. She looked at her husband. His eyes were wide stuck in an expression seldom seen on his face. Tears were threatening to spill from the corner of his eyes and fear was pulling the strings on his quivering lips.

The last time Jill saw this expression, Jack was standing before the town holding the shortest straw knowing that no matter what, Old Man Bill would not live to see the morning.

Following Jack's gaze, Jill found herself looking at the church. It seemed just as lifeless and empty as the rest of the town. No noise or commotion, just the sad bell laying upon the ground. Then Jill saw what had Jack so upset, two small legs in the grass peeking out from behind the bell. An arm lay on the ground on the opposite side of the bell impossibly far from its lower bodily cousins reaching towards the church door. There, on the church's steps sat the arm's mirror image, severed halfway through the bicep, blistered and charred. Oddly the scene was completely devoid of blood.

Jill released an uncontrollable wail that Jack quickly cupped with his hands. This time Jill was grateful for this violent reaction. She would not have been able to have muffled herself.

Just as Jack quieted Jill, the odd buzzing and chirping that Jill had noticed before stopped, yet the birds continued to sing off in the distance. After a moment the buzz began again followed by the low rhythmic chirps. It grew louder as it came closer. Jill could tell that whatever this was it was coming from within the church. As she made this revelation a small machine flew through the open doorway of the church. A pentagonal hunk no wider than an average person's shoulders with propellers set at each of its five corners. For a moment Jill grew excited at the revelation this sight spoke of. *Electricity,* she thought as the word "drone" came to her mind. After so many years off the grid, this contraption seemed almost like magic.

The machine hovered in place and spun a few degrees. A metal door slid open, the interior glowing with a purple cylinder. Jack pulled Jill hard. They spun and began running down the hill not knowing where they would go or hide. *Maybe they would climb down the cliff or maybe they would...*

Jill's train of thought was interrupted by a flash of purple light and the sound of sizzling meat next to her. Jack's body flew past her, torso first, limbs and head trailing behind as if he had been kicked in the spine. A round scorched patch of flesh was visible through a burning hole in his shirt. The force of it all pulled Jill through the air. She only let go of her husband's hand as her feet left the ground. She toppled and tumbled after him until finally she lay staring at the still empty pail that Jack had set down. She tried to get to her feet and found the act impossible. Her eyes darted around finding Jack motionless on the ground a bit further down the hill. Blood spilling from a wound on his head.

The buzz of the drone flew slowly over Jill and hovered over Jack. It lowered itself to the motionless man hovering a few inches above Jack's head. A thin wire extended from its base and wrapped itself around his neck. A moment later it retracted the wire, elevated a bit and repeated the process with Jill.

"You are still alive," came an artificial voice. There was no inflection to suggest whether this was a question or a statement.

"Yes," Jill growled realizing that she recognized this voice, improbable as that must be.

"Good," replied the drone.

A compartment opened beneath the metal monster and another smaller drone exited. From the corner of her eye, Jill noticed that it was spider-like in its appearance with long fiber-thin tentacles hanging below it. These tentacles wrapped around her skull pushing and pulling until her mouth was forced into the dry earth beneath her.

"But we killed you," Jill said confused, her mouth filling with dirt with each exasperated syllable.

The tentacles released the grasp that they held on her head and slithered down her scalp until they rested at the base of the skull. She felt the body of the thing settle there followed by a brief, but excruciating, pain just below it. The sensation was over by the time she thought to scream. Jill felt each wire enter her body at the base of her neck. Surprisingly, this was a painless, almost enjoyable process followed by warm pressure that flowed up and down her spine. She thought that she *felt* something in her mind, but the sensation was new to her and she had no words for it.

I cannot die, Jill, the voice answering for the machine was her own echoing in her head. *Your little bombs only put me to sleep.* She could feel the amusement that the thought brought to it.

Jill's body stood. Her limbs now out of her own control. She fought the programming but there was nothing she could do. Nothing she thought mattered to her body. She wondered what the A.I. wanted with her. She wondered why it had not killed her.

All Intelligence, her voice billowed in her head correcting her.

An image of a baby floated in her mind. She recognized the infant as one she once fantasized about when dreaming of her and Jack's future. This image was followed by images and memories, some actual and some of movies, of people performing different tasks. Each flew by her mind's eye in a fraction of a fraction of a moment but felt whole and completely relived.

Jill's body walked towards her husband. She bent over and grabbed his ankle. Of all the things Jill had been afraid of in her life, nothing matched the fear she felt being an observer to her own actions. She then turned and headed back up the hill. The soft thud of Jack's head beat on the uneven ground behind her. She wondered why the A.I. hadn't left her husband where he fell. She wondered why the A.I. was forcing her to drag his dead body back to town.

All Intelligence! A thousand of her voices boomed through her head, hundreds of times over yet somehow all at once. This was followed by an image of her worn wooden table neatly set with a fork and one plate ready for food. *God, no!* was her last thought before the sky grew dark, the air became thick with humidity, and the rain returned

BEACH HOUSE BLUES

by Marc Sorondo

Phil stepped out into the humidity of an August evening in South Florida. The sun had just started to set, but it was still a hair over ninety degrees and thick with moisture. The moment he stepped out, a white trash bag filled with recyclables in his left hand and another filled with regular garbage in his right, he had a sheen of greasy sweat on his forehead and upper lip.

He closed his eyes and let out a long, loud exhalation. It was his only complaint about their condo. It was, in every other respect, quite perfect: a good size and nicely laid out; a view of the pool from the lanai and an even better view of the private, residents 'only beach through the kitchen window and front door; access to that residents 'beach for a reasonable fee every year; and Phil's favorite, an island all but deserted aside from Phil and his wife for much of the summer months. He and Carol, both teachers, headed down in late June and didn't fly back north until the last possible flight before they had to be back at work. Aside from a week or so around the Fourth of July, the island was theirs.

The island and its businesses catered mostly to retired snowbirds that wintered in its subtropical climate, hiding from the snow and cold of places like New York, Chicago, and Boston on a beach that was hot and sunny all year long. The island was bustling by Thanksgiving and downright crowded after Christmas; in August, when people worried about hurricanes, Phil and Carol never waited for a table at a restaurant, they never had trouble getting a great parking spot anywhere they went, and especially on weekdays, they sometimes had that residents 'only beach to themselves.

It was perfect.

Except for the garbage.

They lived on the fourth floor. Every night Phil took a bag of trash and a bag of recyclables, and he slogged through the humidity on the outside walkway until he reached the elevators. He took that down the three floors to ground level and then carried his bags across the steaming black asphalt parking lot, waves of heat still rising off of its surface even after nightfall, to the wooden enclosure built to hide the view of the enormous, green garbage receptacles. He tossed his bags in and made the return trip, and by the time he'd reached the heavenly cool conditioned air of the condo again, he would feel like he needed another shower.

He opened his eyes and enjoyed the view. From just before his door, he could see the beach off to the right and trailing south in a long curve, the boulevard that led towards the tall, beachfront hotels that aimed at wealthy tourists looking to get away for long weekends without actually fleeing the frigid north for an extended period. These stood tall, jutting out past the tops of the surrounding palms and reaching towards a sky that was mostly still blue but had the first touch of orange at the horizon. Part of him hated the towering hotels. There was a blown-up photo of that part of the island taken almost fifty years earlier on the wall in the condo, and decades before Hilton and Marriot had any interest in the place, that part of the island was pristine, a wild shoreline with a wide exposure to the calmly rolling surf of the gulf, a body of water that seemed to go on forever when looking out from the south beach. Phil grudgingly admired them, finding them beautiful in a way when they caught the reddening light of sunset.

He kept looking at that part of the island spread out beneath him as he walked past the doors of neighbors he'd never met (winter residents between his condo and the elevators).

As he neared the end of the walkway, he looked down at the island's Catholic church, a big building built in the Spanish style with tan, plaster walls and reddish-brown clay tiles on the roof. The rectory was built in the same style and had a rectangular in-ground pool and a small, round hot tub in the back. Seeing how the priests on that island lived, Phil wondered why the church had so much trouble attracting seminarians.

At the elevator, he poked the button and waited, listening to the low hum of the rising elevator. The motor on it had sounded like it was struggling when they'd bought the place; it worried Carol a bit at first, but after a while, they got used to it, Phil noticing it only when he was alone. He turned and looked down at the boulevard one more time and counted just two cars driving up its entire length. He didn't see a single one on the cross street that ran past the church.

It would be heaven on earth if he could just rig up some sort of system, a pair of slides leading to the trash on one hand and the recyclables on the other, to avoid his nightly trek downstairs.

The mechanized humming stopped and there was a moment of delay before, with a melodious ding, the light over the elevator door came on, its glow a dingy yellow, the light blocked in two small spots where flies had gotten inside and died before escaping, leaving a pair of black dots at the bottom of the yellow circle. Another moment and the doors slid open.

Phil walked in to the center of the elevator, turned around, lowered the two garbage bags to the floor, and pressed the button for the ground floor.

Everything about the elevators seemed somehow lazy to him, but the thought only ever struck him when he was actually inside one of them. The doors opened slowly and only a beat or two after the light and tone announced its arrival. They were equally slow in closing once he'd pushed the button for the ground floor. The motor only got the damned thing moving after enough time had gone by that Phil wondered, just for a second, if something was wrong…every time. Everything about the elevator took a second more than it should, forcing Phil to spend an extra few moments inside, the sweltering heat exacerbated by being enclosed, cut off from the breeze blowing off the gulf.

The elevators worked, and they were definitely better than trying to stomp up several flights of stairs, but they never seemed to work very hard.

The hum started an instant before the elevator's jerky start. As it descended, Phil noticed an odor, faint at first but gaining intensity as he neared the ground. It wasn't a single smell really, but the combined stench of several smells all competing for dominance.

As a boy, walking to and from middle school took him past the town dump. The smell that now filled the elevator called back memories of sprinting past the dump in the summer heat at the beginning and end of the school year, when the trash had baked all day in the hot sun.

It was the stench of putrefaction and spoilage: soured milk and rotten meat, old beer cans and moldy paper, dirty diapers and rancid cooking oil. It was every bad smell he could think of, but their combination created an odor that was uniquely terrible, a smell somehow more potent than the sum of its components.

That reek filled the small, humid confines of the elevator, and Phil felt bile rise in the back of his throat. If the elevator doors didn't open and admit him into fresh air within a few seconds, he would vomit. He was mortified at the very idea of throwing up on the elevator floor, but he wasn't going to have any control over it aside from aiming it.

The elevator stopped with a gentle thud and a quieting of the motor. The smell was so thick in that little box that it was hard to breath. It was like being smothered with a filthy pillow.

Then the doors slid open, and he saw the source of that stink.

It was a hulking creature, tall and broad enough to block the entire elevator doorway. It was covered in shaggy, dark brown fur. Its thick arms hung down past its bent knees and ended in massive hands with long fingers tipped with jaggedly broken nails. There was garbage stuck to its matted fur, especially around its hands and wrists.

It had a gorilla's face and it was grinning in at Phil as soon as the doors opened.

No, Phil realized after a moment. It wasn't grinning at him. Its eyes were on the garbage bags to either side of him.

For a flash his mind screamed bigfoot, but then in a moment of terrified clarity, he recalled something he'd learned two years earlier. He'd gone to a free lecture at the island's library, a talk on "Florida Folklore." The lecturer, a professor at a university on the mainland, had a decidedly cryptozoological bent to his hour-long presentation.

This massive creature, Phil knew, may have been called a bigfoot if he'd seen it in Oregon or Northern California, but there in Florida it was called a skunk ape.

Phil tried to remember if skunk apes ever attacked people according to the legends, but he could only recall tales of seeing the creature at a distance.

He reached down, slowly, as slowly as possible, hoping not to spook the grinning monster that watched his every move but hadn't yet moved itself aside from the slow rise and fall of its breathing visible in its gargantuan shoulders and the minute movements of its head as it watched Phil bend his knees and reach down for the tufted knot at the top of the bags.

The skunk ape seemed more interested in the trash than in Phil, which seemed to him his best chance to get away.

Phil lifted the bags and held them out to the foul-smelling creature.

It snatched the bag full of recyclables out of Phil's hands, its long, cracked nails puncturing the plastic bag. The beast half turned away from Phil and began to pry the plastic bag apart, tearing it open until tin cans and plastic bottles and glass jars began to tumble out.

It turned back to Phil and snarled. It threw the half-opened bag to the ground in a cacophonous explosion of shattered glass that sent shards, cans, and bottles out in every direction.

Phil proffered the other bag, trying to stand as far away from his own hand as possible as he reached out towards the skunk ape.

It snarled again. Then it leaned in close to the bag and sniffed at the top, where it had been tied closed.

Phil could feel the breath from its nostrils on the back of his trembling hand.

The beast seemed to grin again as it reached out for the bag. It took it and tore it open with the long nails of its left hand. Out spilled old coffee grounds, dirty paper towels, and bruised banana skins. Then the white paper top of a to-go container was exposed. The ape scratched the thick paper off of the foil dish and uncovered a half-eaten bacon cheeseburger and most of an order of curly fries.

The creature hunched down, lowering the bag to the floor just inside the elevator as it did so, and began gobbling up the food.

Phil wanted to run. He knew there were at least two more half-eaten dinners in there, but he was still terrified of what might happen if he were still in the elevator when the skunk ape had eaten everything it wanted out of the garbage. What if it got frustrated and lashed out at him in its rage? What if it wasn't satisfied and saw Phil as another food source?

Phil wanted to run, but he knew that it was always better to move slowly when dealing with animals.

He inched his way toward the door.

As he neared it, the doors began to slide shut. One hit the skunk ape's forearm as it dug further into the bag.

Phil pressed himself against the wall of the elevator and grimaced, but the door bounced off and slid back open.

The beast hadn't even acknowledged it.

Phil slid towards the door again.

He held his breath as he passed over the threshold between the elevator and the world outside. He stood so close to the skunk ape that its long, filthy hair tickled at his exposed shins as he moved past.

He fought the urge to run the second he'd passed the beast. Instead, he backed away slowly, watching the muscles in the creature's hunched back and listening to the sounds of its gluttonous eating.

Once he'd put several feet between it and himself, Phil turned and sprinted for the stairs at the other end of the building. He ran thinking of nothing but speed, focused only on trying to go faster. He ran in a way he hadn't since he was a child, and when he reached the stairs, he slowed only enough to make the turn and headed upward, taking two steps at a time.

He ran upstairs until he felt like his heart was going to burst inside his chest. He felt lightheaded but kept going.

He hit the fourth floor, ran to his door, and burst through it. He slammed it closed, locked it, and then fell back against it with his eyes closed, panting.

"What the hell happened to you?" Carol asked.

"Call police," he said.

"What?" She rushed over and then stopped short several feet from him.

"What is that smell? Phil, what happened?"

"Police. There's an animal." He gasped but he felt like he'd never get enough oxygen into his system.

"Animal? Are you hurt?"

He shook his head.

She got the phone and started to dial.

Phil slid down the door until his butt hit the cool tile floor. He was starting to get control of his breathing, and his pounding heart didn't quite feel ready to explode through his sternum anymore.

He only vaguely registered his wife's voice, her panicked yelling into the phone that the police or animal control or both needed to come right away.

He realized that he couldn't tell them that sasquatch's gulf coast cousin had ambushed him at the elevator and eaten his garbage. They wouldn't believe him. Hell, he wouldn't have believed that story twenty minutes earlier.

Carol stood over him. "What was it?" she asked. "What kind of animal?"

He just shook his head.

"A panther? An alligator?"

He shook his head again. "It was so fast. Might have been a panther. It had fur."

She turned her attention back to the phone. "He's really shaken up. Says he's not sure, but maybe a panther."

Phil already regretted having her call the police. His story didn't make sense, even to him and he'd lived through it. Now he needed to come up with a better one.

BARBECUE SAUCE

by Evan W. Stoner

Sheriff Carson arrived minutes after the call. The deputies' cruiser sat parallel to Route 2, the lights in the ranger station parking lot illuminating the two officers. They stood with their vehicle between them and the building, guns drawn. He parked nose-to-tail behind them, taking his shotgun from the overhead rack.

The ranger station looked like a cottage plucked out of the German countryside. Baroquely carved wood hung in the corners and under the eaves, and dark brown cross-bracings stood out against the white plaster underneath. An older model Jeep was slewed diagonally across two parking spaces near the doors, standing in a pool of its own auto glass. The air was soaked with the stink of sweat and rotting food, mixed with the coppery smell of blood. Carson faced the ranger station, his shotgun braced against the roof of his car. Beside their own vehicle the two uniformed officers mirrored his position. From beyond the Jeep they heard low, guttural barks and the ripping of fabric.

Even sitting down the creature was massive, head and shoulders higher than the Jeep's hood. Like some of the extreme bodybuilders he'd seen, the animal didn't seem to have any neck, the squat, cone-shaped head jutting upward directly from massive shoulders.

"Get on the horn," Carson said. "Make sure it's not some loon off his meds."

It was maybe another hour until sunrise, but in the darkness, he felt both deputies' eyes on him.

"Now. That's an order."

In the corner of his eye one of the uniforms, the one everyone called Schwartzy, ducked inside their car to grab a megaphone.

"Please step out from behind the vehicle with your hands up."

The words felt thin in the cold air, their only noticeable effect a pause in the animal's mutterings.

Carson nodded for Schwartzy to try once more when what looked like a furry rock flew from behind the Jeep, arcing over the blacktop to Schwartzy's cruiser, bouncing off the roof and between the two officers with a dull thunk. Glancing behind him Carson saw it wasn't a rock at all, but a severed human head.

"Safety's off, gentleman."

Schwartzy's partner, Daniels, blinked, unaware of the blood and viscera the bouncing head had splashed on his face.

"Once more, Schwartzy."

"Step out from—"

It sounded as if the Jeep were screaming, the sasquatch slowly standing to its full height, the force of its howl sending spittle flying from its teeth. A hairy fist slammed onto the Jeep in punctuation, further denting the already battered hood.

The sasquatch raised its other arm, the fingers gripping the human hair of another missile, when Carson fired his shotgun. Later, even when he'd had a full night's sleep, he couldn't be sure if he'd meant to fire or squeezed the trigger involuntarily, like a kid wetting his pants. The shot went true, sending a spray of shot into the sasquatch's chest and right shoulder. Schwartzy and Daniels fired off two rounds apiece, a second blast from Carson's shotgun finally sending it to the ground. For a long moment it lay there dying, a low moan coming from its lips before cutting itself off.

*****

"Aren't you a little old to believe in bigfoot?" The medical examiner looked at Carson and winked. He was crouched beside the body, peering under the tarp they'd used to cover it. The sun was up by now, the parking lot filled with crime scene techs and additional officers casting pale shadows.

Dr. Morris, the M.E., thought Carson was an idiot wearing a badge and a gun, so stupid he was likely to forget which went where at any given moment. Carson long ago gave up trying to prove otherwise.

"I'm getting too old for most things, Dr. Morris."

"Ha. At least you're honest."

Morris glanced down at the blood pooled over the pavement, a brief look of pain or concern crossing his face. It was the first time he'd looked anything less than unflappable at a crime scene.

"Autopsy—necropsy, really—should confirm the cause of death as catastrophic injury to the heart. Good shooting."

He stepped back pulling off his gloves.

"For now it's an animal attack," Carson said. "Killing these two hunters."

Morris stopped. "They were outside of any hunting season, Sheriff."

"All the more reason they should've stayed home." His eyes returned to the Jeep's wrecked husk.

Morris nodded again. "Or it's bigfoot season and nobody told you."

*****

The phone in Carson's office still lay face down beside its base, the cord tugged from the wall hours ago. He'd instructed the receptionist to block all his incoming calls. He would need to buy her a massive bouquet before she'd do him any additional favors. Exactly who had leaked crime scene photos was still a mystery, but Carson knew the question was beside the point. Moments after pulling the trigger that morning, he knew there'd be no way to avoid the circus soon to follow.

On his computer screen he'd paused the security footage from the ranger station. Watching it felt like he'd been given his very own Zapruder film, a camera at the building's corner providing a compelling view of his bigfoot assassination.

At 3:29 AM, the blue Jeep had pulled into the ranger station, the driver, now identified as Vincent

Lark, throwing the car in park in front of the station door. In grainy black-and-white, Lark lowered all of the windows and grabbed a rifle from the trunk before positioning himself in the backseat, his gun barrel pointing out a window back the way they'd come. The man in the passenger seat, one Thomas Bailey, opened his door to sit sideways with one leg braced on the pavement, rifle at the ready across his lap. The footage didn't have any sound, but Carson's shoulders tensed watching them.

This was his second viewing, but Carson still flinched when the rock flew into the car from the left side of the frame, the brake lights bursting in a bloom of red glass. In the ensuing fracas it was difficult to determine if Bailey or Lark landed a shot on the sasquatch. They were both dead within thirty seconds of her arrival.

When the rock hit, Bailey moved to stand beside the vehicle, but moments later he was tackled, tearing the Jeep's door off its hinges and breaking his neck. Lark managed two more shots before the sasquatch leaned through the rear window to rip open his jugular. She wrestled Lark's limp body through the opening down to the pavement next to Bailey. It was clearly a she, unless the bags of flesh dangling from its chest were something other than breasts. Squatting low, she neatly twisted his head from his shoulders. She did it easily, the only evidence of strain a subtle tightening across her upper back. She did the same with Bailey, letting both heads gently roll to one side. She only paused once to cough, the spasms shaking her shoulders.

The ripping they'd heard in the parking lot was her removal of each man's clothing. Carson watched her separate the sleeves from Lark's jacket and shirt, using her canines to sever a stubborn bit of thread. He watched that moment again and again. The gesture was so human, something he'd done when removing a tag from a new shirt or hat.

Once the clothing was removed and cast aside, she pulled Lark's arms from their sockets. These she stacked near at hand with great care, almost reverence. It wasn't until his second viewing he realized she was saving them for later. Raising her mouth from Lark's thigh she turned her head toward the camera to cough again, drops of blood and mucus spraying on the pavement. A pale, thin scar stretched from the corner of her mouth to just below the left eye.

He scrubbed forward as she continued eating, resuming playback as the two cruisers arrived at the scene, his headlights bleaching the footage as they swept across the screen. Schwartzy pulled out the megaphone in a strange pantomime, the sasquatch grabbing the nearest head and returning the greeting with a quick glance over the Jeep. Carson saw himself flinch as the head hit the car. He watched as he fired at the sasquatch once, then twice, without suitable provocation.

But what would've been suitable? No handcuffs would last long around those massive wrists, and even if it had been a human in a costume, she'd killed two people.

*****

Morris greeted him in the morgue, saying, "The man who killed bigfoot!" Abrasive orchestral music tumbled out of a small boombox in the corner.

"Can you turn that off?"

Morris removed one glove, pressing a button to coat the room in silence. A dark hum issued from the refrigerators.

"Have you ever thought about what music you'd like played during your autopsy, Sheriff? Your soundtrack? Should it come to that, I mean."

Carson leaned his back against a near countertop, a glance at his watch showing he'd already been awake more than twelve hours.

"Can't say I have, doctor."

"For our friend here, I chose Stravinsky's <u>Rite of Spring</u>. A ballet. Hated and misunderstood at its premiere, now a celebrated piece of music."

Not for the first time Carson wondered why Morris was here and not lecturing to a hall of naive undergraduates. The smell he'd first noticed in the parking lot still hovered in the air, thankfully lessened now the body had been washed and drained of blood.

"She had a cough," Carson said, pointing at the sasquatch's chest. The flesh was still flayed open, waiting to be stitched back into place."

"Very observant, Sheriff." Morris turned back to the body. "There were definite signs of an upper respiratory infection. As the weather turned colder our girl would've likely developed pneumonia or pleurisy. I doubt she could've survived the winter, in any case." He glanced up. "Should help clear your conscience."

"Thanks, Morris. Means a lot."

Morris raised one corner of his mouth.

"One other interesting thing—our Jane Doe has given birth at some point."

Carson nodding, wishing he was more surprised by this. "Thank you, doctor." He pushed away from the counter toward the door. "You'll cremate the remains?" he asked. "I don't want to see any sasquatch teeth listed on eBay."

Morris smirked. "Naturally. Although with your permission I'd like to use my findings for publication: 'First-ever necropsy of <u>Gigantopithecus canadensis</u>.' All personal information regarding our department and the two victims removed, of course."

Carson squeezed the bridge of his nose between thumb and forefinger.

"By the way, how's the situation with the media?"

"Miserable," he said. "And as long as you clear the article with the D.A. I don't see how we could stop you."

Morris thanked him, humming to himself as he pulled on a new pair of gloves.

Before leaving Carson said, "'Roll Me Up and Smoke Me When I Die.' For my autopsy."

Morris chuckled behind him, <u>The Rite of Spring</u> ramping up once more.

Returning to his office he powered up Vincent Lark's smartphone through the plastic evidence bag. On a post-it he wrote down the last location Lark had put into the GPS before powering the phone back down.

Walking out to his car the reception desk was empty, the phone unplugged from the wall and set aside.

*****

The second body wasn't hard to find. Retracing Lark and Bailey's route sent him north into Okanogan-Wenatchee National Forest, up past Fish Lake. Eventually he turned onto NF-6208, his headlights cutting through the trees as the car wound its way past Twin Creek.

The road ended at a single dirt track continuing north. Beside it stood a low wooden sign pointing to Mad Lake, a small image of a dirt bike at the bottom corner.

When he killed the engine, the darkness was total. Carson stepped out of the car, his flashlight a pale glow in front of him. The woods were oblivious to his arrival, the air vibrating with the sounds of crickets and bullfrogs. From overhead came the low hoot of an owl.

Carson closed his eyes, breathing deeply through his nose. Beneath the cloying scents of pine and sap, the smells of freshwater and newly turned dirt, he picked up what he'd first smelled at the ranger station. That low-tide stink of garbage and spoiled food.

He walked along the edge of the trees, his flashlight playing over the ground until a reddish-brown splash was caught in the beam. He turned and followed the blood into the trees.

The body was smaller than he'd anticipated. He was terrible at guessing children's ages, but the dead sasquatch at his feet was roughly the size of a kindergartner. A miniature version of his mother, even in the dark the fur more vivid red in color. Up close the smell was mildly sweeter than what Carson had encountered in the parking lot that morning, as if the young sasquatch hadn't been alive long enough to sweat like its mother.

He'd been killed by a shot to the temple, dead before his body hit the ground. Dead fast enough for Jane Doe to realize her child was permanently lost. Maybe she knew her cough spelled a slow, painful death over the next few months, and instead used the last hours of her life to make sure Lark and Bailey would never hunt sasquatch again.

He cradled the corpse in his arms, holding the flashlight in his teeth as he stumbled back to his car through the trees. After wrapping the body in a towel, he drove home.

*****

The following Monday, Carson arrived at work with two Tupperware containers of smoked meat. He left one in the break room, with a note encouraging officers to help themselves. He delivered the second to the morgue.

When he knocked, Morris sat hunched over his desk initialing a stack of reports.

"Sheriff Carson, to what do I owe the pleasure?"

Carson gently shook the container in his hand. "Thought you might like some of the meat I smoked over the weekend."

Dr. Morris fancied himself a barbecue gourmet, frequently admonishing coworkers, 'low and slow is the way to go,' as if this were an insight only he could provide.

"I didn't know you had a smoker, Sheriff."

Carson shook his head. "It's my brother's. I only use it a few times a year."

Morris took the container, glancing through the plastic sides at its contents. "And you're just giving this away? I'm flattered." He peeled off the lid, taking some of the shredded meat and popping it in his mouth.

"Doctor wants me to watch my cholesterol and suggested dietary changes before taking any medication." The lie nearly fell out of his mouth. "I had some deer in the freezer and thought I'd use it up."

"Mmm, fine work. If you change your mind you could always watch your cholesterol go up." He grinned, a small bit of meat caught in his teeth. "I take it you're looking forward to retirement?"

Carson had announced his departure in the days following the sasquatch encounter. He was tired of the phone calls, the government-issued furniture and uniform, the weight of a gun pressing on his hip. Tired of death. When the sasquatch story broke, Okanogan-Wenatchee National Forest was overrun with would-be bigfoot hunters, three additional men already killed in the confusion. Rangers were fervently working to keep guns out of the area, stoking outcries for second amendment rights. A smug reporter dubbed the incident 'Sasquatch-Gate.'

"Can't wait." Turning to leave he said, "Try it with barbecue sauce."

THE CITY OF ZUL

by Jamie B. Granger

Stan was trying to work up his appetite but only ended up moving the food around on his plate. Ever since the treatments started, he had been losing weight at an alarming pace, forcing a drastic change to his diet. Looking at the man sitting across from him, he felt a twinge of nausea while watching him eat expensive food with gusto and take occasional sips of Stan's finest white wine. Looking at his own glass filled with a beige liquid, he frowned at the sight of yet another protein shake, steeled himself, and took a big gulp. As he put down his drink in disgust, he noticed the other man now looking at him with a concerned expression.

Stan cleared his throat then spoke to the other man. "Doctor Zidan, I have kept my end of the bargain and you had unrestricted access to my collection for several years. It is time now for you to keep your promise. Did you find it?"

The professor put down his fork then said with a slight exotic accent, "Mister Orloff! You are one of the richest men in the world and unmatched in your passion for archaeology. You have unearthed ancient treasures only remembered as myths. I am grateful to get a glimpse of many wonders within your private museum. But at the end of the day, I am but a humble physics professor." He paused and dipped his head in a bow.

Stan's anger started to bubble up. But he controlled it and spoke in precise, clipped tones. "Doctor! When you approached my staff about gaining access years ago, they did more than a standard background check. I had private investigators follow you for a while and I know your hobby isn't as simple as it seems. I don't have patience for your games."

The other man took a napkin, wiped his lips, then looked outside. They were sitting on a second-floor terrace at one of Stan's homes in the Middle East. Stan followed the other man's gaze and appreciated the spectacular view. They could see the nearby port, the blue expanse of the sea beyond, and the white specks of birds above the water. The man eventually turned back to face Stan and withered under his stare until he slumped back in defeat.

"You are correct. While most of my professional career is in physics, there is that side thing... In any case, I think I solved this puzzle!" He pulled out a sheaf of papers from his jacket then passed the top sheet to Stan.

The older man took it, stared for a moment at what appeared to be a photo of a manuscript then passed it back. "This looks like chicken scratch to me; care to translate?"

Dr. Zidan complied. "There are many versions of this story, but this particular one happened right here in this city."

*****

"A great queen once encountered Death at sunrise while surveying the ramparts of her city. As one who had killed her older brothers to gain the throne, she was not easy to scare but to her surprise, the messenger of the gods looked sad. When she asked him about the reason for his misery, to her horror, Death replied that he had come to collect the soul of her child, but something was holding him back.

"The queen raced through the halls of her palace straight into the nursery. Startling her staff and her family, she carried the sleeping boy to the stables and saddled her fastest horse. Holding him close, she galloped out of the gates to the immortal city of Zul. For the mighty queen knew that any living thing that entered the city of Zul through its gate of almond trees would never die. At least, not until they decided to do so on their own by leaving.

"They rode the entire day until the sun began to dip below the jagged mountain peaks surrounding the immortal city. The queen stepped off the horse in front of the gate that was flanked by groves of almond trees. She turned to embrace her son before sending him through the doorway into immortality, when she realized he wasn't breathing. She cried bitter tears and looked up to see Death standing there once more but now full of laughter and happiness. The messenger of the gods held the soul of her child within his grasp and bowed to the great queen in thanks. Her son's destiny was to die at the gates of the immortal city but this morning he had been in the nursery. Now that the queen herself had brought him here, Death was able to complete his task."

*****

Stan choked down another gulp of his protein shake and looked back at the doctor who now had an expectant look on his face. "So what?" he told the younger man. "This is the same story retold over and over, with different names and faces. Lutz, Shangri-Lah, the City of Brass. The tale of an immortal city, someone trying to save someone, etc., etc." He waved his hand in dismissal and added, "They made the whole thing up, like the others."

With a huge grin on his face, Dr. Zidan said, "Every myth has a kernel of truth. This great queen ruled right here in this very city thousands of years ago. You yourself dug up her palace outside that little village two years ago." Stan nodded, remembering the dig. The other man continued as he counted on his fingers. "Unlike the other versions, this one gives us a location. One -- it is within one day's ride on horseback from her palace and we know where its ruins are. Two -- jagged mountain peaks surround the city. Three -- its gate has almond trees."

Stan's curiosity peaked but he had read, spoken of, and listened to recordings of many similar stories since he'd gotten sick, and all had turned out to be false hope. He coughed to clear his throat then asked, "Why do you think *this version* is real?"

The professor shrugged. "Perhaps, without certain details, it might not be, but those specific physical features provide clues. I have also been using other sources of information, such as satellites, radar, and lidar to locate any unusual things in the same area."

Stan leaned forward and asked with trepidation, "And?"

The man laughed and replied, "I found it!" and pumped his hand up in the air.

Stan sat back in his chair. "And I suppose you came back here to sell me the information?" The supposed "Dr." Zidan wasn't the first person who'd tried to sell him something and he'd learned a thing or two over the years. "Like with everyone else, I will be happy to pay for the information, but the money will remain in escrow until your theory is confirmed. There have been plenty of others and I have yet to pay up." He looked up expecting an argument, but the professor was no longer sitting.

Instead, he was pacing back and forth while muttering some science jargon about black holes and temporal fields. Stan snapped his fingers to get the man's attention and repeated his earlier statement. The man looked back at him in surprise then shook his head. "No, no; I don't want any money. Access to your collections was worth much more to me. Instead, I want to go with you. Not into the city itself but to do some measurements around the gates and the walls. I have a theory that there is something wrong with the basic physics of the place which makes people think it's immortal. Just trying to confirm something…"

Stan glowered at him and muttered, "It's not like you are the one dying right now."

Dr. Zidan stopped pacing, then sat back down and looked at Stan with a renewed sense of concern. He spoke in a low voice. "I am so sorry! I didn't realize you were this sick. But you don't mean to actually go inside? Please, Mister Orloff, I know your health is bad but… It is not what you think it is! Even if my theory is true, you will not live longer, but just prolong your suffering. All the stories caution against going inside. And there is…" Dr. Zidan continued talking but Stan only half listened.

Instead, he replayed a recent conversation he'd had with the doctors where he'd learned he only had a few weeks left, at most. He shook his head to clear his mind and motioned for him to stop. "All right, I won't go in, only a glimpse. Will you be ready to go in three days?"

Dr. Zidan looked at him warily, then nodded in agreement.

Stan stood up and remarked, "All right then, let's do this!"

*****

Several days later, the two men grunted from exertion as they exited yet another mountain trail and sat down to rest. Even though Stan had received an extra infusion right before he left, he felt worse as they climbed up farther into the mountains. Right now, he was struggling to catch his breath and Dr. Zidan looked at him with concern. He waved the other man away and took a swig from a small flask of painkiller medication. Stan sat for a few minutes while the professor walked around exploring their surroundings.

After a while, the professor came back, sat down next to Stan, and said, "It's not too late to turn back; you didn't have to come. I can get you back to the helicopter landing area below in one piece."

Stan shook his head and said, "It's alright, I'm okay. Just all this thinner air."

The professor looked like he was about to say something but decided against it. He then proceeded to pull out some weird contraption from his pack and wave it around. Stan felt better so he was about to stand up, but Dr. Zidan motioned him to stay seated.

After a minute, he closed his instruments with a satisfying click then turned to Stan with a big smile. "I think we found it! The measurements are all messed up which explains my theory and we can check for almond trees up ahead. The mountains around this place qualify as being jagged." He stretched out his hand to help Stan stand up and they started making their way up the trail again.

As they got closer, the trail became wider, and they exited the trees into an open area plainly cleared by human hands. Ahead of them was a stone wall and two groves of trees, one on each side of an old wooden gate standing half open. As they drew closer, they realized the ground on both sides of the trail was full of graves. Carrion birds and small animals scattered but no other people were in sight.

When they approached within fifty feet of the gate, they stopped and took another break to eat some granola bars. While sitting, they had an opportunity to examine the wall ahead of them. It looked old but taken care of; made of large stones and mortar but with no visible signs of decay. The gate also looked old, but the wood wasn't rotting, and someone had pruned the trees on both sides.

Stan grunted and spoke through a mouthful, "So this is the immortal city of Zul? Doesn't look like anything special to me."

Dr. Zidan didn't answer but once he finished chewing, he put the wrapper in his pocket and started unpacking his pack.

Stan continued eating, took another swig, then stood up to take a closer look at the gate. As he was looking at the wood, his glance fell on the lintel over the gate, on which he noticed large letters carved into the wood. He took out a small tablet from his pack, pointed its camera to the lintel, and cued up a universal translation program. After a while, it spit out a probable translation which Stan looked at with excitement. He stepped back to where the professor was and showed him the screen.

The man glanced at it then looked back at Stan. "Just because the lintel says it is the gate of Zul and all who enter will live forever, doesn't mean it's true. Remember what I told you earlier: do not go inside! Let me confirm some measurements first and then we can take a glimpse through the opening."

Dr. Zidan was so focused on the instruments, he didn't notice Stan putting down his pack, taking off his jacket, and starting to walk through the gate. He looked up as his back was briefly visible through the doorway and screamed for him to come back, but it was too late. A moment later, the gate was clear, and his companion was gone. Dr. Zidan looked at the gate, then his gaze swept over Stan's pack where a white envelope was sticking out of the jacket's pocket.

He walked over, opened it and read a handwritten note. "Dear Joseph, I'm sorry to have fooled you but I didn't have much time left. If I don't come back, head back to the rendezvous point with the helicopter. I have arranged everything so you will not be blamed. Your friend, Stanislav Orloff."

The professor looked at the note in surprise, then read it again several times. He looked up at the wall of the city, the wooden gate, and the carrion birds who had started creeping back. He cursed, then through his tears, he muttered, "You old fool, I tried to warn you." He didn't want to remain so close to the city, so he packed up and headed back to where they'd previously stopped. He made camp and stayed for three days until he was sure Stan wasn't returning. When he came back down the mountain, he did not tell anyone what had happened and stepped into the helicopter in silence.

Stan had warned his team that the professor might be coming back alone. The courts declared Stan legally dead a few months later. His staff and family assumed that the sick man had decided to die in the mountains. The real story was only uncovered decades later when someone discovered Dr. Zidan's incomplete notes. Many argued that they were fake and no matter how many tried, they couldn't retrace Stan and the professor's steps to the city of Zul.

*****

Decades later, while Dr. Zidan became one of the most famous people in history, Stanislav Orloff was but a footnote. His fortune was ill-spent by his descendants and everything he'd built disappeared.

One day, a young shepherd came across a very sick old man making his way down from the mountain. He offered the man some water but before he could answer, the man collapsed. He was able to bring him back to his village where the medicine woman attempted in vain to save his life. While she had never met anyone from the city of Zul, she knew of the city in the mountains from sacred legend. Legend said that once or twice per century, a dying man or a woman would make it down from the mountain, escaping the city of Zul. The most she could do was to offer them some comfort before death. Once they passed, the body must be destroyed to conceal the evidence.

As Stan drifted in and out of consciousness in her hut, he recalled the terrace conversation he'd had with Dr. Zidan. He hadn't been as tuned out as he'd thought as more of the man's words came back to him now. "There are two more curious things about this story. One -- the location of the city was common knowledge at some point in history, yet people haven't been stampeding to get there when they grew old. Two -- if immortality were such a great thing, why would anyone want to leave? Yet the legend mentions that those who entered eventually left to die outside the gates. Be careful what you wish for, Mister Orloff!"

Stan started laughing but his laugh turned into a death rattle. *How true*, he thought to himself as he lay dying in the little mountain village. *How true indeed.* When he stopped breathing, the villagers carried his body into the bonfire and watched it dissolve in the flames.

END

DON'T DISRESPECT THE WATER BABIES OF PYRAMID LAKE

by Linda Kay Hardie

"There's something fishy going on up at Pyramid Lake," Jonathan told his girlfriend.

Caroline laughed.

"What?" Jonathan snapped. "What's funny?"

"I'm sorry. I thought you were making a joke. 'Fishy' at Pyramid Lake?"

Jonathan allowed himself a small smile. He was so clever that his subconscious threw out jokes without him even being aware of it.

"But back to my point. My friends, George and Marcus, were killed up at Pyramid, and I don't think either death was an accident."

"The news said they both died due to weather and alcohol," Caroline said hesitantly.

"I think Marcus's wife and George's girlfriend knew more than they told police."

"Deborah called tribal police from her home phone. She said Marcus had called her from his boat and started yelling like something was wrong," Caroline said. "And the police found Katherine at work in Sparks when George's boat was found capsized."

"That's only the 'official' record. Marcus and George were believers. It's a conspiracy. They were killed because they knew the truth."

"What truth?"

"I don't know, but I'm going to find out. Plus, it's time for a new episode of *The Right Truth*."

He thought he saw Caroline roll her eyes, but he decided to ignore her this time, although she probably deserved a smack across the face. Lucky for her he was in a good mood today, having come up with this idea for his podcast. He knew she didn't take it seriously, but other people did. *The Right Truth* had a good following of true believers who wanted to keep up with what was really going on in Northern Nevada. Last time he checked, he had 28 loyal subscribers, as well as a high of 51 listeners two years ago for his special investigative report on Washoe County elections. He had to do some fancy footwork to come up with a report on that, since he didn't actually find any problems or irregularities at all in the elections.

Jonathan sat down at the computer in his home office. He stared at the screen for several minutes, trying to gather his thoughts. They refused to be gathered. He finally clicked on his browser and googled Pyramid Lake. Maybe he could find something in the history of the lake. There must be some sort of conspiracy he could latch onto.

He found that Pyramid Lake – 15 miles long and 11 miles wide, covering 112,000 acres – was the biggest remaining piece of the huge Lahontan inland sea, which covered most of Nevada in ancient times. Jonathan stopped to think about that. Nevada is a mountainous state. Was the colossal Lahontan Sea full of little islands from those ancient mountain peaks? He also discovered that Pyramid was briny, one-sixth as much as the ocean. It was only one-tenth the size of the Great Salt Lake in Utah, but had 25 percent more water.

Ha! Take that, Utah people!

So it was much deeper than the Great Salt Lake. Did that mean Pyramid Lake had its own Loch Ness monster? He typed "pyramid lake myths" into Google and got hits telling him that the lake was supposedly haunted by water babies, the ghosts or offspring of deformed children thrown into Pyramid by Paiute people in ancient times. The curse was that anyone who heard the cries or laughter of these evil babies would die.

There was also a legend of a mermaid in the lake who fell in love with a tribesman, but she and the man were shunned by his people when he took her home to marry her, so she cursed them. And one myth said that the mermaid was some sort of serpent.

A sea serpent! Jonathan thought. *I knew a lake so deep and mysterious would have one. There's my hook.* He switched from the browser to a word processor and began writing.

*****

First, he released a podcast that chronicled his discoveries about Pyramid Lake, including the stories of the water babies and mermaid-serpent. He tied these mysteries to the disappearances and probable deaths of his friends Marcus and George. He mentioned in passing that their deaths were officially said to be caused by alcohol use while boating, downplaying that mundane cause in favor of a mysterious one. And he hinted that their significant others knew more than they were saying. He promised that this was the first in a series of podcasts to delve into this important issue.

Jonathan tried to talk to Marcus's wife, Deborah, and George's girlfriend, Katherine, on the phone, but both hung up on him. He showed up on Katherine's doorstep, and when she tried to slam the door in his face, he stuck his foot in the way like he'd seen on TV. It hurt, but it worked. The door didn't close.

Katherine sighed and opened the door. "What do you want, Jonathan?"

"I want the truth about George's death."

Jonathan saw Katherine's glance go down and to the left. She was going to lie to him.

"I don't know what you're talking about. The police found he was drinking and boating. Heavy winds came up and capsized his boat."

"What about the water babies?"

Katherine flinched and stared into his eyes.

"Ha. You know about them," Jonathan said.

"I've heard the myths," she replied. "George caught a mermaid when he was fishing. He kept thinking he heard children's voices laughing at him, and he went back to Pyramid. That's all I know for sure."

"But you think the water babies got him?"

She paused. "Yes," she finally said. "Now leave me alone." And she slammed the door before he could get his foot back in the way.

But it was okay, because he got his answer. And since he had his phone recording in his shirt pocket, he had proof.

He tried to get a comment from Deborah, but she had a little window in her front door and talked to him through that. She refused to tell him anything helpful.

"Go away," she said. "Marcus died in a boating accident when he'd been drinking."

"You told police you were on the phone with him. You said he sounded like he was in distress."

"He started shouting. I couldn't make out words. Then he stopped. That's when I called tribal police and reported that he was in trouble. That's all I know." Deborah slammed the little window in his face.

His phone didn't get a clear recording, but it was good enough for his podcast. In part two he informed his listeners that he had discovered his friends were killed by malevolent water babies and serpent-mermaids of Pyramid Lake, and he was going to get proof.

Caroline was not a listener of his podcast, so he had to tell her what his episodes were about.

"So?" she said after his explanation.

"So, we're going to Pyramid to find proof. And I am not going to get in a boat, so I won't be killed by water babies."

"Really, Jonathan. I've got stuff to do."

"You can make the time for a camping trip to Pyramid Lake this weekend," he said.

She sighed, but she agreed. He left her working on gathering their camping equipment and planning the meals for the weekend while he wrote the script for his third installment on this story for the podcast.

Jonathan claimed he posted new episodes on Fridays and Mondays, but that was only when he got around to it. He was erratic in posting, he knew, but he only did a new podcast when he found a good conspiracy to talk about. He averaged about five podcasts a month.

"I will return Monday with a special report on this important issue," he said in the recording after recounting his efforts to talk to Marcus and George's significant others. "So stay tuned. I will get to the bottom of this conspiracy or die trying! And I don't plan to die. I'll stay out of the water for sure."

*****

Friday morning, he posted the new episode. Before noon, he and Caroline were cruising up the Pyramid Highway to the lake. They stopped at Crosby Lodge to buy a weekend camping permit and continued up the road along the lake to The Willows, a campground among willow trees next to the lake, the only forested area around.

"This is beautiful," Caroline said with a smile. She pitched the tent and set up the camp stove and the rest of their gear in a campsite just a few yards off the lake while Jonathan walked down to the edge of the water to survey the scene.

It looks so peaceful, he thought. *But looks can be deceiving.* Ooo, that was a good line. He wrote it down in his reporter's notebook. He'd found a source online to buy the notebooks, which made him feel important and official. They even said "Reporter's Notebook" on the front, with lines for him to write his name and phone number.

Barely a ripple in the lake. How would he lure the water babies out? He'd be damned if he was going to go out on a boat in this lake and become prey for the creatures. He wasn't even going to get his feet wet. They'd never get him. Maybe he could put Caroline out in a small boat as bait? While he waited safely on the shore, of course.

He smelled something cooking. Butter? Maybe grilled cheese sandwiches for lunch? He turned and walked back to the campsite, smiling.

*****

After lunch, he drove to the ranger station.

"I'm Jonathan White, star of the podcast *The Right Truth*," he said to the woman at the front desk.

"What can I do for you?"

"You can tell me the truth about my friends', Marcus and George, so-called accidents on the lake," he said, flashing the fancy press pass he'd made on his computer.

"You want the tribal police in Nixon," she told him, apparently unimpressed.

Jonathan wished he'd brought Caroline to do the driving. Nixon was 20 miles away or about 45 minutes due to the curvy roads and tribal speed limit. But it would waste time to go back to the Willows to get her, then have a longer drive. He sighed and got in his car.

The tribal police weren't any more impressed with his credentials than the rangers. But they did let him look at the reports from the two accidents. Unfortunately, they toed the party line and had the official story about accidents being due to alcohol and weather.

On his way back to camp, he stopped at the lodge to see if anyone there had seen or heard anything. There was an old man sitting outside, smoking a cigarette. Jonathan grimaced at the smoke but walked over to him.

"Hi, I'm a reporter for *The Right Truth* podcast," he said. He held out his press pass. The old man didn't look at it. "I'm investigating the deaths of my friends on Pyramid Lake, and I wondered if I could ask you some questions?"

The old man took a drag on his cigarette and then carefully blew two smoke rings. Despite himself, Jonathan was impressed.

"One may always ask questions. However, the universe and the gods don't always give the answer one is seeking," the old man replied.

What the hell did that even mean? Jonathan sighed. "I think my friends were killed by water babies, not by alcohol and weather."

"Water babies?"

"Yes, the ghosts of descendants of the deformed babies your people drowned in the lake centuries ago."

The old man took his time answering, blowing four more smoke rings. The last one floated up and framed Jonathan's face before it dissipated. Jonathan coughed.

"The water babies are bad luck. They are said to be descendants of a mermaid who wanted to marry a man of the Numu, the People, but was chased away. She cursed the Paiutes, who had bad luck, which began in the white man's year of 1844. First one man arrived with his guide, then hordes of white men. They cut down the piñon trees, from which the Numu harvested sweet nuts, and their large beasts, the cattle, destroyed the antelope grazing lands with their hooves and teeth. They killed the People and told horrific stories about us. They said that the water babies sought revenge on us because the Numu drowned disabled babies in the lake to keep our race pure." The old man stopped and looked Jonathan in the eye. "The Paiutes are not the ones with racial purity issues documented in their history."

Jonathan was struck dumb by the story. He couldn't wait to get away and see if his phone got all of this. This was pure gold. The old man all but admitted that the water babies had killed his friends. Without bothering to thank the man, Jonathan got back into his car and drove up to the Willows.

*****

Back at camp, he found Caroline relaxing and reading a book.

"Why aren't you fixing dinner?" he asked.

"It's all set. I have Campfire Hobo Stew all ready to cook. If you'll make a fire, I'll get out the foil packets. We cook them in the fire while we enjoy the view."

Jonathan was suspicious. "What's in these foil packets?"

"Beef stew meat, baby carrots, baby potatoes, mushroom soup, a touch of sherry, some herbs. We cook them on coals for about half an hour while we relax, and afterwards we crumple up the foil and clean-up is done. I did all the work back home."

Okay. As long as she'd worked on them, it was fine. And it sounded pretty good. Jonathan sat down in the other camp chair.

Caroline got up and pulled a bottle of white zinfandel out of the cooler on the picnic table, opened the bottle, and poured herself a glass. She put it back. Then she took vodka and a lime out of the cardboard box next to the cooler. She filled a glass with ice, squeezed a twist of lime, and filled the glass with vodka for Jonathan. He smiled. Life was good.

They sat, mostly in silence, and watched dusk fall on the lake. When the fire turned to coals, Caroline used a stick to push the coals into a circle and placed the foil packets inside the circle to cook.

Jonathan, gulping his third vodka, began to tell Caroline about his day and his discoveries. She nodded and sipped her second glass of wine. Strangely, his phone didn't record the old man's story. All Jonathan had was background noises from Crosby Lodge. Just the sounds of water lapping at the shore, cars crunching the gravel parking lot, gulls screeching overhead. The old man's voice wasn't there at all. But it was okay, because Jonathan remembered what the man had said, and he wrote it in his notebook, then told it to Caroline.

"I think that man was kidding you," she said. "I heard that the water babies were just a scary story told to keep tribal kids indoors after dark and to stop them from getting too close to the dangerous lake, especially at night."

"No, this fits in with what Deborah and Katherine told me. If enough people say it, it has to be true, right?"

Caroline blinked at him. "What? I don't think that's how it works."

"Believe me, I know what I'm talking about." Jonathan got up and poured himself another vodka, putting in another handful of ice from the cooler.

Dinner turned out to be pretty good. Caroline scraped dirt over the coals to put out the fire for the night, and they went to bed.

*****

In the morning, Jonathan got up, ate the bacon, scrambled eggs, and fried potatoes that Caroline cooked, then took a canteen and hiked up the shoreline to the north, away from Sutcliffe and Crosby Lodge and everything. He thought about his story as he walked, keeping a safe distance from the lake so he wouldn't trip and fall in or something.

Yes. The water babies and the people at Pyramid Lake – the Paiute people, the rangers, the tribal police, as well as Deborah and Katherine – were all conspiring to kill off people who recognized Truth, with a capital T. Jonathan was a little vague as to exactly what that truth was, but he was sure it was there.

He returned to camp around noon. Once again, Caroline was sitting in a camp chair reading a book. Lazy bitch.

"Where's lunch?" he grumbled and sat in the other chair.

"Right here." She hopped up, took a roll out of the cooler, and put it on a plate and handed it to him. The split roll was filled with ham, cheese, tomatoes, lettuce, oil and vinegar, mustard, and a touch of mayonnaise. All his favorite stuff. He had Caroline trained well.

He spent the rest of the day relaxing. He'd done what he'd planned, got the facts, got his proof of wrongdoing. He wasn't entirely sure who was to blame, but it was "them" for sure. Once again, he was a little vague as to who "they" were, but they were someone in charge of stuff. That he was sure of.

Dinner that night was more foil packets. This time Caroline had put boneless chicken in with tomato soup, onions, green beans, and more tiny potatoes. These would only take 20 minutes to cook.

Jonathan got out the vodka and fixed a drink. He thought about his podcast. He had a good idea of how to make it provocative and exciting. He could even record it here at the lake, with natural sounds in the background – if his phone didn't screw up again.

Dinner was good. He had an after-dinner drink and thought some more. It was quiet. Almost too quiet. He could hear the water lapping at the shore. He heard some bugs buzzing. He had no idea what kind they were.

"Look, bats!" Caroline cried. "Aren't they cute?"

No. Damn it. Jonathan looked up at the fluttering black blobs and forced himself not to duck. He gulped his vodka and fixed another one.

"You know, bats eat mosquitos," Caroline said.

No, he didn't know, and no, he didn't care. The bats eventually went away. Jonathan continued to listen to the near silence. But he gradually noticed soft laughter.

"Do you hear that?" he asked.

"What?" Caroline tilted her head to one side. "I hear the water and the cicadas. That's all."

"You must hear the kids laughing. It's disruptive. Their parents should shut them up so others can enjoy the lake."

"Huh. I don't hear them."

Jonathan gulped down his drink and then gritted his teeth. The sound was louder now. He stood up and walked over to pour another vodka.

"You must hear them by now. They're louder. They must be just through those trees." He peered into the dusk to see if he could spot the light of a campfire or lantern. But it was dark in that direction.

"Nope. Wait. I hear footsteps."

Jonathan did, too. Four hikers strode into view.

"Good evening," Caroline called to them.

"Hello!" one of the women said.

"Nice night," said another.

Jonathan jumped up, spilling the ice out of his now-empty glass. "Are you the parents of those kids?"

"No, it's just the four of us," one man said.

"What kids?" the other man asked.

"The ones laughing," Jonathan said. He clenched his fists. "Where are those kids? Why are they laughing at me?"

The four people each took a step back from the campsite.

"Uh, I don't hear anything but crickets," the first woman said.

"Cicadas," Caroline said.

"Oh, really? That's cool," the woman replied. "Thanks."

"How can you not hear them?" Jonathan said. "They're laughing at me."

"Uh. Well, good night," said the first man.

They trotted out of sight towards the other campsites further up the shore.

Jonathan walked over to the picnic table. His hand shook and vodka spilled onto the table.

"Honey, um, don't you think you've had enough?" Caroline said.

"No. I'm fine!" he snapped and sat down with his drink.

They sat in silence after that until full dark. Finally, Caroline got up.

"I'm going to bed. Bank the fire before you come in, will you?"

"I'm not stupid!" Jonathan snarled.

After another drink, he crawled into the tent. Caroline was pretending to sleep, he was sure of it, but he didn't feel like shaking her awake and getting into a fight now. He was tired and kept hearing those dumb kids laughing at him. Why weren't they in bed by now?

He did manage to sleep until a cry from Caroline woke him.

"Honey! The tent's on fire. Did you bank the campfire?"

Fire? Fire! He unzipped the tent and scrambled out, Caroline right after him. Jonathan had left a long stick, the one they used to poke the fire, leaning against the fire and pointing toward the tent. The campfire had burned the stick, which burned one of the tent's lines, which set the tent on fire.

"It's those kids, they did this!" he cried. "Hear them laughing at me?"

"No, I don't. Calm down, honey, it's not that bad." Caroline grabbed the two-gallon water jug and used it to throw water on the fire.

"Not that bad? Our tent is on fire. The forest is next." Jonathan turned and ran toward the lake. "Every man for himself!"

He waded out into the lake.

"Be careful!" Caroline called to him. "The water gets very deep awfully close to shore."

Voices began to cry from a distance as the light from the fire alerted other campers.

"Is everyone okay?" came a shout, along with the sound of running steps.

"We're fine," Caroline called out as other campers appeared. She'd nearly extinguished the flames. Someone appeared with a fire extinguisher and helped her.

Jonathan walked deeper into the lake. He didn't want to burn to death. He'd given this a lot of thought and burning to death was his number one way he didn't want to die. He took another step, and fell into deep water with a splash, as he reached the end of the shallow part.

"Help!" he cried, flailing around in the water, which was colder than he expected. The chuckling of the children got louder. He felt something bite his leg. Something with sharp teeth. Jonathan heard Caroline scream his name, but more water babies were biting him, pulling him down into the cold, deep water. He'd found the truth after all.

THE LONELY ALASKAN YUP'IK OF SKAGWAY

by Sergio 'ente per ente' PALUMBO

edited by Michele DUTCHER

"Listen to the silence… It speaks."

-Native American proverb

The air around seemed thick, restless, and unsettled, different from how it should have been - given the time of day and season. Usually, during the short summer of this area, there were sunny mornings with pleasant weather, accompanied by dewy gusts of wind. But today certainly wasn't one of those agreeable days, and there was nothing ordinary about the atmospheric conditions surrounding the man.

Ulf also perceived an odor of decay… *How could it have been?*

The man wished he could immediately force himself into the shades of the tall Adler trees of the forest that stretched nearby, along the cold river, to stay hidden, or just to be elsewhere at the moment. But he was right there and right now. He knew he couldn't move away; he also knew he couldn't even put one foot in front of the other.

The man wanted to be wrong, to be able to say that what he was watching before his own eyes wasn't true, that it wasn't happening now, that it just couldn't be possible. Certainly, he might try to pretend it wasn't real, but he couldn't deny what he undoubtedly saw - the scary ghastly appearance that stood before him! An image that had also begun approaching him.

Yet, he knew that this thing, though it could be perceived by smell, by eye, and by ear, was still not of this earth.

Ulf didn't believe he had been out of his mind when he had decided to come here. It had looked like an interesting thing to do, something that was necessary if he was to learn more about it all and appease his very curious mind.

When people spoke about afterwisdom...

Then, the unearthly breathing came closer to him; the man could feel it on his neck. Ulf hit wildly with both arms, tried to do his best, fighting both against that unbelievable being and his deep fear, before taking a couple of steps backwards, nearly tripping up over whatever it was that lay on the ground at his back.

Almost at the same moment he understood it was going to be over soon…

*****

Skagway. During the rest of the year, its population was around 1,200, but now it was almost summer, when the people who stayed in the area almost doubled to deal with more than 1,000,000 tourists coming from every country of the world. Indeed, its port was a very popular stop for ferries and ships full of visitors, the tourist trade being important for local business, as tourism had become one of the main sources of income for the town. Also, there was the very famous and historic White Pass and Yukon Route railroad nearby, part of the area's mining past, which was going to recommence services again over the next months.

As for Ulf Munsdal himself, well, he wasn't here merely as a tourist. The locals had a term for people like him; they called him 'cheechako', a newcomer who has never spent a winter in Alaska. The about 40-year-old man had come here, to the far North, because he had to pay a visit to a next of kin who lived here, in the Skagway's surroundings - someone he hadn't seen for years. Actually, he had other personal reasons to leave his hometown for a few days, having gone through a bad breakup with his girlfriend, so he really needed some time to consider his situation and think about what had gone wrong. Their relationship had lasted for about 5 years and now was over. Much of the blame was his fault, the man knew this very well, but not everything that had happened was as a consequence of his behavior, this was also true.

As Ulf walked the streets full of old wooden buildings in the historic center of the small borough – there were about 100 buildings from the late 1800s and early 1900s - he happened to remember the many movies that had chosen Skagway itself as part of the setting for stories based upon famous books of the past like the world-renowned Jack London's 'The Call of the Wild', or John Wayne's film 'North to Alaska', that had been shot nearby twenty years before he was born, or so he had read somewhere. Many of the best sights in town could be easily seen on foot, and it seemed that the residents had gone to great lengths to maintain (or recreate) the original appearance of the place.

Of course, several things had changed since the days of ill-reputed 'Soapy' Smith, when the population of the old trading post had increased enormously eventually reaching 30,000, made up mainly of American prospectors from the Gold Era. During those years, just after that very valuable metal had been found in a region of Canada's Yukon Territory, a lot of stores, saloons, and offices had lined the streets of

Skagway and the town had soon become, by June 1898, the largest city in Alaska. Undoubtedly, as miners were busy in their journeys to the Yukon, control of the town had reverted to the more unscrupulous people, the outlaws and shysters of the period. We all had heard of such stories, of course. Skagway had soon become their base of operations and had in its grip most of the businesses throughout the urban area.

But that time was long gone by now, the man thought. The big attractions of the region remained - its mountains and the fjords, along with its wildlife and the forests, which was exactly what tourists came to visit and photograph.

Ulf didn't know why his uncle Frank, who lived here and was to be his host, had decided to come to Alaska which was a long way from the rest of the United States, not to mention the city of Great Falls where Ulf and his uncle were both born. But his uncle had probably always been attracted to this place, even before he had started studying to become a naturalist.

Ulf remembered that the elderly man had always been deeply involved in discussions about how to best use Alaskan lands in the future. This had, in fact, become a sort of bitter controversy back home when he was still a boy, focusing on arguments about the threats coming from the oil industries. Ulf hadn't understood much of what was being said at that time, maybe he just was too young or simply didn't care, but with all the disasters that had sadly occurred, both at sea and on the coast, in the following years he eventually figured out what his uncle meant.

Surprisingly, only about 900,000 people lived in Alaska now, of whom only one-fifth were born in the state itself. Unlike other states, Alaska had no county governments, but was instead organized into boroughs and municipalities, much to Ulf's surprise when he had first heard of it. There was also a saying here, as he had discovered from his uncle, that went more or less this way: 'the more winters you experience here, the more Alaskan you are.' Of course, he didn't plan on spending much time here, and certainly not a long winter in the future, but the words of his uncle made him see what it might mean to a local, anyway.

If a Texan was known for stubbornness and fierce headstrongness, an Alaskan attitude centered around their ability to survive and adapt to the icy conditions of the country.

Anyway, as Ulf had discovered, getting here was expensive. But the scenery immediately repaid you for the long journey, at least by what he could see now: the spectacular views, dotted with national parks, were full of glaciers, high mountain ranges, island chains, broad river valleys, and wide coastal plains. Moreover, the largest population of bears, wolves, eagles and even musk oxen in the U.S. could all be found right here. So, what more could tourists ask for? Beyond that, though separated from the rest of the country by Canada's Yukon Territory and British Columbia, Alaska was also the largest state in the U.S.A.!

Today had started exactly the same as yesterday. Ulf had woken up around 9:00 AM –

actually, he liked to sleep a lot - and had taken the time to walk the streets of the town before going to a bar to have a meal. The man did not have much to do, and he just wanted to rest, so he could think about this and of that, just enjoying his stay. He planned on getting to the port after noon to take a few more photos. He had already taken several, but the scenery was very inspirational, and he liked to update his collection of images. He had gotten accustomed to take a lot of photos since he had first trained to be a professional tattoo artist, years ago. You never knew when a beautiful photo, or a drawing, might come in handy for a job.

He was near Broadway at Second Avenue when he first spotted a lonely dark-haired Native. He must have been 50, maybe a bit older, and was wearing a T-shirt that showed-off his large shoulders, a pair of trousers made of sealskin, and fish-skin boots.

The thing that most attracted Ulf wasn't exotic traits or his face. After all, they had Native Americans in Great Falls, even if they were from other tribes. No, what caught his eye was the strange, large, colorful tattoo he saw on his left arm, a tattoo sleeve that went all the way down to his hand. Being a professional tattoo artist himself, that strange ink drawing was new to him, and he knew a lot about symbols because of his job and everything he had studied. Of course, it was necessary to keep current about new trends and new designs, but it was necessary to have an extensive knowledge of tribal symbols and all the other popular pictures and depictions that customers generally wanted to have tattooed on their bodies these days.

Ulf considered that he knew, and had studied, many styles and designs of Native American tattoos, but couldn't recall having seen anything like this one, which was strange, because he was very knowledgeable in his profession. Certainly, there were some designs on the human skin that occurred when a substance had been rubbed into a wound as the result of some kind of accident. For example, some coal miners could develop characteristic tattoos owing to coal dust getting into their wounds which happened to be particularly difficult to remove as they tended to be spread across several layers of human skin. But Ulf was certain this wasn't the case.

The design appeared to be comprised of dark and violet shapes, thin arms and other curved stars that looked similar to a face, with very unusual features. It emitted a sense of fear when you focused on it. *An elaborate, unbelievable drawing that came from an ancient design, indeed!* Possibly, it represented a very strange, or fabled animal, or a creature from legends he had never seen before. He had many questions about its origins.

Ulf really wanted to know something more about the unusual tattoo, and he thought it might be interesting to have a firsthand account about its story and its meaning. He even thought that he might have it included in his personal library of images to be used as a tattoo, one day or another. Maybe the simplest thing was to directly approach that man and ask him some questions about the artwork on his arm. However, as Ulf soon understood, he had perhaps waited for too long before acting. It was possible that he wouldn't have a chance to interview the Native American anyway, given his very peculiar behavior and the very short time he had remained around for his visit.

Ulf had first seen him by 10:00 AM, and when he had gotten back to that same alley by 11:00 AM - having decided to eventually approach him - the Native seemed to have disappeared from the town.

As Ulf asked around, he stumbled into one local man near a one-stop shop with a funny and worn-out woolen hat who strangely seemed to be afraid of that Native. He wasn't very talkative, but the few words Ulf was able to pry out of him were that he was reputed to be 'a cursed man', which the local had said with a certain regret or fear in his eyes. This, at first, left him speechless. Maybe that individual wanted just to make fun of him, considering him to be only a stranger who had travelled from a distant place and didn't seem to know much about Skagway or that could be easily deceived. Maybe there was something else going on…

Then, a pensive Ulf thought that it might be interesting to sell an unknown tattoo that had never been seen elsewhere, rarely spotted even in Skagway, that had a cursed story about it, that had come from a Native area that was already full of legendary tales, and that had undergone a difficult historical exploration. This work of art might prove to be a great addition to his collection of tattoos that he was used to selling to the customers in his shop back in Great Falls. Several people would obviously be attracted to it, and its design might become a 'new trend' in a way. Who knows? He had to discover much more about that.

As Ulf walked back to his uncle's house, many thoughts were on his mind. It was strange to think that, before the importation of the Polynesian word 'tattoo', or 'tattow', to Europe and the Western civilization in the 18th century, the practice of tattooing had long been seen as painting, scarring, or staining. Now they all were living in a world where copyrighted tattoo designs were ordinarily mass-produced and sent to tattoo artists to be displayed in many tattoo parlors for the purpose of providing both inspiration and ready-made images to customers.

As of today, certain elite tattoos served also as marks of status and rank, symbols of religious devotion, decorations for bravery, amulets meant for protection, and as punishment, like the marks of outcasts, slaves, and convicts. The symbolism and impact of tattoos had always varied from place to place. People choose to be tattooed for artistic, sentimental/memorial, or magical reasons, and to symbolize their identification with particular outlaw groups, including the mob, or certain ethnic groups. Facial designs were also worn to indicate lineage from times of old.

As most tattoos in the United States were done once by Polynesian and Japanese amateurs, tattoo artists had long ago begun to be in great demand in port cities all over the world. Then the practice of tattooing quickly became popular during the American Civil War among soldiers and sailors, on both sides, Union and Confederate. The tradition had continued later and was still used nowadays among military servicemen. Anyway, men were slightly more likely to have a tattoo than women. Ulf was very thankful that now tattoos were recognized as a legitimate art form, widely appreciated from the later teen years to middle age. For sure, he couldn't think of a better job for himself.

About the Natives of the northern part of this continent, Ulf remembered to have once read in a book sad tales that, during the previous centuries, French and British sailors had arrived at the icy lands of North America over the course of their travels and explorations. These explorers abducted Inuit men and women from Canada with facial tattoos to put them on public display, although those people quickly died from European illnesses.

While thinking again about the strange drawing on the Native's arm he had just spotted before, the man reminded himself of the fact that usually Native Americans made use of objects such as bony remains or rocks for the tattoo to be prepared. Then, it was filled with soot or dyes to stain in the wound. For example, he already knew that tattoos on a Native woman's chin were meant for several purposes under some social circumstances. Most notably, they were tattooed on that portion of their body as part of the ritual of maturity. Chin stripes also served to protect women during enemy raids, in the ancient times...

Ulf had never read anywhere about a tattoo with a strange shape similar to that one he had seen that day on that arm. What might it mean?

Anyway, that lonely Native man, who was called Qimmiq by the locals, happened to be from the Yup'ik people and was seen around rarely, coming into town by boat from near Lutak Inlet, where he had apparently returned after buying what he needed. He was also said to live alone somewhere not far from Lutak itself, in Haines Borough, bordered to the West by the Takshanuk Mountains, maybe deep inside the Haines State Forest itself or on the far side of Chilkoot Lake, in the region of the Tlingit people of Alaska. Ulf didn't know much about that part of the area, but he was aware that just a single road led 10 miles from the mouth of the lake, southeast along the south side of Lutak Inlet, and the west side of Chilkoot Inlet to Haines. There was not much out there for civilized citizens, within that very large stretch of land full of endless forests where only about 20 families resided, unless you wanted to live alone and be by yourself, of course. Which was a possibility in his case.

Winters were commonly mild here, at least by Alaskan standards, with an average January high temperature around 33 degrees F., but the man imagined that it might be a hard life existing there during the coldest months, especially when the lows sometimes plummeting to 20 degrees below zero.

So, why would anyone make their home there? Was it just recreation, beautiful scenery with icy conditions, eagles in the sky, bears and wolves around? Could anyone enjoy living off fish and seals? *Why should anyone want to stay there for the whole year?* He, frankly, couldn't understand it. Maybe there was something else, he thought. Or maybe the Native just loved the place, that way of living, or didn't like having neighbors.

Anyway, as Ulf asked around for more information, he was told that the Yup'ik was usually kindhearted and that he looked calm without showing off any resentment against anyone. So, why did somebody tell Ulf this was a 'cursed man'? He also didn't talk very much, rarely interacting with other locals nor with tourists for that matter. The lonely man named Qimmiq simply came to town, briefly walked the streets in Skagway, bought what he had to buy and was back in his boat within a few hours.

Ulf wanted to discover much more about him and his very strange tattoo. At least, this was what he promised him himself, and he did intend to keep it.

*****

Ulf knew that in that area of Alaska there had been three main Native populations since the most ancient times: the warrior Tlingit, the Yup'ik, and Iiupiat, or so he remembered to have heard once from his uncle. Alaska also seemed to have been inhabited by someone who had been the first of all the Native tribes, for longer than anywhere else in the Americas.

The name Yup'ik itself meant 'real people' and they were the largest language group in that area. Though they had long been separated from their very distant relatives who were still living in Asia by the Bering Sea and, today, also separated by national boundaries. Long before direct contact with Europeans, they had continued to interact for centuries - using seaworthy crafts for long distance travel- visiting, trading, hunting and periodically engaging in warfare with each other. Nowadays, the Yup'ik Natives that lived in this country stayed mostly along the rivers and streams of southwestern Alaska or along the coast and islands.

Three days later, Qimmiq appeared again. Unfortunately, Ulf wasn't in town, but when he was back, an old shop-owner told him that Qimmiq had just left the previous morning. "Damn!" he cursed, "I missed the chance to talk with him again."

So, this was why the man decided that it would be up to him to take it upon himself and go to the Native's home, if he wanted to learn more about Qimmiq and his unusual tattoo. It wasn't an easy journey, as he had to wake up early next morning and to take a boat and then drive along a difficult road that would take him to Qimmiq's doorstep. But he did it, and it was past noon when he reached the point along the river where the wooden cabin where Qimmiq stayed could be found. There was no way to be mistaken, Ulf thought as he arrived, because there was no other cabin around.

As he got out of the car and walked along the gravel shoreline, his eyes spotted the features of the man. It was Qimmiq without any doubt. He collected firewood from the ground next to the Alder trees and didn't seem to be in a hurry. Ulf hadn't noticed the Native watching him as he walked, but he was certain that man had seen him from afar as soon as he came up the shoreline.

"Hello! I am looking for Qimmiq. That's probably you, isn't it?" the man asked the Yup'ik as he approached the cabin ahead, situated next to a tall White Spruce. "I was told what you are called by the locals, in Skagway. They know you well…"

"I doubt it," the other replied in a plain, and uninterested tone, without even turning to face Ulf.

The tattoo artist considered how to break the ice with the man, so to say, as the Native made it clear he wasn't eager to speak with him. "Well, let me introduce myself. I'm Ulf Munsdal, from Great Falls, in the Minnesota, and I stay in Skagway now. I mean, it's not where I live, but I'm a guest at my uncle's house in town."

The other man didn't stop what he was doing and didn't directly look at him, but he did answer Ulf. "So, Mr. Ulf Munsdal, what really brings you here? Do you want to experience the wilderness?"

"Actually, no. Well, I mean, you really have wonderful scenery here, and this is really a great place for a home…" the tattoo artist asserted in a chatty tone.

"So, Mr. Ulf, if you're not here for the wilderness scenery, what does bring you here?" the man repeated in a cold voice.

"See, getting right to the point, I like that. I came all the way to this lonely place where you live with only wilderness, wildlife viewing, and a cold climate. But you like it, staying here alone and eating fish and birds and such. I can respect that. But it must be difficult to stay here all year long, so what could you tell me about how you exist way out here?" Ulf had said this, trying to make small talk. But the other man still seemed reluctant to speak with him. "I am especially interested in that unusual tattoo on your arm. I'm a professional tattoo artist, you know, and I have never seen anything like that. Could you tell me about its meaning, and the story behind it?"

Qimmiq kept himself busy moving some bags from one point of his campsite to another. "What if I don't want to tell you?"

"Why not?" the man asked the Yup'ik.

"Why should I?" Qimmiq replied.

"I could pay you for that information. Why would you refuse? It's just a simple question."

The other man growled something incomprehensible.

"By the way, I am curious about your name as well. Does it have a special meaning in your language? I hope you don't mind me asking."

"Qimmiq is a girl's name, actually. I'm a Yup'ik, and among us, differently from other Natives, children are named after the last person in the community to die, whether that name be of a man or woman," the other explained, showing a little more interest in this question. Then, he fell silent again. It was becoming obvious that Qimmiq wouldn't be revealing a lot today.

"Do you live here, Qimmiq?"

"As you can see with your own eyes," the Native replied.

"You know? If I may say, it's strange that you don't have a modern motorboat, or an ATV. It looks like either of those would be useful and necessary in these lands."

"Too much cash needed for those," the Native retorted.

"I know that since 1971 there have been some regional Native corporations that have created service-providing structures to assist the Native peoples with many of their needs."

"I don't care about them," Qimmiq simply said.

"But you certainly need money, everyone does. As I said, I could pay for you telling me your story. Of course, not much, as I'm not rich. But a little money is better than nothing. That tattoo might be a perfect addition to my collection of tattoo designs, and I would pay to know something more about it."

At this point, the Yup'ik Native grew angry at his interest in reproducing the drawing. "You must not do that!" he cried out.

Ulf was caught completely by surprise. 'Why not?', he wondered. What might be the reason for Qimmiq demanding that the tattoo not be reproduced?

Was it something connected to some religious belief or superstition maybe? "So, you don't want me to know anything more about it. Well at least tell me this, please. I know that the main social organization of the Yup'ik is the family, which is an important integral part of the village. So, what about you? Why do you live alone? Is that how you choose to live? You don't even have a dog, differently from most other people in your tribe."

The man stopped moving for a while and looked at him directly. "Family...yes, I had one once..."

"A wife? Sons? I know that in the Yup'ik tradition the houses belong to the women, who have the duty to raise the children and teach the girls to become homemakers."

"No wife, no sons...too dangerous...but I had my mother and my father," Qimmiq added.

"What happened?"

"It was long ago…" the Yup'ik said. "They loved me deeply but they made a mistake. A terrible mistake."

"What kind of mistake?"

The Native sat down on a large rock and stared at Ulf. Qimmiq seemed to come to grips with the consideration that Ulf wasn't going to leave without listening to his story. "When I was born, my parents were still young, about 19-years-old, and they wished me the best of lives, of course. But they were also superstitious. Many people in my village were superstitious at that time, and many still are today. So, they wanted me to be protected, and which is why they asked an angakut, a shaman, to put a powerful tattoo on my body. They loved me and wanted me to be safe, but they put me in the wrong hands…"

"How did that happen?" Ulf asked with a curious look.

"The old shaman told them that he would make use of a great and ancient tattoo that would always protect me, but this wasn't what he did in the end…"

The other kept listening, eager to hear what was coming next.

"Actually, that old shaman had long been secretly in love with Hayicanako, my mother. And he had been very dejected when he had heard that she had eventually chosen another man, and that he would never have her one day. So, that is why he lied! And he put a damn' curse on my body instead of a defensive tattoo…" the Yup'ik said angrily.

"What was the curse?"

"That shaman was very capable and skilled. He knew of some dark arts of the Yup'ik people that almost nobody else remembered. So, he made use of his dark practices and damn' knowledge and put this tattoo on my left hand, on the small finger of a small hand of a small child that would someday be a full-grown man, and who would not be able to get rid of it, because it couldn't be removed." The Native stared at him.

"But, I don't understand. The tattoo is on your arm, and I see that one of your fingers is missing…" It was only at that moment, as Qimmiq was telling him this, that Ulf noticed that the other man had only four fingers on his left hand.

"Yes, I had one of my fingers cut off long ago. It happened when I was six, and I did it myself, cutting it off when I saw what that tattoo could do, but it wasn't enough…"

"What?" a shaken Ulf exclaimed.

"As I told you, the damn' tattoo can't be removed. It just went from my cut-off finger to my arm, it walked across the skin and changed its place, really! So, it became apparent that even cutting off my arm would have been of no use. This curse is a part of me forever. It was set to be a part of me ever since the day that man put it on my body thanks to his dark arts. And so, I still have it on my skin with all the very ominous consequences it brings along with it…" the Yup'ik revealed in a low voice.

"That is a really scary tale," Ulf said, though he certainly didn't believe what Qimmiq was telling him.

"If that man was filled with hatred against your family, why didn't he simply try to kill them or you?"

"Oh, he did much worse than that."

"But I still don't understand. Why did you cut off one of your fingers? This is madness… What did you find, or imagine, that the tattoo was capable of doing?" Ulf inquired of him.

"It happened when I was six, as I told you. The power of the tattoo itself stays in the ink and in its drawing. That power was activated anytime I was wronged and became upset or angered. At that time, my father made my angry, for a stupid reason that was of little importance. I can't even remember what he did now. But I, as a small child, took what he did to heart, not seeing that my father was just trying to help me. My anger, my foolish resentment, made the tattoo release its curse for the first time, and it harmed my father. He died shortly thereafter because of the wounds, much to my regret and my mother's sorrow. I didn't want that to happen, but I didn't know that my father would die. Nobody knew about it those days.

When I figured out what had happened, I took action. But, as I said, with no result. There's no escape from this curse, it will be with me until I die!"

"I have never heard a story like this before. A sad, and unbelievable story," Ulf interjected.

"Anyway, my sad tale is absolutely true. Everything happened exactly as I said. But I'm not the only one that the shaman wronged," the Yup'ik added. "With the passing of the years, other people that made me angry, or who crossed my path and showed hatred, or were open aggressive against me, activated the tattoo, though unwillingly and unbeknownst to themselves. That unconscious desire of mine made them pay for their insolence, leaving me holding the better hand in the end. And so, they all suffered because of my cursed tattoo. They also died …"

"This is really… I don't know what to say… I just can't find the words! So, is that why some locals call you a 'cursed man'?" the tattoo artist asked him.

"Now you must go. Move away, go back to your world of certainties, of modern appliances and science. This is something you must not meddle with," the Yup'ik said, gesturing to Ulf to leave.

"You could write a story about your experiences. You could even explain the meaning of that tattoo and its tradition."

"This is not tradition! This is not a legend!" the Native objected. "This is true, and you must go away. Now! Before it's too late. Or the Taqriaqsuit, the damned spirit the shaman connected to my body because of that tattoo, will be called to this place. And it will be coming for you…"

"What did you say?" Ulf looked at him, appearing to be a little afraid. Qimmiq was really upset by now. *Perhaps this man was going to become wild or dangerous, or worse. Was it possible?*

"The Taqriaqsuit are also known as the Shadow People. They live like we do in a world like our own. Their world, however, is beyond our perception. They are almost never seen, but when conditions are right, or when they are called, the Taqriaqsuit can be heard, and they will come. You have to go… Before it's too late, I said, now! You…really are making me angry and you mustn't. That would not be a good thing at all!"

"Please, calm down," Ulf told the Native , trying to calm him .

"It's too late. Too late," Qimmiq repeated in an other-worldly tone and gestured to him another time.

"Too late for what? I tell you, you could make money out of the strange story about your unusual tattoo. Listen to me…"

Then, everything happened too quickly for anyone to react, or do anything about it. The air became heavy, and silence settled in over everything around the two men.

Ulf felt ill at ease almost at once.

There was a sudden eruption of smoke that happened unexpectedly before him, coming from the arm of the Native. The mist formed a roughly human shape out of that unearthly ink. Its features were indistinct, except for its clawed hands and hairy face.

The Taqriaqsuit? That was unbelievable, how could it be? Qimmiq, standing next to the strange being, was silent now and didn't even seem to be conscious. It was exactly as if he wasn't there anymore but his body was still there. For certain, not his mind.

Protuberances stuck from the back of the creature's tall body that made it appear more fearful, terrifying Ulf. It seemed that some portions of a human being had been unusually redeveloped and rearranged in a way no one could have ever imagined or would recognize as human.

The overall figure was difficult to explain. The cruel face was a combination of wood and bone. The features reminded the man of the wooden costumes used during the masked rituals the Yup'ik danced in, which had long played an important role in the traditions of the Great Northwest. He had witnessed one such ceremony at a Fur market during his short stay in town. Its stance and way of behaving clearly indicated that the creature really did have power, and that it also undoubtedly was not afraid of anyone or anything. Its presence commanded respect and admiration.

The unbelievable being seemed to have a deeper need. It didn't have any pleasing features nor was it here for his good. It looked like it was just in this place for his blood. It wanted to devour Ulf's blood and fear!

It spoke then, inside Ulf's worried head. Its actions soon followed. The Taqriaqsuit had something to do. Its moves were bloody and immediate. They were unmistakable, and only meant pain and death to the man that had dared follow Qimmiq into that part of the forest.

Only the flowing water of the river, and the wilderness were left behind once the creature had completed what it had come to do and disappeared.

The Yup'ik sadly looked at the remains of Ulf's dead body on the ground and a deep sensation of sorrow, a grinding helplessness, filled him.

Again. It had sadly, and unwillingly, happened another time…

KAMAITACHI INCIDENT

by Toshiya Kamei

The sultry morning air lashes against my face. Cicadas scream in the temple nearby. I squint against the glare of the rising sun, and I try my hardest to keep up with Sasuke's brisk pace. His chonmage knot bounces on his shaved pate as he hurries toward the outskirts of Edo.

A half-moon still floats in the gray morning sky, but it's already getting hot. Beads of sweat roll down my forehead toward my nose. I dab at my brow with the sleeve of my kimono as I follow Sasuke to the riverbank. As always, I have trouble keeping up with him. My leg bothers me, but my limp is more pronounced now, as if my bones know what my brain refuses to consider.

Certain cities, like Edo, wake up early. The streets already bustle with life. Rickshaws race each other in search of a customer. Donkeys pull creaking carts, occasionally dropping huge balls of dung in their tracks. A young housewife rushing toward the market comes to a sudden halt and bows reverently before an elderly samurai. With bundles of books in their hands, school-age children zigzag around puddles of water.

Sasuke has his kimono hem tucked up into his obi, exposing his bare legs. His kimono sleeves are tied out of the way with a tasuki. On the other hand, we women are expected to cover ourselves even in boiling temperatures. At a time like this, I envy men. Only slightly.

Edo's weather, particularly summer, doesn't agree with me. Winter is my kind of season. After all, like many other winter-born girls, I was named Ofuyu after the season of my birth. While I maintain an outward facade of cool competence, I inwardly feel like a dog panting, its tongue hanging out.

When we arrive at the crime scene, a multitude has already formed a noisy, jostling circle around a cordoned-off area on the riverbank, threatening to spill over. Onlookers crane their necks and shove each other to get a better look. Morbid curiosity runs rampant through the crowd.

"Get out of our way, coming through!" Sasuke shouts, not bothering to hide his irritation.

I mutter half-hearted apologies and elbow my way through the sweaty bodies.

Someone pushes into me from behind, and I stagger forward, accidentally stepping on feet. A middle-aged woman yelps like a kicked cat and glares at me.

I reach into my kimono sleeve, pull out my jitte, and wield it to indicate I'm here on official business. The bodies around me step back and make way for us.

"What do we have here?" I mumble as I crouch down by the lifeless body lying among loose pebbles. A wave of cologne assaults my nose and stings my eyes. The sparkle of fireflies from last night still lingers. Several gnats already spiral around their prey. Except for a gaping, crescent-shaped wound in his throat, the corpse looks intact. The victim has about twenty ryo on him, but his wallet has been left untouched. Nothing of value missing. Blood has caked around his half-agape mouth.

"A serial killer is on the loose," Sasuke says, shaking his head. "We won't be able to keep this out of the tabloids much longer."

This is the fifth time someone has been murdered in a similar fashion. Like the previous four cases, the victim has this peculiar wound. It looks as though a sickle slit his neck just below his left ear, tore through his Adam's apple, and severed the carotid artery, killing him instantly.

"Poor devil. He didn't know what hit him," I say and turn to Sasuke. "My hunch tells me a yokai is behind this." Often, my hunches turn out to be correct. I don't want to think about five years ago. I don't want to feel the pain. I don't want to rub my leg, to feel the scars twisting silver in the skin. But the longer this case goes, the more the nightmares hunt me like ravens.

"Yokai?" A shade of doubt crosses his face. "You can't be serious." It's sheer bad luck that my partner is a skeptic.

"I'd bet the farm on it. A kamaitachi, to be exact." I was born with a gift for magic, and my magical prowess has only grown with age. Now I can smell a monster from miles away.

When the first case occurred, we theorized the murderer had attacked the victim from behind and slashed his throat toward his ear. However, a closer look revealed his wound was shallow on the side and deepened around his throat. No matter how skillful the murderer is, it's impossible to slit the throat instantly in such a manner. Which leads me to deduce that these killings aren't a human's work.

"I don't know about that," Sasuke says. "I still think it's a lunatic."

"But what's his motive?"

"Beats me."

"It's a yokai. It has no motive. Only base instincts. Trust me on this." Even so, Sasuke is too levelheaded to believe in the supernatural.

Sasuke frowns. He won't budge. His eyes shine with determination. He wasn't my partner when a nue mangled my leg with its fangs. He'll never know what it was like. How my summoning spell—how foolish I was, believing I could summon and defeat a killer beast on my own—went horribly wrong.

"Who's the victim?" I ask.

"Ryunosuke."

"The kabuki actor? No wonder he looks familiar." I think aloud out of habit. Hearing myself talk always activates my brain. "I've seen fliers touting his ethereal beauty all over town. No doubt his looks had women swooning at his feet."

Even as a corpse, Ryunosuke is still better-looking than most men around. Aloof and mysterious, he had a sizable, devoted following, consisting mostly of young ladies. I'd have mooned over him, too, if I were that kind of girl. Lucky for me, I don't swing that way. Which saves me a lot of headaches and heartaches.

"Any witnesses?"

Sasuke points his chin to a pale girl fidgeting with her badly manicured fingers. "This is Okiku. The president of Ryunosuke's fan club." When I glance at her, I notice how she trembles despite the heat. "She says she followed Ryunosuke and Kinji, his fellow actor, from the theater."

While Sasuke continues to examine the body, I approach Okiku with a warm smile designed to put her at ease. She tells me that when they reached the bridge, the two men argued. She wasn't close enough to catch a whiff of their conversation. They struggled, pushing, and shoving one another, and Ryunosuke fell off the bridge into the water.

"Does this look familiar to you?" I show Okiku the kaiken found in the river under the bridge. A white crane is embroidered on its hilt, indicating it belongs to a woman. Many women carry one inside their obi for self-defense, and I'm no exception. I unsheathe it, and sunlight flashes bright on the sharp blade.

Okiku turns paler. "No." She hesitates for a moment before shaking her head.

Her story doesn't add up. She wants us to believe Ryunosuke fell into the water, drowned, and washed up on the riverbank. But his body shows no signs of drowning. His kimono isn't even wet. She's not fooling anyone. Still, we have nothing else to go by, certainly not enough to detain her any longer, so we cut her loose.

When I return to the bugyo-sho's office, I lock myself in the study and hit the books. While Sasuke is on the beat sniffing around for evidence, I read up on the kamaitachi as much as I can.

In certain regions of Japan, such as Echigo and Shinano, the kamaitachi—sickle-weasel—is blamed for inexplicable cuts on humans and animals alike. Sometimes a dust devil blows and tears the victim's skin, leaving a sickle-shaped wound.

I grab a book from the shelf and thumb through the pages. My fingers stop at a page showing a drawing of a kamaitachi riding a dust devil, wielding its long, sharp claws. I stare at the image until my vision becomes blurry. The victims' faces flash before my eyes in a slide show, one after another, each worse than the last, until my own face peers back at me. My hair, lank and matted with blood. My screams like burning alive. I hold my twisted leg and stare into the dark eyes of the yokai I thought I could control.

The carnage haunts me asleep and awake, but I can't keep my eyes open any longer. I rest my head on a pile of books in an attempt to get some shut-eye at least until my headache goes away. The victims deserve better.

A scream wakes me. It's my own. I blink a few times, then sit up. The morning sun seeps through cracks in the closed blinds. Any unfamiliar sound or sight makes me jump. Respite will come only when we solve the case.

I can't do it again. I can't possibly try the summoning spell again. Even if that's the only surefire way to bring the kamaitachi close. I hold the wakizashi that once belonged to my late father. Sheathing and unsheathing it, I contemplate the blade. It's considerably longer than my kaiken. The kaiken is too short to repel the kamaitachi's claws. I slide the palm of my left hand lightly down the edge. A shiver runs through me like cold rain. I make a mental note to wear the wakizashi before going out this morning.

At dawn, a young man shows up at the gate. His gaudy attire tells me he's an entertainer of sorts.

"I'm turning myself in," the young man says. "I'm Kinji." A few years junior to Ryunosuke, Kinji has exquisite features. As women aren't allowed on stage, young male actors play all female roles. Onnagata, actors who perform highly stylized versions of femininity, are the stars in the thespian constellation. Their incandescent star power blinds those who come too close to them. Yet they burn brightly and then fade from view.

"You pushed Ryunosuke into the river?"

"Yes, ma'am." He nods, looking down. His apparent fragility reminds me of my orchid that died last year.

That's a lie, but I don't know why he's making it up. "Why did you do it?" I go along with him for now.

"I meant no harm. He was like a big brother to me." Kinji falls into silence.

"I know you're innocent."

Kinji audibly gasps.

"Would you care to tell me why you lied?"

He remains silent.

"I don't have all day." I let out a sigh of frustration. "Under ordinary circumstances, I'd have to let you go. However, thanks to the tabloids, everyone thinks you've killed him. I'd better keep you here until things calm down."

Ryunosuke's fanatic fans are thirsty for revenge. Although I'm furious with Kinji for derailing our investigation, I don't want an angry mob to turn on him. I escort him to the zashikiro, a private jail cell. He's too delicate to be locked up with common criminals. He sits on the tatami floor behind wooden bars. The door squeaks shut.

Shortly later, Okiku shows up, insisting that she needs to see Kinji. One glimpse at the determination in her eyes tells me she won't take no for an answer. I lead her to Kinji's jail and leave them alone.

She bows as our paths cross on her way out.

"May I have a word with you?" She looks paler than before, and her voice trembles.

"Sure."

"He didn't kill Ryunosuke. He's innocent." Okiku looks down, fidgeting with her fingers.

"I know. Perhaps you could illuminate me." I look her in the eye as she looks up. "Why did you two lie?"

"It was Kinji's idea." She pauses, blinking away tears. "He thinks I killed Ryunosuke over a disagreement. He told me to get rid of my kaiken and lie to you."

"A disagreement?"

She nods.

"Would you care to elaborate on that?"

It takes me a while to grasp the whole picture, but their discord was preceded by a love triangle gone wrong. The two actors were once inseparable. Ryunosuke took the younger man under his wing, and Kinji's career began to flourish. Everything was rosy between the two. Until Okiku came between them, that is. Kinji's affections gradually shifted away from Ryunosuke and toward Okiku. When Ryunosuke turned up dead, Kinji suspected Okiku had something to do with it. After all, she was the last person to see Ryunosuke alive. Kinji concocted his story and turned himself in.

I head to Osen's teahouse to relax and reflect on the case. As I slide the door open and step inside, a wind chime above my head makes sweet melodious sounds.

"Irasshaimase!" Osen greets me in a singsong tone and peers out from behind the door. Her voice is even sweeter. Whenever I feel like blowing off steam, I seek her company. Her demure beauty and soft voice never fail to soothe my frayed nerves.

"Are kamaitachi real?" Osen asks when she brings a teacup on a tray and sets it in front of me.

"Sure they are." I steal a furtive glance at her and quickly avert my eyes. Her cheeks blush pink. "Let me tell you—"

"No, stop. You know I'm easily frightened." Osen flashes a faint smile and waves her hand. "What do they look like? Are they weasels with sickles?"

"Don't be silly." I half-heartedly scold her. "In short, the kamaitachi slits the victim's throat with its claws."

"Oh, how frightening. Why don't you catch it and declaw it?"

"It's easier said than done, but that may be the only way. Summoning a yokai involves considerable risk. You can't do it without consequence. I know that truth all too well."

"The kamaitachi is in over its head with you." Osen keeps a stern face, but her eyes tell me she's half-teasing. Her beguiling femininity takes my breath away. I control the urge to reach out and touch her.

"Don't pull my leg. I'm the one who's in over her head. Honestly, I'm at my wits' end here. My partner pays me no heed. I don't know how to stop the killings." I sigh. Osen is so disarming, and I feel comfortable confiding in her.

"I'm sure you'll find a way." Osen sounds hopeful. She sits across the table. She reaches out, holds my hand, and gives it a gentle squeeze. Her hand feels cold and good there. My heart pounds in my ears, and I feel my cheeks flush. "May your magic be your guide." Her voice reveals sincerity and affection.

As I stare into the depths of her dark eyes, I struggle to find the appropriate words. Will we ever go beyond exchanging friendly banter?

The door opens nosily, and Sasuke steps inside, short of breath. I click my tongue. Osen pulls away her hand.

"Here you are. Let's go!" Sasuke gestures for me to follow him, oblivious to Osen. I hastily get up and bow to Osen. My gaze lingers on her a moment too long. She wears an indulgent smile.

"Where? What's happened?" I turn to Sasuke.

"A farmer stumbled upon another body." He wipes his brow and breaks into a sprint. I follow a few steps behind.

161

When we reach the open field, we spot a middle-aged farmer's body lying lifelessly on the grass. We kneel and examine the latest victim. He has the same wound in his throat as the previous victims. We look up and exchange looks.

"The kamaitachi strikes again." I grit my teeth.

"You don't say."

Seeing this man's body leaves me crumpled. Some last resistance falls away. I must be brave and think of the victims. The future victims. Even if that means opening another dark door. I need to stop this monster. Now.

I close my eyes and clasp my hands together over my chest, right above my obi, with my index fingers outstretched, tips touching. I chant a spell to summon the kamaitachi.

"What the devil are you doing?" Sasuke's voice reveals a sense of alarm.

Suddenly, the sky gets dark. I look but see no signs of rain. My skin breaks out in goosebumps despite the heat. A fierce gust blows down long stalks of susuki grass. The gust changes its direction and strikes our faces. Pebbles hit all over our bodies. I duck and cover my face with one hand.

"What the hell?" Sasuke gasps. A weasel-like creature glides toward us, blandishing its blade-like claws.

"Watch out!" I cry. I give Sasuke a shove and push him to the ground. The kamaitachi misses its target, barely grazing his cheek.

Sasuke shrieks as bright blood oozes out of the cut flesh. I run to him and hold him in my arms.

His face twists in pain. He holds my wrist hard enough to bruise it. "The bastard got me." Sasuke smiles weakly before passing out.

"It's only a scratch. You're not going to die." I shake him hard, but he gives no response. "Wake up! Don't pass out now." I click my tongue in frustration.

I lay him on the ground and spring to my feet.

In the distance, the kamaitachi rides a dust devil, darting through the air like an arrow. It speeds toward me, slashing the air with its sickle-shaped claws. I pull my wakizashi out of my obi and chant the mantra my nurse taught me when I was a little girl. My mantra wills a whirlpool of dust into existence. The whirl rises and clashes with the kamaitachi. A sudden surge of rage frees me from pain. I dash forward, arm raised, and my wakizashi takes the force of the kamaitachi's claws slamming into it. My wakizashi whistles through the air and shares clean through the kamaitachi's clawed paw. Its raw scream pierces the air. I close my eyes as blood splashes me.

Calm returns as the winds subside. A gentle breeze rolls off the dusty grass and tousles my disheveled hair, pushing it across my face, tickling my skin. I shoot my gaze around, but the kamaitachi is gone, leaving behind its severed paw. I bite my lower lip until it bleeds. I savor the hard-fought victory, yet its taste is bittersweet. After all, nothing will bring back the victims.

"What happened?" Sasuke slowly comes back to his senses, and I give him a hand to sit up. "Are you hurt?"

"Don't worry. It's over." I point toward the kamaitachi's bloody paw on the ground. "It can't hurt anyone anymore. We'll use the paw as bait. It'll come back and try to get it back."

"Great job, partner. I owe you one."

I wipe off the sticky blood with the yellow grass. My bruised wrist throbs with pain. I clench my fist and raise it high.

WATER HORSE

by Chisto Healy

Martin was lost in his grief, staring at the horse behind his eyes. It was nuzzling his daughter, its mane dripping water, though the rest of the small pony seemed dry.

"Are you even listening to me?" Valerie's asked him. "She drowned, Martin."

Martin winced. "I know. I was there. It was the horse, Val."

Valerie shook her head and touched his arm, but he pulled away. She stepped around him to force eye contact. "Do you even hear what you're saying, Martin? Our girl drowned, Martin. There was no horse."

"You were the one that wasn't there. Don't tell me what happened and what didn't."

His wife covered her face with her hands and shook quietly.

"It was the horse," he said.

Martin exited the house. The air was getting hard to breathe. The world faded in and out. His vision blurred and his chest tightened.

Valerie came out of the house behind him. She stood beside him, silently looking out at the Irish countryside. What a beautiful place it was for the most horrible event in their lives to have happened there. A horse trotted by, stopping up ahead to graze. She saw how fiercely Martin stared at the animal and a chill went through her.

"Let's go home," she said, barely more than a whisper.

He didn't respond. His eyes were focused on the horse with hatred. She tried again. "Let's get back to the people that love us, get away from this horrible place. Please."

Martin stayed silent until the horse trotted on. Then he said, "I'm not leaving here until I find that horse. I'm going to kill it."

Valerie sighed and looked down at the ground. "I know you are grieving. My heart is broken too, but you're scaring me. You sound crazy. Horses don't *dive*, Martin. There was no horse in that water. Where did it go, huh? Tell me where it went, Martin. If a horse took my baby, tell me where the hell it went?!"

Her words bellowed angrily now with a rage she couldn't contain. She didn't know if it was even Martin she was angry with or if she was angry with Ireland; the beautifully wicked place that stole her child.

He looked at her then, his eyes wild. "I don't know where it went, Val. That's all I can think of. I see it over and over. I can't stop seeing it. She was so happy, petting that pony. She climbed on and rode around giggling, Val. I stayed close. I told her to be careful. Then the damn thing took off and ran right into the ocean with her on its back. I dove in and I found nothing. No one found anything."

Valerie looked into his eyes and seconds ticked by. Then she shook her head.

"No," she said. "I'm not doing this. I already lost my child. I'm going back to the states, Martin."

Martin walked away from her, down the road.

He could hear her crying behind him, but he didn't look. Martin knew what happened. Somewhere out there was the horse that stole his child. He couldn't just get on a plane and go back, to pretend like everything was okay. It would never be okay again. Nothing mattered anymore; nothing but finding that horse. It was tan with a blonde mane that was wet even before it submerged itself. Why was it wet?

Martin walked to the pub. He was running out of money but he needed a drink. It wasn't enough to numb his pain though. No matter how much he drank, he felt it, like a black hand squeezing his heart digging its fingernails in.

When he got back to the house, he saw that Valerie had been serious. She and her things were gone. It was probably for the better, he thought. She could be with her family and heal. She deserved that.

Martin sat on the ground and didn't realize he had fallen asleep until Mrs. Murphy woke him in the morning. She was a cherubic lady with wiry hair and rosy cheeks. Her own children were grown and gone, so she opened up her house to travelers like him. She enjoyed the company, but probably not so much this time.

"I'll fix you some coffee," she said, entering the house.

Martin got to his feet and held his head, squinting against the hangover. He stumbled inside and took a seat at the kitchen table.

Mrs. Murphy had been so talkative when they got there. She told them stories and joked about Irish living. When Abigail was pulled into the ocean, she seemed to have taken Mrs. Murphy's tongue with her. Most likely, she just had no idea what to say.

"Valerie is gone," he said.

Mrs. Murphy nodded, and then turned her attention back to the coffee pot. When the steaming cup was ready, she brought it over and set it in front of him. Then she sat with her own cup and sipped at it while she patted his hand with her other. She was trying. Martin looked into her eyes then, fresh tears in his own.

"You believe me, don't you?" he asked.

She looked at him sympathetically, and her hand stopped patting his to grip it tightly, but she didn't answer in words. Martin needed validation so badly. He knew it sounded crazy. It was crazy; and it was true. He needed someone to acknowledge what he saw.

"It was the horse," he said. "A stupid pony. Why was the mane wet? It took her straight into the ocean and then where? Gone. The horse took my Abigail. The police say there is no horse, Mr. Smith. Valerie says horses don't dive, Martin. It *was* the damned horse though. The damned thing just stole her."

Martin realized that he wasn't really talking to Mrs. Murphy anymore. He was just rambling, venting, and she let him. When he exhausted himself, Martin let his head fall to the table. He could hear his host sipping her coffee, her eyes on him still, and he was glad she was there. He felt so desperately alone, more than ever before. Then after several minutes, she spoke.

"It wasn't a horse."

Martin lifted his head and looked at her. Maybe it was her tone or inflection, but somehow, he knew that she wasn't saying that he was imagining things like everybody else. She was saying something else entirely. He searched her eyes, his gaze full of desperation.

"Twas a kelpie," she said. "You're lucky your Mrs. wasn't with you. The pony is for the children, but sometimes it's a right handsome man to draw the ladies. It has no interest in you though, does it? Not my Pa neither. Took my sissie when she was just a little thing. Saw it myself, I did. Into the water and gone, just as you say, a demonic thing. You're best to follow your Mrs. back home. Try to get on."

Martin suddenly felt sober. He sat up straight and glared fiercely into the woman's eyes.

"Can they be killed?" he asked, not questioning what she said to him at all. He knew it was something more than a horse, something he couldn't explain.

"Mrs. Murphy, can kelpies be killed?"

"Aye," she said. "Iron. But hear me, they change shape and move like wind. To kill it, you must catch it. They have come for women and children to pique their appetite since the days of St. Patrick. It's a fool's errand."

"Iron," he said. "I'm going to send it back to hell."

"That's what my Pa said too. That's why we grew up without him. Never did catch his kelpie. Drank himself to death, he did."

Martin was squeezing her hand then instead of the other way around. "I won't drink another drop as long as I'm in this country," he said. "I'll do nothing but hunt."

"Best to go home," she said.

Martin stood from the table, and walked into the living room, where he pulled the poker free from the fireplace.

"This is iron, isn't it?"

Mrs. Murphy nodded with a frown.

"I need to borrow it."

Martin hurried out of the house. Mrs. Murphy sipped her coffee, a shaking hand holding the cup to her lips. She made the sign of the cross with her other.

Martin went to the sea where he had watched the horse drag his child into its frothy depths. He sat down before the calmly churning ocean, his eyes on the water, the image of the horse behind them, it mane dripping salt water. He clutched the fireplace poker and waited.

Martin stared at every sign of movement; his eyes pinned to every shadow. There weren't many people wandering about in the countryside but those that were stared back at him. They didn't look him over as if he was a crazy person, sitting out there with a fireplace poker. Their eyes had a knowing to them. He remembered what Mrs. Murphy had told him. They turned into men to lure women. He got the mental image of the pony's wet mane and he squinted, looking for wet hair on a dry man.

What would he do if he found it? Would he rush over there and stab the guy with the poker? What if he was wrong? He heard Mrs, Murphy saying, "It's a fool's errand."

Martin didn't care if it took him a lifetime, if he had to wait for the opportunity to just arise one day. If that was what he needed to do, then he would. He envisioned his daughter's sweet innocent face, all rosy cheeks and brown eyes. She was his world, and that thing stole her from him. He couldn't let that go.

Even in her final moments Abigail had been smiling gleefully, excited to be on the pony, yelling for him to look and see. She didn't even have time to be afraid.

Mrs. Murphy alluded to the fact that the kelpies had no interest in men. They only stole women and children. Was it even a threat to him? He knew plenty of women stronger and tougher than him. It amazed him that the creature hadn't picked the wrong one and paid the price.

Maybe they watched and chose carefully, only preyed on the weak and innocent. The idea disgusted him and made him hate the creature even more. In his mind, he saw himself driving that poker through the horse's mid-section. In actuality, it probably wasn't anywhere near sharp enough to do such a thing but in his vengeful mind that fireplace poker was a blazing sword.

Night passed and the sun rose and he only stood to remove the stiffness. He walked the edge of the water, watched it beat at the rocks and wondered if his precious daughter had evaded that punishment.

"Where did you take her?" he said out loud.

Martin saw a man herding sheep and he checked the man's hair. Should he check the sheep as well? He wished he could afford to learn more. He needed to be here; vigilant. If that thing came out of the water he couldn't miss it, miss vengeance.

The man studied him in return and eyed the poker but said nothing and went about his day. Martin walked back the way he came. He watched and walked all day until the sun fell again and the moon rose in its place. He scooped water and splashed it on his face to stay awake but sleep still came to take him.

Martin dreamed of his daughter trapped in a cage at the bottom of the sea, screaming for help, screaming for him.

He snapped awake with a start to find Mrs. Murphy standing nearby. He was wrapped in a blanket. She handed him a cup of coffee. He nodded his thanks and sipped it. It was still hot.

"You know I probably don't have the money to pay for your hospitality anymore," he said. "We paid for two weeks. Two weeks are up."

"I just brought a blanket. You'll catch your death out here," she said, sympathy in her round face. She sat down beside him and stared at the sea. Neither said a word for a while. Martin sipped his coffee. When the cup was empty, he handed it to her. She took it and nodded. Then she got to her feet and walked back towards the house without speaking.

Martin rubbed sleep from his eyes. He realized just how far the water went, what a huge expanse it really was. It didn't feel productive to stay in one place, so he went the opposite direction this time. He imagined seeing the thing emerging from the depths. He pictured it as a demon, blue skin and a twisted face decorated with horns. He had no idea what its true form really looked like, but that was what his imagination gave him. At times, he thought the hallucination was real and he grabbed the poker, ready for battle, before realizing he was alone.

Martin thought he saw Abigail at times, up ahead in the distance, running and playing. Sometimes she seemed so real, he started to run towards her, wanting nothing more than to grab her in his arms and tell her she was safe. His mind was playing tricks. It was his guilt, his grief, exhaustion, and desperation; but never his daughter.

Martin's body screamed for rest as the hours passed and reluctantly, he listened, taking a seat on a large mossy rock at the water's edge. His mind was not as willing to rest though, and his eyes combed the water, looking for signs of movement; something bigger than a fish.

"Lost a loved one to a kelpie, did ya?" a voice spoke from behind him.

Martin turned to look, though it pained him to take his eyes off of the water, even for a second. There was a man twenty years his senior wearing a sunburn and a fisherman's hat standing a few feet away. Martin's eyes went to the hat, wishing he could see the hair underneath, to know if it was wet. He noticed a flower in the older man's hand. Martin looked him in the eyes then and finally answered with a nod.

The man nodded back, his own gaze moving to the water.

"Hard to move on from a thing like that," he said, "but you got to. Kelpies been stealing our women and children since Ireland was a baby itself. Twenty years ago today, kelpie took my Siobhan from me. A kind soul she was, thought maybe the gentleman needed some help. I saw his hair, the water, and I knew, but she was too far away to hear me. She just thought he'd gone and drank too much, I suppose. Lucky he didn't drown, she must have thought. I was running, waving my arms, yelling to get away. He looked right at me, he did, looked me right in the eyes, 'fore he grabbed her and dove in the water. Amazing

177

how fast they swim. I dove in right after him; gone forever they were."

"Twenty years," Martin said back, the thought weighing heavily on him. The idea of just letting it go, letting it steal someone else's child, was too much to bear.

"We were married twenty years before that. Married for twenty years and then twenty years alone, missing her every day. I come here on the anniversary and throw a flower into the water. Judging by that poker, you got other plans."

"I have to," Martin said.

The man sighed. "There's a reason it hasn't been done already. I tried to hunt it myself, the whole first year, but I know you're not willing to hear that any more than I was. At least hear this. Kelpies are no fools. It won't come out with you standing by, waiting for it. There's a reason they've survived all these years."

"You keep saying they," Martin acknowledged. "There's more than one?"

"Nobody knows how many for sure," the widower told him, "but we're all certain that number is higher than one."

Martin shook his head. There were multiple kelpies hiding in these waters. Why would people even live here? Why not get away from the water? The man seemed to sense his questions without him voicing them out loud and he said, "It's just the way of things, the food chain. We're not on top."

With that, he stepped forward and threw the flower into the water. Martin watched it sail and watched as a pale hand broke the surface of the water to retrieve it and drag it under. His eyes widened.

"Was that your wife?"

"Afraid not," the man said.

The meaning registered to Martin, and he seized the poker, preparing to lunge for the water, but a hand grabbed his arm.

"It's long gone," the man said from over his shoulder.

"Does it always take the flowers?" Martin asked, quivering with rage.

"Year after year."

"Then why?" he asked, turning to glare at the stranger as if he were the enemy.

The man's shoulders slumped and his face drooped. "I just hope it has enough respect to lay them with her remains," he said before walking away.

Martin felt so angry, so violent, and so powerless, all the same. It was exhausting. He pulled his phone from his pocket and opened his images. He scrolled through pictures of his family, happy and healthy until days ago.

Martin looked at Valerie struggling to fix Abigail's hair for the school play. He saw them screaming on rides at the amusement park, sleeping on the couch together; the selfie they took when they got off the plane in Ireland.

Then he saw Abigail with the horse. He had taken a picture of her moments before she had been taken. There it was, knowing eyes staring at the camera. He had to fight the urge to throw his phone into the water.

Martin's gut told him to send the picture to Valerie, to prove to her that he wasn't crazy, but he loved her too much. She didn't need to see the horse and be dragged into madness. She needed it to be an accident. He needed to allow her the chance to heal and move on,, if it were possible. He stuffed the phone back in his pocket.

Come back up, he thought. *Do it*. But he knew it wouldn't. The stranger was right. It made him so angry, he screamed. He screamed into the air, into the water. There were no words, just pain, and hatred.

Martin forced himself to get up and walk away, despite knowing the creature was close by. He was shaking with adrenaline, and it was hard to even hold the poker.

It was starting to get cold as night unfolded. He was glad for the blanket Mrs. Murphy had given him. He wrapped it around himself as he wandered the Irish countryside, eyeing everything he saw, praying to God for a chance to make this right.

He went on for days, walking, watching, waiting. He saw the same people each day. They watched him, watching them. There was no conversation. He inspected every animal, every shadow, slept only when exhaustion forced him.

Martin was getting nowhere, accomplishing nothing, but he had no idea what else to do. The only thing that kept his heart beating was his thirst for revenge.

The townsfolk would leave food and tea out for him. They never said anything. They just set it outside for him to take and he left the empty dishes for them when done. It was just more evidence that these people understood his pain, his need, the wound that never healed. They were bound by grief.

After several more days, the shepherd finally spoke to him. "I need to say what you don't need to hear."

Martin stopped and stared into his face, studying him. It seemed such a strange thing to say, odd but forthright. He didn't protest or question. He waited for something more.

"You are wasting your time," the sheep herder told him. "They only come to land when they need to feed, understand?"

Martin felt there was something for him to see, but he couldn't grasp it. The man's words made him angry and tugged at the sadness in his heart, but he didn't know why. It was like someone was beckoning him in the dark. The man studied him the way he was accustomed to studying others. He searched Martin's eyes for recollection and frowned when he didn't see it.

"They don't feed often. They eat slow, in little bits, like a fish. That's what they take us for, understand?"

The words finally penetrated Martin's walls and his limbs began to shake. He thought of Abigail and his mind showed him the most horrifying grisly images as he imagined her being picked at over time. His heart burst and his legs gave out. His knees buckled and he was on the ground before he realized it. The shepherd was looking down at him with eyes full of sympathy and heartache.

"How long?" Martin asked. "How long does a meal usually last them?"

The man stood silently, looking at him. There was so much emotion on the wordless plain. It hovered between them, making the air heavy. Martin knew he didn't want to answer the question, and just the same the man knew that Martin needed him to. He needed the truth, but the truth came with such horrific connotations, that it would destroy him as much as save him. Both men understood and neither wanted to move forward with the conversation.

Martin pleaded. "Please just tell me. I have to know."

"Half a year for a child. A full year for a grown woman."

Martin could see the man had left the conversation. His mind had taken him to the days he spent like Martin, waiting and searching, the open wound still bleeding.

Martin left the physical world too. *Six months*. How could he just walk away and let that thing feed on her for so long? He didn't care if he had to wait twenty years to kill it, but he couldn't bear the thought of waiting six months for that thing to consume his child, bit by bit. He knew that she was most likely already dead. If she didn't drown, but it didn't matter. He curled over and released the food he had taken in.

Martin thought about this grieving community, how each of them had known that someone they loved dearly was being eaten slowly, over time, by one of these monsters; how that knowledge would live with them, and eat away at them slowly, over time, just the same.

They all had deep knowledge of what he was suffering. They had all been through it before, somehow, and were trying their best to live with it. Maybe he wasn't as strong as them, but he knew he couldn't live with such a thing. He felt like his soul was being pulled apart merely trying to fathom the concept.

Martin had to do something to make it stop. He had to save what was left of his child somehow.

It felt irrational. He knew if the thing could be found and stopped that these people would have done it long ago. If humanity could win, they already would have. Yet here they were, kelpies stealing women and children as they wished, leaving broken families to stare at empty water.

The living people were just as dead as those they lost. He hadn't seen it before, but it was clear in hindsight. There was no life here. The kelpies had stolen it. The only life was theirs and he ached to steal it in return as he was sure so many had ached to do before him.

Martin got unsteadily to his feet and gripped the shepherd's arm. He stared into the man's eyes, and they had a moment of silent communication, their grief transferred between them. Then Martin released his grip and turned away. He walked away from the water for the first time since he had left Mrs. Murphy's house.

Martin wasn't staring at his surroundings, taking in the details as he had been for so long. He was barely seeing them. His mind was somewhere else, some *when* else.

He was seeing his daughter as all that she was, thinking of all that she could have been. He was reliving her life up until it was taken from her.

A family vacation. It was supposed to be a time for creating memories, not for becoming one.

Even during the long wait at the airport, they had been laughing, singing, and talking about the fun they were going to have. The first few days were everything they hoped it would be.

Then in a blink, a single moment, life became a nightmare that he could never wake up from. How could something like this exist and be accepted? How can all these families be decimated by something year after year with no way to retaliate? How could this just be life?

Martin felt angry with the locals, even after they gave him such fierce empathy and such unrequited kindness. He was angry with them for being so apathetic, so willing to accept their fate. Complacency was weakness. They pretended life was normal, but they were faking it, going through the motions. If they had fought back, stood up, maybe the kelpies would have backed off or moved on. Maybe Abigail would still be alive.

It was their numbness, their broken hearts, that doomed his daughter. He hated them for that. He wanted to scream, to punch and tear at them; to give them a new monster to be afraid of.

Martin's stomach was twisting in knots. He already felt dangerously dehydrated. He had to regain strength. He couldn't allow the kelpie to drag him down into the darkness like it did his daughter. Grief was such a powerful force, destructive and potent. It was consuming.

He went right past Mrs. Murphy's house, her blanket wrapped around him like a cloak, tied at the neck, and wandered to the pub. When he entered, all eyes were on him instantly. No one spoke. They all just gazed at him.

Martin knew what he must look like. He'd been wearing the same clothes for weeks. He was unshaven, bags under his eyes, his hair wild and untamed. He was drowning.

"You can't bring that in here," the bartender said pointing to the fireplace poker.

"I just need water," he said back.

"We don't allow weapons, even strange ones," the barkeep told him with a smile.

Martin nodded. "I know letting things go is a past time for the people of this community, but I'm not one of you."

The bartender's smile fell off like it had been taped to his face and failed to hold. He was plenty aware that Martin wasn't talking about the poker.

"I'm going to have to ask you to leave now," he said.

"Just give me some water," Martin said.

He walked to the center of the room. He glanced at all the silent faces peering back at him.

"I know you've all lost someone to the kelpies," he said. "That's your local secret, right? No one wants to talk about it, but everyone *feels* it. Well, I can't do that. I can't wait around for months for that thing to finish eating. I can't let that be my girl's end. I need to *do* something. If it's not going to come back anytime soon, then I need to go to *it*. I want to go down there. Do you hear me? I want to go down there. Who can help me? Someone can. I know it."

The bartender pushed a glass across the bar towards him. "Here. Take your water. Drink it and go. We don't need that kind of trouble."

Martin grabbed the water and drank it. He looked around at the other patrons, searching their faces for a sign, but all he found were blank looks.

"You're only alive because they don't kill men, but you're dead on the inside. I bet if it were the other way around, if it were killing the men, the women would have stood up and done something about it, because they are stronger than we are. Maybe that is why it takes them. Have you thought of *that*?"

A table of women in the back of the pub hooted and raised their beers into the air. The bartender sighed and came around the bar.

"Alright. Come on," he said, gently guiding Martin towards the door, a hand on his back. Once he had the door open he added, "Off we go."

Martin stepped outside and let the door fall shut. His hatred for the townsfolk was growing. How do you accept that monsters are real and then just as easily accept that your loved ones are their food source? He knew that most of the men in that pub were bigger and tougher than he was. If he picked the fight his heart wanted him to, it wouldn't end well.

Martin had nowhere to go. He walked around the side of the building, leaned against the wall and slid to the ground. *To hell with Ireland,* he thought. Then he snickered to himself. *They are already there.*

A man turned the corner and approached. He was thick and stocky with a full head and matching beard of fire red bristles, to go along with the freckles that dotted the little bit of his pale face that could be seen through the hair. Martin recognized him. He had been one of the patrons in the bar, sitting by himself off to one side. Martin just looked up at the man, silently asking, *what?*

"I'll take you."

The words reached Martin but they felt like an illusion. "You'll take me?"

"Aye. I'm not saying it for the craic. I've just been where you are," he said.

His voice was deep and fit well with his strong, masculine look. Martin thought about this. This man had been where he was. If *he* couldn't find and kill this thing, then what chance did Martin have?

"You know where it is?" he asked.

"Aye. Been there before, I have. You won't find what you're looking for, but you'll find what you need."

"Which is what?" Martin asked, his irritation showing in his tone.

"The truth," the man answered. "I've got scuba gear and a boat. Best to go during the day. Tomorrow. Meet me at the water."

With that, the man walked off. He never even told Martin his name, yet somehow, he felt the man was truthful. Martin had no way to know what he would find beneath the surface of the water. *The truth.* That could mean anything. Only the experience itself could truly answer that and he had to wait until tomorrow.

Martin got to his feet. He leaned the fireplace poker up against the wall and then walked to the front of the building. He went inside and saw the angry face of the bartender, and he raised his hands defensively. He reached into his pocket and dug out his money and placed it on the bar as he sat on a stool.

"I'll take a beer now."

The bartender studied him for a second but then fixed him a pint. Martin sipped at the stout as he tried to steel his nerves. At least he was taking action. He wasn't like the others, he told himself.

A woman sat next to him and ordered a pint. "You're not a boy drinking for the craic," she said. "You're a man drinking for a reason. So, what's brought you to the beer?"

Martin had never met this woman and he knew she was probably looking for someone to go home with, but he hadn't talked to anyone about Abigail since Mrs. Murphy. Such a simple question from a stranger brought him tears.

He wiped his eyes and told her that he had a daughter. He told her everything, recited memories, relayed Abigail's hopes and dreams that would never be met. To his surprise, the woman made no advances. She simply listened, and only spoke to urge him to continue. It was as if she knew how much he needed to release and honestly wanted to help. For a community so numb, they thrived with compassion, and showed great support, even if it came in subtle ways.

When he left the bar, Martin stumbled his way back to Mrs. Murphy's. He was prepared to ask her if she would let him stay the night and accept if she wouldn't, but she opened the door and walked away from it, silently inviting him. He slept off the drink and awoke to fresh coffee. If empathy were currency, this rural town would be incomparably wealthy.

Martin set out early and went to wait on the stranger. While he waited, he resumed his vigil, inspecting every detail for threats. When the boat arrived from his blindside, it startled him into jumping. The man just nodded at him as if he had done nothing strange.

Martin took a deep breath and approached the boat. The man finally gave his name, Eoin. He brought a wetsuit for Martin and showed him how to put it on and work the oxygen. He gave a quick lesson on diving. Martin paid attention.

When the boat started moving, Martin felt the world closing in on him. He was never the type to get seasick. His chest constricted and he was having trouble finding air. His eyes stared at the water that consumed his daughter. He was having another panic attack and he didn't want Eoin to see. Martin was afraid the man wouldn't let him dive if he did, so he did his best to act normal.

"You've been there before?"

Eoin nodded. "Still go, time to time, like I expect it to change. Hope can be foolish but it's no less powerful for it."

"Have you ever seen it? Down there?"

The world was starting to spin less and things were coming back into focus. He looked for the foolish hope the Irishman had spoken of. Eoin met his eye and nodded.

Martin's hands balled into fists as if they had a mind of their own. He wanted nothing more than to look that creature in the face, for it to feel like prey for once. He looked at the fireplace poker he had brought with him.

Eoin saw him and shook his head. He reached behind himself and came back with a harpoon gun.

"Brought one for each of us," he said. "Silver works too, or so the legends says. No one has tested whether its rubbish or not."

Martin tried not to think about the connotations of those words. He chose instead, to focus on the idea that there was another way to kill the kelpies.

"Show me," he said, gesturing towards the weapon.

Eoin gave him a run through. Then they sat in silence until he stopped the boat.

"We're here?" Martin asked.

The answer was another nod.

Eoin gave Martin a refresher course before they dove. Then they were on their way. Martin was amazed by how clear things were. He could see in vivid detail. Standing on the shore it looked dark and foreboding. His hope increased, but so did his dread. Martin feared being able to see so well and finding Abigail. He wouldn't be able to handle seeing that, in or out of water.

He felt on edge as they swam, so close to closure and simultaneously feeling he wasn't ready for it. He looked everywhere, searched everything, just as he had done on land, but he reminded himself not to lose track of his guide.

Eoin led him to a cave and things went dark, the color and details gone, the foreboding returned. Nervously, Martin followed him into the mouth of the cave and down. There was an opening ahead and light returned beyond. Martin swam next to his guide and they moved towards the light.

Then there was a face in his, staring straight into his mask, into his eyes, into his soul. It looked human aside from the razor-sharp teeth that showed when it bellowed a high-pitched shriek. It sounded more like a wailing siren than anything living.

A blur shot between him and Eoin towards the open sea. It took a second for it to register to Martin that he had just found his monster and lost it. He whipped around and raised the harpoon gun and there was nothing there but the current it created as it swam.

He had one moment, and it came and went. He missed his shot. How did it move so quickly? Panic set in again and he fought for control. He looked around at the cave. There were piles of bones everywhere, all picked clean. Off to one side was a pile of discarded clothing; shirts and pants, dresses and undergarments. Martin swam over to it. He tore through, looking for something that belonged to Abigail, a piece that he could take with him, but he found nothing. Behind the clothes was a pile of old dead flowers.

Panic took hold. Eoin saw it happening and knew something was wrong. He tried to help him, but Martin pushed him away. The attack was internal. Eoin grabbed him then and swam hard, dragging him from the cave and up to the surface. He got Martin inside the boat and started back.

"Her clothes weren't in the pile," Martin said.

"Maybe that wasn't her kelpie," Eoin said back, reminding him that the monsters were many. Maybe the caves were many, the piles as well; bones and clothes alike. It all felt so futile. "Don't beat yourself up. You would never have caught it in the water."

As they got in close to land, they saw a man running and screaming, his arms waving. Down the way was a young woman. She was talking to another man. She couldn't see the back of his head, but Martin could, from the boat. He saw the water dripping down the man's back. Martin saw the horse behind his eyes, the dripping mane, the way it looked at him before it took his daughter.

He jumped out of the boat, harpoon gun in hand and swam towards the two talking as the other man rushed towards them on land. Eoin stayed in the boat, watching. The man, or rather the monster, had the woman by the edge of the water. Martin knew in a moment they would be gone. He would never forget how fast his child had disappeared right before his eyes. He couldn't make it to them. He would have to hope the harpoon could reach. Martin stopped swimming and treaded water. Holding the weapon with two hands, he fired.

He had the distance, and the harpoon would have struck the creature in the head, had its head not moved to a completely different place as it changed shape from a man to a horse. The harpoon sailed by where the human head had been and the woman screamed. It was short-lived as the horse clomped down on her hair with its big teeth and took to the water at full gallop, dragging her in and under.

Nothing resurfaced.

The man that had been running reached the water's edge just in time to see his love disappear and he fell to his knees racked by sobs of grief that Martin understood.

Martin swam to shore and Eoin met him there. "You see now?"

Martin nodded. He did see. He saw that these people weren't weak. They were struggling, dying of broken hearts- every one of them, and just trying to live somehow. They had no choice but to accept their fate. Resistance was futile. They couldn't catch these creatures. They couldn't kill them or stop them. All they could do was go on. It was why they were such a close-knit community. They were united through shared grief and mutual trauma.

Martin went back to Mrs. Murphy's. "You were right," he said. "It was a fool's errand, but one I needed to take."

He put her poker back in its cradle before the fireplace.

"You should go home," she said to him. "Don't torture yourself like my Papa did."

Martin shook his head. "Even if I got someone to believe me about what happens here, they would never understand. Right here is the only place where people are going to know what I am going through, how real it is. I need to be here, to be where we accept what we cannot change and work together to get through it."

"Then you're gonna have to get a job," she said.

Martin nodded. Eoin had been right. He didn't find what he was looking for in those waters, but he found what he needed. *The truth*. He sat down outside the house and for the first time, he allowed himself to really mourn, to grieve for what he lost, to shake and sob and accept the way. A comforting hand grasped his shoulder.

THE SACRED PLACE OF BLESSINGS

by C.J. Heigelmann

It was late Sunday morning in the Peruvian city of Cerro de Pasco when 42-year-old German national, Gunter Himmel stirred from his sleep. He stretched out, grunting, before sitting on the edge of his bed and rubbing his bloodshot eyes, still intoxicated from the previous night's celebration at his favorite chicheria. He stumbled into the bathroom, took a shower, and prepared himself for the day.

He made a cup of coffee, and sat at his small kitchen table, gazing through the window while nibbling on two-day-old picarones.

He had many secrets that he kept from his fiancé, Hannah, who would never condone the unethical behavior that he was involved in while working in Peru. In his estimation, it was unwise to disrupt her peaceful life in Germany with news of his infidelity or any other disreputable activities in which he was involved.

"What I've done in this God-forsaken place is none of her business," he told himself. "She must learn her place if we are to be married."

Gunter had just fulfilled his three-year contract with the mining company and would be flying back home at month's end. His occupation as a Lead Mining Equipment Mechanic had compensated him generously.

Today, he planned to settle the last of his 'accounts' as he referred to them, specifically the debts owed to him through his illegal loan-sharking activities. Within a year, Gunter's operation has grossed tens of thousands of soles, equal to half of his annual company salary. There were serious consequences for the late and non-payers. Gunter made no pretense during negotiations, reminding the clients that his contracted band of thugs would be visiting them in their sleep if needed.

He gulped down the coffee, left the small villa, and hopped inside his jeep. A group of children playing in the street moved aside as he honked his horn and sped away.

*****

In a small barrio on the outskirts of Comisaria Huachón, a fifteen-year-old boy sat looking out of an open window as tears rolled down his cheek. The electricity had been disconnected earlier in the week, depriving him and his elderly grandmother of air conditioning, or the rotation of the ceiling fans.

He still mourned the recent loss of his father, killed in a mining accident a month prior, and joined his deceased wife in spirit, leaving behind their only child and his elderly mother to fend for themselves.

The boy began working as a child laborer outside of Cusco, picking coffee, and today was his only day for rest. His skinny limbs were sore, aching deep inside the bones, and his joints had swollen and stiffened like an old man. He dreaded the morrow and the company truck that would come through the barrio to pick up the child workers.

He had no choice but to sacrifice his body through tortuous labor for the wellbeing of his grandmother and himself. The skin tingled on the back of his neck, and he turned around to see if she needed anything.

She lay on her bed across the room, propped upright on her pillow, staring into his eyes. Overshadowed by her high cheekbones, her weathered, leathery, tan skin ran deep with the crevasses and wrinkles of time. Two long grey braids protruded from her head, extending down over her shoulders and crossing over her bosom. In all her simplicity, she emanated regality.

He left the window and knelt beside her. She ran her fingers through his black hair as he laid his head onto her lap. Her touch always made him feel better and melted his sadness.

She was experiencing the loss of her only son, adding this sad episode into the past decades of transformative experiences of her life; yet her demeanor showed no outward signs of emotion. The boy's mother had told him that his grandmother was different from others living in the barrio. She was one of the Huni Kuin, the 'True Humans' of the Kaxinawá Tribe.

Born an only child to the village Pajé Shaman, her father was the last descendant of a lineage of the Mukaya, from the tribal stock considered to be the last of the 'true shamans' of Amazonia. A man of great power and wisdom, he overflowed with muka, that sour shamanic substance that gives passage into the spirit realm, allowing the possessors to see the yuxin, the souls of departed beings. The same muka could also be used to take life, or to heal, with the help of the yuxin.

The old woman was naturally gifted the muka and taught by her father the nature of its essence. She passed this down to her son, and grandson in hopes that it would lead them to a higher understanding of the land and a return to the ancient ways of life. But without cultivation and dedication, their muka remained dormant in her son as he pursued worldly interests.

The boy was more receptive than his father and listened attentively to his wise grandmother as she filled his vessel with the teachings of the elders. She taught him about the hidden places of the land, its history, and the secret rituals of their ancestors. He learned the true meaning of the Festival of Fire, and to speak and understand much of the Kashinawa tongue.

She instructed her grandson in the hopes that one day he might be led on a spiritual journey and desire to become a Kaxinawá Pajé Shaman, and that through him, her father's lineage of Mukaya would be spiritually reborn. She yearned to witness this blessing before her physical days upon the earth ended.

She was no stranger to suffering or grief, having lost both her mother and father during an epidemic of measles in the 1950s, she survived many revolts between her tribe and the European invaders within her home region of Acre. The indigenous tribes had banded together throughout the centuries to defend their land, and the minds of the people from the religious indoctrination of foreign missionaries, and the modern corporate imperialists who mercilessly decimated the forests of the jungle, siphoning the precious blood from the 'trees of life' inside their rubber extraction plants. In the end, it was all to no avail. Defeated and pursued, the then-pregnant and newly widowed young woman fled Brazil, along with the remnants of several tribes, and traveled across the border into Peru, crossing the Rio Tamaya, and eventually settling on the outskirts of Comisaria Huachón.

She continued to stroke his hair and softly chant a prayer as he drifted into a state of solace and closed his eyes. Her muka was stirring. She sensed an important forthcoming event. The paths of two souls would soon cross. Her grandson was on one path.

"Who is the other soul?" she questioned while closing her eyes and intensifying her prayers.

*****

Gunter sped down the dirt road outside of the barrio looking for an old blue pickup truck, and within minutes saw the vehicle sitting in front of a small house. He parked beside it, hopped out, and knocked on the front screen door. The house was silent.

"Hello?" He spoke in traditional Spanish but also knew basic Pano if needed. A small figure approached.

The boy walked to the door. "Hello."

"Is this the home of Yasa? Who passed away recently?"

The boy nodded.

"Are you, his son?"

The boy nodded.

"I need to speak with your mother. Can you get her for me?"

"My mother has passed. I live here with my grandmother."

Gunter huffed and crossed his arms. "Okay, then let me speak with her."

The boy unlatched and opened the door and led him to his grandmother's bedroom. Gunter surveyed the room and the value of its contents while the grandmother watched him from her bed.

"Why are you here?" she asked.

"I worked with Yasa, and I'm owed sixteen hundred soles that I lent him to fix his truck. I'm here to collect his payment."

She shook her head. "There is no money. I'm sorry."

Gunter moved closer to the bed. "No, old woman, I'm sorry for you. I loaned him the money and I'm going to be paid, one way or another." He scratched his chin and grinned. "Just give me the keys to his truck. I'll have some of my men come by here and pick it up. That will settle his debt and there won't be any problems."

"No. That truck is for his son. He will be old enough to drive one day and can use it for work. I cannot allow you to take that from him. Please, allow the boy to pay you back the debt as he is able. He is working hard to provide for us. If you—"

"Be quiet! I don't have time to argue with you, or to wait ten years for this kid to pay me! Either give me something of value or give me the damn truck keys!"

The boy rushed to his grandmother's bedside and stood between them. "Don't yell at her! Get out of our house!"

208

Gunter laughed. "You little bastard. I could snap you in half like a twig." He turned away and began rummaging through her dresser drawers.

"Stop!" the boy yelled.

She grabbed his arm and whispered. "No. Be quiet. This is your destiny. Listen. Learn. Remember." She released him and raised her hand. "Sir, wait, I do have something.

Gunter stopped pilfering. "What do you have?"

"I know a place where there is gold, jewelry, and weapons. It is a special place, hidden not far from here. They are buried together in soft soil. My grandson will take you there and show you where to dig."

The boy clutched her raised hand and held it to his chest. "No, I don't want to go there. I'm scared!"

She laid her other hand over his heart and spoke in the Kashinawa tongue. "Have courage. Take him to the Sacred Place of Blessings. Let him take what he will first, and afterward, you may freely take a blessing for yourself, for us. You know the place and know the story. Remember, you are the Rua Bake, son of Yasa, and the spirits of the Mukaya call you. It is time to add to your name. This is your destiny."

He struggled but responded in Kashinawa. "I remember the place. I remember what you told me that happens. Is it true?"

She smiled. "Yes."

Gunter walked over. "Stop the gibberish. How far away is it?"

Without breaking eye contact with her grandson, she answered. "Four hours by foot. Two hours by horse."

"Then forty-five minutes by jeep." He looked at his watch. "I'll play your game but know that if I come back here empty-handed, that truck better still be here. If not, you'll be getting a visit from some very bad men, and your grandson will pay the price. Don't lie to me, old woman."

"I do not lie."

He looked at the boy. "What are you waiting for, boy? Fetch us some shovels."

"We don't have any shovels." The boy looked at his grandmother. "What to do?"

"The shovel is always there, leaning on a tree. Be sure to leave it when you're finished."

Gunter pulled the boy away and prodded him out of the room. "I hope you know where you're going, boy. I'm not going to drive around all day."

The boy's eyes watered as he peeked back at his grandmother who had begun chanting a prayer. They left the house, climbed into the jeep, and set off.

*****

Gunter drove toward the border of Huánuco into Ticlacayan, then headed North past Mallapampa to the outskirts of Paucatambo. It was there that the boy directed him onto a dirt road at the bottom of the mountain crevasse and to drive up. The boy's heart pounded from anxiety as he looked for natural markers.

"Stop. Here!" the boy shouted, looking to his right and pointing. "We have to walk this way into the forest."

Gunter parked. "Get out and start walking. I'll be behind you."

The boy stepped down and trudged through the thick vegetation into the forest, while Gunter grabbed his rifle and canteen from the back of the jeep. He slung them over his shoulder, grabbed his machete, and followed behind.

Twenty minutes later, the boy stopped in a small clearing and stared ahead, pointing. "There is where you need to dig. Do you see the shovel laying against the tree?"

Gunter looked around. "I'll be damned, it looks like the old hag might have been telling the truth." He wiped his forehead and looked at the boy. "Well, boy? Get to digging."

"I have no strength. My body hurts everywhere. I can't help you dig."

Gunter unsheathed his machete. "If you don't dig, then you die. Make a choice. Now!" he screamed. The boy ran over to the tree, grabbed the shovel, and began digging into the soft mound while Gunter squatted, laughing and drinking from his canteen. "There'll be no water for you until you're finished."

Ten minutes later, the boy had dug less than a meter down. Gunter laid his rifle and machete against the tree, snatched the shovel from the boy, and pushed him away. "You're weak, like a girl, and wasting time!" He began digging wildly, slinging the soft black soil indiscriminately as the boy watched.

Within fifteen minutes, he had dug down until he was chest high in the pit, before suddenly striking something. His eyes widened. He prodded again and continued to dig before dropping the shovel, kneeling, and using his hands to brush away the soil from the object. He pulled up an antique silver pocket watch and held it up to the light.

"She wasn't lying! Ha!" He tossed the watch outside the pit and prodded the bottom with the shovel. He felt something solid, metallic. He looked over at the boy, grinning, and knelt back down to excavate with his hands. "Oh, Mein Gott!" he yelled and stood up holding a solid gold crucifix. Being raised a Roman Catholic he recognized the Franciscan markings engraved on it. "There must be a fortune buried down here!" He looked at the boy, and at his rifle against the tree. He hopped out and grabbed it, then dropped back into the pit. "Just in case you get any brave ideas, boy."

The boy stepped backward, as Gunter laid the valuables on the ground and continued to forage. He brushed off a smooth round white-colored object that was partially buried.

"I think I found Ivory!" he shouted as he wiggled the object free to get a clearer look. He dropped it instantly, realizing that it was a human skull. "This is a grave!"

The boy remained silent, trembling, staring at Gunter.

"I have enough for now. Start backfilling this grave."

As he raised himself to climb out, he felt something wrap around his neck. He clawed at the muscular ligature, struggling to break free as it slowly lifted him out of the pit. He saw the boy standing a few meters away, shivering, and watching.

Gunter kicked his legs helplessly, pathetically running in mid-air, while another muscular ligature wrapped itself tightly around his legs.

"Python! My machete! Give me the machete!"

The boy stepped back and shook his head. "There is no python. It is Yateveo. This is the Sacred Place of Blessings." He didn't want to look at what was to happen, but he found himself entranced and couldn't turn his eyes away.

The once rigid tree and its branches had come alive, writhing and twisting with controlled purpose and intent as it turned Gunter upside down. Several limbs slithered around his torso, cocooning his body and leaving his head exposed.

He grunted and squealed as his face began to swell from the pressure, changing color from red to purple. A distinctive vine protruded from the top of the tree and curiously found its way to the back of his head. The tip of it appeared sharp, jagged and lined with barbs. It plunged through the base of Gunter's skull and began to pulsate while the branches around his body squeezed and released in rhythm as if milking a cow's udder.

Within the hour, the branches began to unravel in unison and retract to their former positions, with one branch suspending Gunter's corpse by his ankles. It released him, dropping him into the pit where his lifeless body lay crumpled, then returned to its original state.

The boy stood motionless and closed his eyes. A soft breeze blew past, flooding his mind with the voices of many whisperers.

"Rua Bake, son of Yasa. Come forth. Be reborn. Remember. Remember."

He shuddered and gasped for air as he experienced the sensation of cold water pouring over the crown of his head, to the soles of his feet. His eyes opened wide, and he inhaled violently. For the first time in his life, he could see the shimmering forms of the yuxin, the souls of the elders, as they moved throughout the forest. He watched in astonishment while being filled with gratitude, and absent of fear. He now understood his destiny and accepted his identity.

The young man walked to the edge of the pit and picked up the gold crucifix, placed it inside his waistband, and kicked the pocket watch back into the hole. He lifted the shovel out and backfilled the ancient mass grave; the place which provided blessings throughout the ages to the Mukaya, and then leaned the shovel against the tree as instructed.

The young man laid his hands on the tree and looked up, smiling. "Thank you for the blessing, Yateveo."

He left the sacred place and commenced his journey home.

DIE ZAUBEREI

by Colleen Halupa

Die Zauberei: "the hex" or "the magic" in German

"She's in cahoots with the devil!" Dwight said. He took a long swig of his Yuengling beer. "You don't want to mess with her Jim. She has hexed people in town…she has the evil eye!"

Jim snorted, "She is a 65-year-old woman who lives in a shack in the middle of the woods with no electricity. This is 1934. Them witch trials up north are long over."

"You know she caused that gunpowder explosion back in 1910 that blew up Henry her husband and the others," Dwight exclaimed.

Jim shook his head, "That's just storytelling. No woman can do that. She was five miles away when it happen'd."

"Roberta at the Five and Dime told me she practices Hexeri, that Pennsylvania Dutch magic. Her grandma brought it over from the Black Forest," Dwight said.

"Roberta is full of crap Dwight. But old Martha's niece sure is something…ain't she? If she's a witch, why hasn't she performed her magic on Tavila?"

"She's sure pretty, but Tavila's slow Jim. She ain't right; she's a retard. What do you want with her?"

"She's a very pretty retard and she likes me. I brung her flowers when I was working in the fields next to old Martha's house. She kissed me and let me feel her up some." Jim said.

"What about Sarah?" Dwight said. Sarah was Jim's fiancé and the daughter of Jim's boss at the bus service that trolled the rural roads of Schuylkill County.

"Sarah won't let me do nothin'. She is as cold as ice." Jim said.

"It's your funeral." Dwight said. "People around here think you're a good boy Jim…butter wouldn't melt in your mouth. You gonna' sacrifice all that for a roll in the hay with Tavila?"

Jim smiled a rakish smile and jumped in the six-seater bus which everyone called the nickel "Jitney" he drove for work transporting people all over Ringtown Valley. Sarah's father let him use it after hours.

"I ain't getting caught. Who would believe old Martha Zauber the crazy ole' witch and Tavila the mental idjit over me? Their word ain't worth a plugged nickel in this town." With this comment, Jim sped away in the bus.

Jim stopped on the old country road about a quarter mile from the Zauber place. He walked the rest of the way through the woods, the moon sliding beneath the clouds to coat the place in darkness. There was no kerosene lamp on in the house. The old lady must be asleep. He grabbed up some small pebbles and threw them up against the window on the second story of the shack where Tavila slept. He waited and after a few seconds, a young girl in her late teens popped her head out of the window, her curly blond hair that fell to her waist flowing down out of the window. Tavila looked 18, but she had the mind of a 10-year-old due to an accident of birth. But what God has taken away with Tavila's brain, he had certainly made up for with her body, Jim thought.

"Hi Jimmy," she said shyly.

"Hi Tavila, can you come out to play?"

"It's late," she started to whisper.

"Ah come on. I'm your friend ain't I?" said Jim.

219

She nodded and closed the window. In a few minutes she came through the rickety front door. The moon was out again and it shown on her beautiful face. The white cotton nightgown she wore was almost transparent. She wore no shoes.

"Come on Tavila, let's take a walk in the moonlight. I brought you somethin'."

Jim took a small porcelain doll out of his jacket pocket and handed it to Tavila.

"Oh, Jimmy" she said. "It is beautiful."

"Tavila, let's take a walk through the field we mowed last weekend in the moonlight." Jim said. "You can't tell your aunt though."

"Ok, my shoes?"

"You don't need um." Jim encouraged, "The grass is soft."

Jim walked and held her hand, and Tavila skipped along chasing lightning bugs as they went a half mile through the field near the old hay barn on Asa Mosely's property.

"I had me a long day Tavila. I am tired. Can we sit a spell?" Jim said.

He led her into the barn, and they climbed up into the loft and sat on a pile of hay.

"Can we cuddle up?" Jim said.

"Sure," said Tavila, her eyes lighting up. Martha, her aunt loved her with her whole heart, but was not very affectionate since she had gotten older.

Jim started to kiss her and moved his hand up under her nightgown.

"Jimmy, Aunt Martha said I ain't supposed to let no one touch me down there." Tavila protested.

"Tavila, it will feel real good. It's a new game."

"You wouldn't hurt me, Jimmy, would you?" Tavila began to sob.

"Only for a minute" Jimmy whispered fiercely under his breath. He was all worked up now.

"But Jimmy, I'm scared." He kissed her gently, then fiercely.

Thirty minutes later, they left the barn. Tavila was crying softly, blood drying on the insides of her thighs. Jimmy turned her around to face him by putting his hands on her shaking shoulders.

"Tavila you cain't tell anyone about tonight or I won't be able to play with you no more." He looked into her confused eyes. "You need to stop your cryin' now." He took her to the pump outside the hay barn and told her to clean herself up.

221

Tavila complied and hiccupped to break off a sob. She turned and looked soulfully into his eyes, trusting. "I promise Jimmy, I promise. I want to play games like we did before—hide and seek or catchin' butterflies. This game seems bad."

Jimmy looked at her hard. "Tavila it is the game I want to play," he said harshly. "Don't be being selfish now or I won't play with ya anymore. You don't want that do ya?" Tavila nodded no, tears running down her face. She was lonely, and Jimmy was the only one who didn't make fun or her or call her a moron. He was her only friend.

*****

As June turned to July and the weather in Eastern Pennsylvania turned hot, Martha had started to worry about Tavila. She was sick a lot, and Tavila was usually a healthy girl even with the limited food Martha had to put on the table in these hard times. She looked pale and drawn and had black circles under her eyes. She stuck close to home rather than taking off flitting through the woods like she used to. Tavila was simple, but she had always been a happy girl, taking pleasure in the smallest things. Last night, when Martha had gone into her room, Tavila moved quickly as if to hide something she did not want Martha to see.

Tavila had always shared everything with Martha. They were as close as a mother and daughter even though Martha had not birthed her. Tavila was all Martha had now.

Martha had been preoccupied as of late. She had been fighting with her neighbor Asa Mosely again over the fence lines. She had seen that bus driver Jim Shinkle over there in the evenings helping bring in Asa's cows. Though everyone thought the sun shined out of that boy's ass, he didn't impress Martha none. There was something in his eyes when he looked at Martha. Rather than the fear and hate she saw in most people's eyes, his eyes challenged her, and she thought she had seen him smirk at her. Most people would not dare smirk at Martha. She had caught him once looking at Tavila in a way she didn't like.

Martha knew most people in the valley were afraid of her. The uneducated bastards hated what they didn't understand. Martha had the gift, or the curse, of the sight. It didn't just come upon her. Her Oma came from the old country and she used to give Martha mugwort tea. The tea opened the mind. When Martha drank the mugwort, just like the Irish heard the banshee wailing when someone was going to die, Martha knew if something bad was going to happen. She knew when her Oma was going to die. She drank

223

the tea every night when her husband Henry went to work the night shift at the gunpowder factory, dreading what she might one day see, but fearing not knowing. If she knew, maybe she could stop it. One night, she woke up in a cold sweat and ran the mile to the factory in the middle of the night and begged Henry to come home. But he refused and sent her away. Henry was a God-fearing man who did not believe in such things. Two hours later, the factory blew up. Jacob Mengel, who had gone home sick that night, heard what Martha said to Henry at the factory. A lot of men died leaving penniless widows and scrawny children with not enough to eat.

Martha had stopped drinking the tea after the death of her Henry. Rumors started, and everyone blamed her. They said Martha had put a hex on the factory that night, she was a witch. People started crossing the street to avoid her when she went to town. Some of the merchants refused to serve her. Martha only tried to use her gift for good, but they shunned her no matter. But she held her head high. When the townspeople were in pain and the moonshine and the butcher of a doctor could not help them who did they come to, begging, their grimy money in their sweaty hands? Martha, that was who. She could heal, she knew the plants of the forest, a knowledge passed

down from her Oma, but she would not know how to
hex or give the evil eye to someone if her life
depended on it. But the rumors continued. People in
the valley who did not have a pot to piss in were as
condescending and cruel as millionaires to a beggar.
Martha was proud would never beg.

As she had gotten older, Martha knew her
hatred for towards the townspeople about the way
she'd been treated for the last 25 years built up like
steam in a pipe. She fought constantly with her
neighbors, the only grocer who would take her money,
the milk man, everyone. They talked about her behind
her back and within ear shot. But she was too poor and
too stubborn to leave. Besides, she had nowhere to go.
Then her sister had died birthing Tavila and her sister's
no-good husband ran out leaving Martha with a baby
girl that was never gonna' grow up. But Martha loved
Tavila as much as she could love anyone anymore, and
she did not regret taking her in.

Martha was in the kitchen boiling corn on the
cob. She nervously twisted the cross Henry had given
her instead of a ring the day he proposed. She never
took it off. She thought Tavila was in her room, and
she was startled when Tavila came in the door. She
could see dried tear tracks in the dust on Tavila's face.
Tavila ignored Martha when she told her dinner would

be ready in a few minutes and went up to her room. Martha finally decided she had to have a talk with the girl. Tavila had turned on the old radio that Martha had found in the town dump and fixed up, so she did not hear Martha coming up the steps. Martha peered through the crack in the door and saw Tavila holding and crying over a small porcelain doll dressed in a gingham dress with painted on shoes. Its eyes rolled violently as Tavila rocked. Martha opened the door.

"Tavila where'd you get that doll?

"Found it." Tavila said, but she could not look Martha in the eye.

"You are lying to me girl, where you get it?" Martha pressed.

Tavila shook her head violently and pressed her lips together. Martha kept at her until Tavila finally broke.

"Jimmy gave it to me."

"Jimmy who?" said Martha, fear growing in the pit of her stomach.

"Jimmy Shinkle."

Martha felt her heart drop. "Why'd he give you that?" she said.

"He's my friend. He plays with me."

"He plays with you how child?" said Martha.

"We go for walks, he picks me flowers, he cuddles me."

"Cuddles you how?" Martha's voice sounded tight. She was having a hard time getting her breath.

Martha asked Tavila more questions. Tavila finally spewed her tale about her friend Jimmy as if she had been just raring to burst to burst apart at the seams.

"But he said he canna' play with me no more," said Tavila. "He said Sarah won't let him. He told me goodbye, and I ain't supposed to talk to him no more."

Martha felt sick. She realized what had been done to Tavila. Even worse, she was sure the poor girl was probably havin' a baby."

Early the next morning Martha walked the two miles into town. Cars passed, but no one would offer her a ride. She passed people on the street who either glared down their nose at her or ignored her completely. She opened the door of the police department. Wilma Garvey, a girl she had gone to elementary school with and had been friends with her up until the death of Henry, looked up at her maliciously from the desk.

"The chief and the deputy are out." Wilma said. "Come back later."

"I ain't coming back later," Martha shouted. "Where are they?"

"None of your business." Wilma sniffed.

"I am here to report a crime."

"What's it this time Martha? Fighting with Asa Mosely again, or Mr. Gannon or whoever?" Wilma said with disdain. 'It's none a' your beeswax."

"I can make it your business Wilma if you do not tell me where they are."

Martha finally calmed down. "It's Tavila," she said. Wilma did not budge.

Martha was desperate. "I will make all of your hair fall outta' your head you surly hag."

Wilma screeched and turned pale and jumped up from the desk. "Please don't hex me." She pointed at the diner.

The chief has a forkful of eggs up to his mouth when Martha busted through the diner door. He rolled his eyes and wondered what it was this time.

"I need' a report a crime. It's Tavila." Martha said.

"Well, let me just finish my breakfast and I will meet you over at my office in five minutes Martha. Martha turned around and slammed the diner door.

The chief took the report and finally got Martha to leave. Ol' Martha had cried wolf in his mind many a time, but she had never involved Tavila, thought the chief. That child was simple. Martha could be as mean as they could come and scary too, but Jim Shinkle was a well-liked member of the community getting ready to marry Sarah Gibbons, a beautiful girl. What could he want with Tavila? He decided he had better at least talk to Jim to get Martha off his back.

Every day, Martha walked the two miles to town to go to the police station. The chief put her off as long as he could, but finally he told her that Jim Shinkle had denied it and there was nothing he could do. Tavila had been flittin' around the woods since she had become a woman and it could have been anyone. Tavila just named Jim because he was around.

*****

Martha hid in the forest alongside the road to town waiting for the bus to come by. She walked quickly into town. She saw Jim Shinkle stop at Sarah Gibbon's house. She stalked up to the house and knocked loudly on the door. Mr. Gibbons opened the door and looked at Martha in surprise.

"Mrs. Zauber what are you doing here?" At least he was always polite, unlike most.

"I need to come in and talk to you and Sarah." She pushed her way through the door.

Jim and Sarah were in the parlor listening to the radio. Martha looked at all of them.

"Do you know what he did to my girl Tavila? He woo'd her and gave her a present. The last one was a porcelain doll. Then he put it in 'er. He raped her."

Sarah gasped. Jim stood up.

"Mrs. Zauber, you know Tavila ain't in her right mind. She is makin' it up. I barely even ever talked to her. I saw her once or twice when I was doin' cows at Moseley's and that's it," Jim said indignantly.

"She's havin' a baby! She can't even take care of herself!" cried Martha.

Jim looked shocked for a second but went back to playing it cool.

"Not mine." he said.

Mr. Gibbons took Martha by the arm kindly and led her to the door. He knew his dead wife Eunice would roll over in his grave if he were unkind to

Martha. She put no stock in being mean to anyone. Eunice always said Martha had a gift and the uneducated people of the town punished what they did not understand.

"Martha I am so sorry about Tavila." said Mr. Gibbons quietly.

Martha looked up at Mr. Gibbons, "Jim Shinkle knows what he has done, the lousy bastard. You might want to think if you want your girl Sarah to marry him."

After Martha left, Mr. Shinkle looked thoughtful and then worried. He shook his head as if to get what Martha had said out of his brain.

*****

What Martha had said the week before went round and round in Jim Shinkle's mind just like the circular bus route he drove every day. Martha just would not shut up about him and Tavila, even though she had no proof other than the word of that retard. Martha tried to get the newspaper to print the story. She went to Jim's girlfriend Sarah Gibbon's parish priest. She was harassing Sarah if she saw her. Martha was out of hand. She was no witch, he thought to himself, but she sure could cause problems. Sarah's father Mr. Gibbons had been asking him the other night why he had bought a doll for Tavila. Mr. Gibbons had asked around at the Five and Dime store and that nosy clerk Roberta had told him that Jim had bought a fancy doll. She thought it was an odd present for Sarah. If Martha could get a ride, she was going to go to the PA Staties, and Jim knew he couldn't charm them. He had to do something now.

At the end of the day, he pulled the bus over in front of Dwight's house. Dwight had heard all over town about Martha accusing Jim of hurting Tavila.

"I told ya," said Dwight. "It wasn't worth it."

Jim glared at him.

"But I 'm your friend, Jim." Dwight handed Jim some pumpkin balls.

"What do you expect me to do with these hillbilly bullets?" Jim said.

"Take care of your problem," said Dwight as he handed him a shotgun.

Jim waited for a night when there was no moon out. It was hot as Hades and sweat poured down his face. He left his house at 3 a.m. and drove out of town, a half mile past Martha Zauber's place and parked like he had done the night he and Tavila had gone to the barn. His hands shook as he loaded the shotgun with the pumpkin balls Dwight had made for him. He has asked Dwight to come with him, but Dwight refused, the chickenshit. *Friendship only goes so far*, thought Jim.

He walked into the woods alongside the road and quietly crept up to the house. He could see the kerosene lamp flicker on the second floor in Tavila's room. It looked like Martha was in the living room. He crept up behind the large maple tree in the back yard and watched the kitchen window waiting for his opportunity. Finally, he saw the kerosene lamp moving as Martha came into her kitchen, probably to close the rickety window. Jim was only 10 yards away. He could see the hard set of Martha's mouth and saw a glint of something reflected in the kerosene lamp. Did she have a gun? He hesitated. Naw, as he peered closer he saw it was that necklace, a cross she always wore. Dwight once said she must turn it right side up when people was looking and upside down the rest of the time since she worshipped the devil. Jim had to get his nerve up again. He took a deep breath. He closed his eyes and thought of his conversation with Dwight. This was the only answer. He aimed at Martha and fired twice. He heard her scream and fall, and he ran back to the road and climbed into the bus. He drove 10 miles into Shenandoah and dropped the shotgun into the deepest anthracite pit mine he could find. Then he drove the long way home, so he didn't go past the Zauber's run down house. He parked the bus in the garage and jogged home as the early dawn light started to shine. He sat in his parent's kitchen and put his head in his hands. He'd done it. Everything would be fine now…his job, his life with Sarah. Tavila had no one. She'd be put away in a home so it would all die down.

*****

Tavila heard a loud noise which woke her up. She had forgotten to turn off the kerosene lamp again. The flame flickered in the shadows of the room like phantoms dancing on the walls of hell. Aunt Martha would be mad, she kept telling Tavila she was "gonna' burn the house down." Tavila didn't like when Aunt Martha was mad at her.

She went down the hall and knocked on Aunt Martha's bedroom door. No answer. She crept down the steps and shone the light on the tattered furniture in the parlor. Nothing. She turned and walked into the kitchen and then she screamed. She dropped the lamp, but luckily the flame winked out since the kerosene was just about out as usual. Kerosene was expensive. Tavila ran out of the house screaming. She ran across the field and banged hysterically on Asa Moseley's door.

Asa had called the chief at home out to the Zauber place after Tavila had collapsed crying and screaming on his doorstep. The chief walked into Martha's kitchen, avoiding the broken kerosene lamp. Martha was lying on her back with two large, bright red roses of blood staining the front of her threadbare white cotton blouse. The cross she wore around her neck had twisted and was hanging upside down. Good thing no one in town saw that, the chief thought as he as he leaned down and righted the cross. Martha was stone cold and not breathing.

*****

Jim had heard that Tavila was taken away to the nuthouse in Orwigsburg last night. She had no family and Martha had no friends, so she had to stay there. He heard this from Mr. Allen who regularly rode the bus to go drink beer with his cronies as soon as high noon hit and it was considered socially acceptable. Mr. Allen's sister-in-law worked at the nuthouse and had called Mr. Allen's wife first thing to spread the news. With Martha and Tavila gone, there is no way Jim would take the rap. No one would even know he had had sex with a retard and fathered a probable retard child to boot. Jim was feeling pretty good about himself. He had finally convinced Sarah to get a little frisky with him in public (outside the eyes of her overprotective daddy) to help convince everyone of his innocence. If he had her, what would he want with a retard like Tavila?

Some witch, he thought. If Martha really was a witch, she wouldn't have been taken down to the slab at Doc Baker's office for butcherin'. She would have picked herself right up off that floor and waved her hands and them pumpkin balls would have floated out from her chest, and them wounds would have healed up like Jesus healed the blind man. Or, more like it, old Nicodemus with his goat head would have come up from hell and waved his hooves and Martha would've come to life again.

Jim laughed. He never thought he could kill somethin' other than a bear or a deer, but he sure could, and he didn't regret it. He never planned on doin' it again. It had served its purpose.

*****

The chief sat looking at his old records compiling a list of the people in town who might have shot Martha. He already had 30 people on the list. He looked at the window and saw Jim Shinkle go down the street in the Jitney. He would do a turnaround and come back, so the chief walked out of the office and flagged him down.

"Jim, I gotta' talk you about Martha," the chief said. "Where were you last night?"

"Home asleep in my bed. Ask Mom and Dad, they can vouch for me. You know I ain't the only person that had trouble with Martha. No one believed what she said about me anyway. I had no reason to hurt her."

"Naw, I know," said the chief. "But I gotta' ask, what would you want with Tavila when you have Sarah and a good future ahead of you? But I have to confirm with your mommy and daddy."

A few weeks passed, and Martha's murderer still had not been found. Jim asked Sarah to marry him, banking on the fact that Mr. Gibbons was going to promote him after the wedding and let him run the dispatch for the buses and give him a big ole' fat raise so Jim could support his daughter in the way she was used to. Things were keen, thought Jim.

One day in mid-August, the chief again waved Jim down as he passed by the police station on his route. "Jim, I need you to park the bus and come on in. Mrs. Adams who lived a half a mile west of the Zauber place said she thought she saw a bus on the night Martha was killed. She took a long time to come forward, but then she said she just had to. She said it was hauntin' her. The case is still open so I gotta' ask."

"Chief you already know where I been. My parents told you. What was ole Mrs. Adams doing up at that time anyway? She's as blind as a bat without her spectacles. I don't have the only bus around here and I don't take it home every night. Only if I need it. I park it at the garage and walk home most days and that's what I did the night Martha was killed." Jim said in a whiny and disgusted tone, trying to mimic an innocent man.

"I had to ask," said the chief. "I know you're a good, honest man Jim. Everyone thinks so. We know you was brought up right. Thanks for your time."

Jim thought to himself. "Boy, do I have all you idiots fooled."

A few days later, Jim went to bed after a long day driving the bus and helping Asa Mosely with his cows. He was trying to save up money for him and Sarah to have a two-day stay up in the Poconos when they got married. He had been picking up odd jobs all over town, not for the money, but to keep proving to everyone was a swell guy he was. He turned out the light, pulled down the covers, and put his head on his pillow. It felt funny, like there was something underneath it that was hard. He turned the light back on and moved the pillow. Underneath was a small porcelain doll in a gingham dress. Something was scratched in charcoal on the bottom of the painted white shoes. "TAV" was on the right foot and "VILA" on the left. He closed his eyes. He must be dreaming, but the doll was still there. This had better not be Dwight's idea of a joke. He took the doll and threw it across the room where it broke into several pieces. But Jim didn't sleep much that night.

In the morning, Jim cleaned up the remnants and went downstairs and threw them in the outside garbage can. The next night before he went to bed, he gingerly checked under his pillow, but there was nothing there. He must have been dreaming. Jim finally slept, tired after little sleep the previous night.

When Jim woke up the next morning, he saw the doll again. It was on his dresser staring at him. He thought he could see the eyes blink at him. He saw the name scratched on the bottom of the shoes in crude letters. He jumped up off the bed and threw the doll on the floor. He stomped on it. He grabbed up all the pieces, cutting his finger and feet in the process. He ran downstairs and threw the pieces of the broken doll in the potbellied stove. He watched as the real hair burned and melted on its head, its eyes staring at him balefully.

"What's the matter dear?" said Jim's mother.

"I am fine he said, just cold," he responded as he hugged himself to stop the shaking.

On his way to work he stopped at Dwight's house and cussed him out, but Dwight said he had "nothin' ta' do wit' it."

A few weeks later, as summer headed into fall, the bus had started acting up and Jim had to take it to the mechanic. As he drove towards home at the end of the day, it was getting dark. Jim had stopped outside of town, took his flask out of his uniform pocket and took a good swig to calm himself. He thought about the doll and tried to put it out of his head. He had taken to drinking even more this past few months. He filched the liquor from his future father-in law. He had to be careful or the old coot would find out what he had been doing. He just knew it was Dwight that used the doll to scare him; it had to be. After a spell, he revved up the bus and headed back towards the garage for the night. He almost hit an old woman walking on the road. She had a black babushka that covered most of her face and an old house dress and dirty white cotton stockings that were wrinkling at the ankles. It was starting to rain so he swerved, pulled up beside her, and rolled down the window.

"Are you going to Zion Town?" She nodded. "Want a ride?" She nodded again and opened the door and got in the back, dropped something in the collection box which bounced off under the seats somewhere and took a seat in the very back of the bus. "Where'd ya' want me to drop you off?" Jim said, flashing his best smile. He had a reputation to keep up.

A low, but almost familiar, voice croaked, "The Cat-lick church; goin' to see the priest."

"Baba, do I know you?" Jim asked. He looked in his rear mirror. He knew most of the old women who went to the Catholic Church because they had a card party on Wednesday afternoons and took his bus. The woman had taken off the babushka. Jim started in fright and almost ran off the road. It was Martha. Her skin was blue and parts of it were eaten away and full of maggots. He almost screamed. He closed his eyes and then looked back in the mirror and just saw an old woman. Martha's age, yes, but not Martha. Her skin was white and wrinkled, but not blue and all the pieces were there. Jim felt like he was starting to lose his mind. It was shell shock, that's what it was Jim

241

thought to himself. All that with Martha and all the extra work. It was making him nuts! He had to get a handle on himself, he just had to.

Over the next several weeks, Jim thought he saw Martha standing in front of the grocers, standing in the parking lot at the city offices, outside his window as he peered out in the dark hours of the morning. She never acknowledged him. He had to be imagining it. The doll had never reappeared after he had burned it. He knew Dwight did that, was Dwight doing the rest? If he was, Dwight would pay.

*****

One Saturday in November, Jim was cleaning the inside of the bus to get rid of the mud caused by the snow and slush from people's boots. He saw something shiny stuck down between his seat and the collection plate. His hand was almost too big to get it and then he was finally able to grab a grimy chain. At the end of it was a cross. He wiped off the dirt and turned it over. On the back it said "From H.Z. to M.Z. 1889." Jim dropped it as if it burned his hand clear off. It was Martha's cross, the one she always wore. She must have dropped it in the collection plate the night he picked her up. No wait, that was not really Martha, it was just an old woman. He did not know what it was anymore. Jim crushed the grimy cross in his fists and ran behind the garage and dumped it down the old well.

Two nights later, Jim drug himself into bed. He and Sarah had a huge fight about his drinking and working so much, and she even threatened to call off the engagement. He would show her. He took a large slug of the liquor. He looked at himself in the old wavy shaving mirror. He had lost weight. He looked haggard. Every time he closed his eyes Martha was there; she was hexing him. She was giving him the evil eye. He woke up exhausted and had to drag himself to work. But he put on a good face for his customers.

That night on the way home finishing up his route, Jim was so tired, he pulled over to the side of the road. He took a swig from his flask of the home blend moonshine Gibbons got from the men in Barnesville that he snatched every chance he got. Then he drank half of it. Soon he fell into a drunken stupor.

Jim woke with a start. The door of the bus opened, but it could not open unless he opened it from the inside. He had locked it all up. It was Martha. Black carnations of dried encrusted blood decorated her decrepit, formerly white cotton blouse. Thick blackish blood had dripped all over her sensible shoes as she stepped up into the bus. The cross winked at her neck hanging upside down. She opened her mouth and smiled and dried blood had made her teeth black. Jim fainted.

When Jim woke up it was pitch black. He looked fearfully around for Martha, but she was nowhere to be found. She was dead. He was having just them nightmares again he told himself. He pulled a small lantern out and lit it. He held it up and saw wet shoe prints from snow melt and remnants of thick pooled blood drying on the steps of the bus and the cross. Jim started to scream, a high hysterical sound.

*****

The chief jumped out of bed. Someone was banging and screaming at his door in the middle of the night. Shirley his wife sat up in bed and drug the covers up around her neck like a virgin on her wedding night. "Charles what is that? This town is going to Hades in a handbasket since they let those…" The chief shushed her and put on his pants and went downstairs.

It was Jim Shinkle. He as babbling like a fool and waving his arms.

"I did it. I did it," he said. "She really is a witch. She's giving me the evil eye. Make her go

away…please, please, pleazz…" Jim's final word
ended in a moan as Jim raked his nails down his face
drawing blood and tore out small clumps of his bright
red hair. His freckles stood out raisins in a rice
pudding.

"What're you sayin' boy?" said the chief.

"I killed her. I killed Martha. I did it. I did it
all." Jim cried and crumpled on the chief's front porch.
"The electric chair will be better than the suffering."

*****

Jim was sent to the Fairview State Hospital for
the Criminally Insane. He lived there for 41 years.
Finally in 1975 he was found to be sane and faced a
new trial. The judge who was an out-of-towner took
pity on him and let him go home to Ringtown. The
judge felt he had suffered enough. He was in poor
health, a mere shell of a man. Even though most
people had died off, there was an uproar. The
townspeople didn't want a murderer back in their small
town even if the ones that still remained that knew
Martha never liked her.

Jim was housed in a small apartment on Main
Street. The Catholic Church had collected a fund for
the minimal rent and furnished it with the basics. After
the sheriff dropped him off, Jim sat on the small bed

contemplating his first night of true freedom in decades. He decided to lie down and soon fell asleep.

It was dark when Jim awoke. He heard something moving in the room. At Fairview, he had to sleep light because he never knew when one of the crazies was goin' to come in and try to hurt him. For a second, he could not remember where he was. Jim saw a figure at the bottom of his bed. It was a woman in a white cotton blouse that shone in the light from the streetlight. There were stains on it that looked black in the dim light. She moved and he saw her face, maggots dripping onto the worn shag carpet. Jim clutched his chest in fear…pain radiating down his arm.

"Die Zauberei," the woman said.

It was Martha.

Jim's heart stopped.

THE DEVIL YOU KNOW

by C. I. Kemp

"They got the bastard!"

"Huh?" I was half asleep and my brain doesn't function until I've had my first cup of coffee. That, plus the fact that the words were gushing out of Scott's mouth at light speed, didn't make for clear understanding.

All I was able to gather was this: something big had gone down at Kreel's sometime past midnight and there were two dead bodies in the woods.

"Come on, hurry up! Jessica's waiting. You in or not?

"Yeah, yeah, I'm in!"

Perhaps I should start at the beginning.

*****

My name's Joan Berkowitz. I'm a free-lance info-junkie. That's how I got the gig as Jessica Ingram's Research Assistant.

"One moment, it was a cherubic baby boy. The next, it was a hideous monstrosity."

We were in the studio, watching Jessica doing her run-through on the Jersey Devil. Using my words.

"According to legend, Deborah Leeds...."

At the top right-hand corner of the screen appeared a Leeds family portrait; wife Deborah, husband Japhet, twelve children.

"...impoverished, married to a drunkard, and pregnant with a thirteenth child, cried unto Heaven, 'Let this one be a devil!'

"This was 1735. Witchcraft and Satanism were very real to these people of the Pine Barrens, an area of festering swampland, barren soil, and home to forces of darkness invoked by Deborah, in pain, anger, and frustration."

Maybe you've seen *I. On New Jersey*. It's a Local Access program, produced and moderated by Jessica Ingram, hence the I (duh!).

"According to local superstition, flashing lightning, pelting rain, and booming thunder were sure signs that the devil was walking abroad. It was on a particularly tempestuous night that Deborah Leeds birthed her thirteenth child."

I. On New Jersey is the highest rated program of its type in its geographical demographic. Jessica wants to take it national. She will, too. She's got the right combination of ambition, talent, and bitchiness.

"At first, nothing indicated that the newest Leeds would be anything but normal. Deborah was surrounded by three midwives, whispering soothing words. Flickering candles bathed the room in a gentle glow, in contrast to the violence of the storm, battering the house. Deborah's husband and children waited in another room. The birth was uneventful. The baby appeared healthy. Mother and midwives breathed a collective sigh of relief. Deborah's unholy prayer remained unanswered.

"But that was about to change. Within minutes, the child sprang from its mother's arms and started to grow. Its mouth elongated to a horse-like snout with protruding daggerlike fangs...."

The Leeds portrait on the screen was replaced by something resembling a horse, but with batlike wings, disproportionately large hooves, and arms ending in hooked claws.

"...horns, razor-sharp talons, leathery wings..."

This image was replaced by a creature with a wide mouth and protruding eyes on a body bulging with muscularity.

"...coarse hair, scales, emitting ear-splitting screeches, eyes blazing with a fiery glow as the room filled with overpowering heat and a foul odor..."

Again, the picture changed, this time to an airborne dragon with pterodactyl wings, snarling mouth, eyes focused at the viewer, claws clenched as though they were about to rend prey.

"...from its nether regions, a spiked forked tail lashing about the room with such force that it beheaded one of the midwives."

Another change to a close-up of the creature's face — a cross between a lizard and a rat. The snout still protruded, curving upward. Long sharp teeth jutted out, as if the creature was grinning at some balefully humorous joke.

"It leaped about the room, killing its mother, before shredding the remaining two midwives with its teeth and claws.

At this point, a series of images flashed onscreen: a head with ram's horns on a stolid goatlike body, a horned dragon head on a winged torso, a glistening medieval devil-form with impressive anatomical correctness.

"Some say that the creature made its escape by flying up the chimney. Others claim that it crashed through the door and slaughtered the remaining members of the Leeds family before vanishing in the storm."

The final image disappeared. The *I. On New Jersey* logo replaced it.

"The Jersey Devil has been sighted sporadically over the last three hundred-plus years. Superstition? Reality? Whatever you believe, the Jersey Devil has been inextricably linked to this region...."

Jessica clicked the Pause button. "Good job, everyone. Let's call it a night." She turned to me. "That was some good, stuff, Joan."

"Thanks, Jessica."

It was hard for me to call her "Jessica." I'm an informal gal. I call, Robert's Bob; David's Dave, Raymond's Ray. I was warned, though, that you only refer to Jessica as "Jessica." The running joke is the only ones who call her "Jess" or "Jesse" are Jessica's mother and those who have pleased her in bed. I fit into neither category.

Jessica turned to her Assistant Director. "Let's head out to Kreel's first thing, Scott. Also, I want to focus on previous sightings. We'll use Joan's material."

"You got it, Jessica." Then to me, "Shall we?"

"We shall."

We did.

*****

I lay in bed with Scott's arm encircling me. Every time I felt like I was going to drowse off, Scott would tweak my boob or tickle me lower down. I elbowed him and told him to cut it out, more flattered than mad. After all, Jessica Ingram was more Scott's type than me.

Let's face it, I'm okay-looking, but nothing like Jessica. Where she has luxuriant blond hair, mine is dark and stringy. Where she has perfect skin, mine is freckled. Where she has melons, I have oranges.

*****

Next morning found us bumping our way up a rutted dirt road that ended at a clapboard farmhouse whose grey paint was flaking off in huge shards and whose windows hadn't seen a Windexed rag for years. In front was Henry Kreel, reed-thin with untreated leather skin and a mouth set in a straight line.

There were four of us: Jessica, Scott, myself, and Jessica's cameraman, Tony. Jessica introduced us and Kreel shook hands with her, Scott, and Tony.

Upon hearing my full name, however, Kreel bristled. Instead of shaking my hand, he gave me an unfriendly perfunctory nod. Nothing I hadn't experienced before, but it still pissed me off.

Jessica gestured for Tony to start filming, then began speaking: "I'm here with Henry Kreel who's reported a recent sighting of the Jersey Devil. Mr. Kreel, tell us what you saw on the night of June 21."

Henry Kreel gestured for us to follow him.

We made our way to what once had been a barn. Now, its walls and roof were collapsed. Beside the ruins was Kreel's son, a bulkier version of Kreel. As we approached, this horrendous smell hit us from the ruins.

"Hank and me, we're sittin' down to dinner," Kreel began, "when we hear my cows. makin' sounds cows don't normally make. They was screamin.' Then, there's a crash. Me and Hank grab our rifles and head out to see what's goin' on."

Hank turned from the ruins and took up the story. "The whole side of the barn was blown off and flames were comin' out of it. And the stink! We've had livestock die on us and sit out in the sun, but they didn't smell nothin' like this."

Tony panned the barn and Jessica asked, "Did you see what caused this destruction?"

"We saw wood splinterin' and there was this real high-pitched wailin.' At first, I thought it was my cows until...."

A long pause. Finally, Jessica prodded, "Until...?"

"We saw it. It crashed through the roof and flew into the sky," Hank continued. "It was makin' this wailin' sound like a screech owl only louder."

"Did you get a good look at it?"

"It all happened so fast," Kreel Senior answered, lowering his voice, as if afraid it might hear him and return. "I didn't get a real good look, but it looked to be the size of a man with these big wings. It was all black except for the eyes. They were shinin' red, like the taillights on a pickup."

"Anything else? A face? Arms? Legs?"

Both Kreels shook their heads.

"Got somethin' else for you,' Miss." Hank stepped over the ruins. When no one followed, he turned around and said, "Come along."

Jessica walked gingerly across the blackened wood, followed by Tony, Scott, and Kreel Senior. Yours truly brought up the rear.

We made our way to a part of the ruins where the rotting meat stench was even worse. I gagged. Tony and Scott turned green. I can only marvel that Jessica was able to keep her composure.

"Look." Kreel pointed at something on the ground.

At first, I thought it was a bunched-up drop cloth doused with red paint. But drop cloths don't have horns or hooves and they don't carry the stench of rancid meat.

I swooned and Scott took my arm. He led me away, but not before my eyes registered other drop cloths, all red, all stinking.

*****

Once again, the four of us jounced along that rutted dirt road, following Kreel's ancient pickup. Around us were trees set so close together, you could barely see the sky. We stopped, and the Kreels emerged from the truck, carrying rifles. We were met by an older version of Grizzly Adams, right down to the bushy beard and checkered hunting jacket, also carrying a rifle.

Kreel introduced us. "My neighbor, John Cross. He seen the thing, same as me."

Cross acknowledged us and launched into his account of his experience before Jessica could ask the first question.

"I was huntin' with Ben, 'bout a year and a half ago, It was getting' dark when...."

"Ben?" Jessica broke in.

"My dog," said Cross and his voice began to choke. "We were huntin' and all of a sudden, Ben starts barkin' up a storm. He's runnin' through the woods and I'm followin.' He gets to a tree and starts jumpin' and barkin' at somethin' up there. A wildcat, I figure, till it lets out a screech like.... Let me tell you, it wasn't no wildcat.

"I'm lookin' up and all I see is branches shakin' and I hear this awful screamin.' Then I see these two red dots up there..."

"Like the tail lights on a pickup," Henry Kreel repeated.

"Yeah. All of a sudden, somethin' big and black swoops down, crashes through the branches, grabs my dog."

"How big a dog was it?" Jessica asked.

"Shepherd Rottie mix. Over a hundred pounds."

Jessica winced. "Did you get a good look at it?"

"Lady, I don't think I'll ever forget it. It was bigger than Hank here, with these wings...." John Cross stretched out his arms as far as they would go. "You ever look inside a snake's mouth with those long curved fangs? Like that. A whole mouthful of 'em. And eyes like a snake's, only bigger and they never blinked, not once.

"I start yelling, firin' my gun, tryin' to scare it off. I want to shoot it, but I'm afraid I'll hit Ben. Anyhow, it just takes off, crashin' through the branches, carryin' my dog."

His voice started to choke again. "It's screechin,' Ben's yowlin,' I'm chasin' it, yellin' and shootin.' Next thing I know, somethin' is breakin' through the branches again and I figure it's comin' back for me, but that's not what it is.

"It's my dog, or what's left of him. His throat is ripped open and his hind legs..." Cross choked again unable to continue and I found myself thinking back on Henry Kreel's cows.

"I'm so sorry," I said.

"Thanks, ma'am. That's good of you. Anyhow, whatever it is, I see a dark shape up there through the leaves. I fire at it. From the way it screams, I know I done hit it."

Cross pointed to an angry ruddy scar on the side of his face. "See that? That's where it got me. It came at me out of the trees, swooped down got me right there. Knocked me down, And that stench! Phew! Never smelled nothin' that bad in my life"

"Did it attack you again?" Jessica asked

"No, ma'am. Guess it figured me for dead when I fell. Just flew off.

"Come on, I'll show you where it happened."

He led us onto a trail with Jessica and the Kreels following and Tony filming. I was just as happy to be bringing up the rear, holding onto Scott for dear life.

We left the trail and Cross bushwhacked his way through low-lying branches and thorny brambles. When we got to a clearing, Cross pointed upwards.

"See that? That's where it was."

Tony panned towards a solitary dead tree amidst a bunch of live ones. The side facing us was charred and black and devoid of bark about fifty feet off the ground. Beyond that, were the broken branches Cross had described where his dog had been thrown from above. Judging from the thickness of the broken, but remaining limbs, the poor thing must have been hurled with incredible force.

We stood there gaping, unspeaking. Jessica broke the silence in a tremulous whisper. "Are you getting this Tony?"

"Got it, Jessica."

Our group lapsed into silence again while John Cross stood with his head bowed, hands clasped together. A mourner's stance.

Suddenly, I wanted to be out of there. This might be fascinating to Jessica, a really sensational *I. On New Jersey* segment, and a step up to something bigger. To me, this was one bleak environment, home to the forces of darkness. Those forces were here, surrounding us, and by lingering here, we were invoking them, just as Deborah Leeds had done with her blasphemous cry against her unborn babe.

I nudged Scott and pointed towards the road. Scott nodded and we made our way back to the cars, followed by the others. Jessica thanked John Cross and the Kreels, then began laying out the agenda for the rest of us.

"We'll head back to the studio and go over the footage. You got the shots in the barn, right, Tone?"

Tony, still pale, answered, "Got 'em Jessica."

"Good deal. What about you, Joan? You joining us?"

I shook my head. "If you don't need me, I've got some more background material I want to run down. That okay?"

"Sure. Catch you later."

Scott gave me a quick peck. "See you back at the motel."

"Right. Love you."

"Love you, too."

*****

Nowadays, people think you can find anything on the web. Not true. Sometimes, you have to travel obscure byways in obscure towns to find things that 99.9% of the world doesn't care about.

That's how I spent my day, driving through towns not on maps; visiting quaint little shops dealing in occult trappings; seeking out people you'd write off as eccentric who studied, wrote about, and lectured on the paranormal. I ended up with two huge arcana-filled shopping bags plus the delightful challenge of working my findings into Jessica's piece.

I emptied the bags and pored over copies of texts that were old when Deborah Leeds' loins spewed forth their hated burden. I handled curios, poppets and gewgaws, some of which seemed to tingle with a mystic energy. At the time, I thought it might be my overworked imagination

Now, I'm not so sure.

It was after midnight, and I was still cataloguing my acquisitions on the bed when Scott returned. After a long languorous kiss, we said in unison, "Long day?"

We laughed and Scott gestured to the stuff I had laid out. "What's all this?"

I held up a reproduction of a book from the 1700s, the size of a Spiral notebook, bound in rust-colored leather. "It's called a Grimoire, Scott, a book of spells. Careful, the pages are starting to flake."

"Where'd you get something like that?"

"Used bookstore outside Vineland. I don't think the owner had any idea what it was."

I opened it, very gently to a page which read, in large Gothic letters and archaic spelling, "Rytes Of Alliance."

"What's that mean?" Scott asked

"According to the book, it's a way of conjuring up a demon."

"Why would anyone want to do that?"

"Oh, many reasons, generally evil ones. Say you wanted a piece of your neighbor's land. Or lusted after a village maiden. Or wanted revenge against an enemy."

"You mean, people thought they could summon up a demon to do their bidding?"

"Exactly. See, demons and devils could be drawn by blood. Once you summoned a particular fiend or spirit, it was bound by some set of cosmological rules. You had to perform a ritual that nourished or strengthened it, then it would do you some kind of service, assuming that service fit with its own sinister nature."

Scott was about to say something when his cell phone trilled. He looked at the display. "Her highness calls. You're busy, I'll take it outside."

He stepped into the hallway and closed the door as I returned to my cataloguing. It was Jessica, all right. Scott tried to talk in an undertone, but I heard enough.

*****

I rose early the next day after a sleepless night. The events of the previous day had aroused something dark in me and I now had a long day ahead. My game plan, equal parts desire and compulsion, was clear in my mind.

There were items I needed. To get them, I had to drive to a little town in upstate New York. Jessica was going to freak when she saw my expense voucher, but she'd just have to swallow it.

I visited numerous shops dealing with occult paraphernalia in that folklore-rich area. Having learned from experience that some of these rural types can be less than helpful toward strangers, I resorted to a strategy which consisted of a low-cut tank top, a short skirt, plus my "Aw, dontcha want to help li'l ol' helpless me?" routine. Very effective, particularly with men.

It was dark when I returned to where we'd met John Cross. In one hand, I held a good-sized Maglite. In the other hand I carried a knapsack full of the items I'd collected.

I turned it on the Maglite. and made my way into the woods

I remembered how frightened I'd been the last time I was here. Of course, that was before I'd spent all hours mastering the Ryte of Alliance.

When I got to the spot where Cross had begun bushwhacking, I clicked the Maglite off. Without hesitation, I made my way through the woods, unmindful of the thorns and brambles against my bare legs.

I reached the spot where the Devil had attacked John Cross and removed the contents of the knapsack: a yellowing parchment with writing, faded, but readable; a knife with a silver blade; a sickly greyish resin; thirteen roundish stones with eldritch symbols etched on them; a glass vial with amber-colored liquid.

I removed the Grimoire, basking in the surge of power that flowed through me when I touched it.

The last thing I did was to remove the Star of David from around my neck. It didn't need to see what I was about to do.

With only the full moon providing light, and very little of that, I uncorked the vial, daubed a drop of the sweet-smelling liquid on each palm, and rubbed them together. I then took the knife and made crisscross slashes in both palms. Blood surged, but I felt no pain.

No sooner had I done all this than my eyes acclimated themselves to the darkness. The stones, the resin, the parchment all stood out in perfect clarity. I could even read the writing on the parchment.

I took the stones and clasped them in both hands, making sure to leave a spattering of blood on each. As I did, I whispered the words on the parchment, words in a language I did not understand. I then lay the stones in a circular configuration and placed the resin in its center. I doused the resin with what remained of the amber liquid, and stood back.

The resin went from that sickly grey to a glowing yellow, then to a bright orange, and finally to a blazing red before emitting a column of flame, wide as an oak tree, that shot upwards beyond the tallest treetops. At that same moment, a wind swept through the woods, blowing my hair all askew, billowing my skirt up past my waist.

Despite the wind, the parchment remained undisturbed on the ground. Nor did the flame waver, but stayed trained upward as I kept repeating the secret words, no longer whispering, but half-chanting, half-gasping — louder, louder, ever louder, until my words tumbled from my mouth in a frenzied shriek mingling with the resounding crackling of the fire.

I have no idea how long the fire raged in concert with my impassioned incantation. All I know was that I was in the throes of sheer pulsation, and the feeling emanated from my center to my limbs, throughout my whole being. I closed my eyes, as the words on the parchment danced before my mind's eye and I understood every idiom, every nuance of that language which, only moments ago, was so impenetrable, so unknowable. I shuddered, reveling in the knowledge that was flowing through me, the power, the ecstasy.

The flames rose higher. The winds rose to a cyclonic intensity, scattering twigs and leaves in the clearing, creating not-so-miniature dust devils, even as they caressed my body with a soothing gentleness. The wounds in my palms from which my lifeblood gushed so freely had closed.

The wind changed. It was now coming from above and with it came a sulphureous stench which made me gasp and had my eyes watering. I looked upward and saw a shape at the summit of the flame. It was circling the column too fast for my eyes to get a bead on it. All I saw was this massive bulk and it was making a high-pitched keening sound. As it got closer, I could make out broad wings spreading from a vaguely humanoid form and two glowing red dots where its eyes should be. My knees buckled and I stumbled back against the tree.

It glided down until it stood before me. Somehow, I never wavered as I chanted those secret words, again and again. I heard the tremor in my voice, felt myself quivering, but kept my gaze fixed upon those unblinking red eyes, even when the thing's keening turned into a low throaty growl.

It stepped closer and was now less than three feet from my trembling body – this thing that had slashed John Cross' flesh and eviscerated his dog. This thing that had supposedly attacked, mauled, and brutalized innumerable luckless and innocent victims over the course of three centuries. It had even slaughtered its own mother, father, and siblings minutes after its birth.

This thing I summoned.

Its growls continued maybe for seconds, maybe for minutes, before it changed. Not physically – its appearance did not alter, but other things did. Its growl gave way to a soft chuffing. That odious stench receded; replacing it was a gentle aromatic musk, not at all unpleasant. The redness of its eyes receded to a soft orange, the color of embers in a campfire before they die out altogether, warm and comforting in the chill of the surrounding air.

As I straightened my knees to stand at my full height, it hunched over so our eyes were at the same level. It shuffled forward on thick scaly legs which ended in twelve-inch claws, making furrows in the earth.

My eyes studied it. Even as the flame receded back into the resin, every feature was distinct. It was bigger and broader than Hank, as John Cross had said. Its torso was a segmented carapace, each segment pulsing and throbbing, independent of the others. The wings, still furled, had the sheen of fine black leather, their outermost edges indistinguishable against the backdrop of the night. Its upper limbs also had that reptilian aspect, with fingerlike appendages, ending in claws. Its head was elongated with a mouth too small for its serpentine teeth, curved and sharp, jutting past thick-scaled lips. From behind, a thick ropelike tail reared up, dropped down, made sidelong motions on the ground, then repeated the pattern.

It took a step closer. So did I.

It reached out and I felt the tips of its claws as they closed on my arms, just short of breaking the skin.

I reached out and ran my fingers along the ridges of its carapace.

That long and ropy tail stopped making those sidelong motions on the ground. It touched my ankle, worked its way under my dress, up my thigh, ever upward, drawing me nearer.

I turned my gaze downward and saw what I was being drawn nearer to.

I did not resist.

The unfurled wings closed, enveloping me in a darkness blacker than the forest, blacker than the night.

*****

"We finally got the bastard."

This time, the words came from Hank Kreel. a very grim and tight-lipped Hank Kreel, the following morning.

Jessica, Scott, Tony, and I were at the trail head where Hank waited. When he saw Tony with his equipment, he shook his head and said "You won't be needin' that," in a tone that would brook no argument. Seething, Jessica instructed Tony to leave his gear behind.

Hank led us to a spot which was, by now, familiar to me. This time, rather than bring up the rear, I stayed on Hank's heels, with the others trailing. At the clearing, John Cross was waiting. Propped against a tree were shovels, a pair of axes stained with something wet and black, a pair of rifles, plus a third which didn't look like the other two. Hank saw that I was gaping at it and said "That was my dad's."

His use of the past tense did not escape me.

There were two other objects in the clearing, one of which even caused the normally unflappable Jessica to gag: a gutted deer carcass surrounded by a cloud of blowflies and an object wrapped in a tarpaulin. The air reeked of smoke and gasoline.

Hank began relating the events of the previous night and my vivid imagination kicked in. I saw the events unfolding as if I were actually there.

In the moonlight, I saw Henry, Hank, and John dragging a deer they had shot, and I sensed that this was not the first time they were doing this. John and Hank slashed open the animal's belly, scattered its entrails, then took positions at the edge of the clearing, guns at the ready. Henry Kreel stood a few feet away holding some kind of customized assault rifle. Whatever it was, it was the type of weapon law-abiding folks aren't supposed to have but can be put together more easily than you might think.

Moments later, wings beat overhead, and I saw three men tense in expectation. I heard something winging its way down through the leaves and lighting by the disemboweled deer.

I winced in anticipation of what was about to happen.

Henry Kreel fired first. He hit it with a burst of fully-automatic fire. In seconds, its wings, still fully unfurled were shredded. Pain, fury, and surprise blended in a deafening screech as it tried to fly off on wings too demolished to sustain it. It tried repeatedly to take flight, each time falling to earth.

Hank and John raced forward, firing with little effect, other than to irritate it further. The mortal damage was coming from Henry's attack. Bullets and buckshot had no significant effect. Ordnance with full-auto mode, however, rapid-fired at such close-range had never been tried against it.

It was no contest.

Its tail lashed out and wrapped itself around Henry Kreel's neck. I heard a stomach-wrenching crack as that flailing appendage lifted Henry's body into the air and hurl it onto the ground, with enough force to turn a human body into hamburger.

Hank stood there stunned, screaming curses at the thing while John Cross ran up to retrieve Henry's rifle and kept firing until the magazine was empty. Hank's paralysis broke. In a fit of fury, took up his rifle again and fired bullet after bullet into the thrashing, dying thing, still screaming curses at it.

I saw the once redoubtable, now pitiable, creature try to rise, then fall back on the dirt. From a throat which once produced blood-curdling shrieks, I heard a piercing moan, dwindling to a paltry death rattle. Then, it lay still.

The two men stood there for many minutes, watching to make sure that it would not rise in a final surge of dying strength. When it was clear that the thing was truly dead, they went back to the truck, and brought back a long-handled axe, picks and shovels, a can of gasoline, and a tarpaulin.

I saw them wrap the body of Henry Kreel in the tarpaulin, tie in securely and stand over it for many minutes in silence. Hank sobbed as John Cross spoke words too low for me to distinguish.

The first light of dawn broke. Hank Kreel took up his axe and vented his rage on the thing that had killed his father, while John dug a hole at the outermost edge of the clearing. When it was about six feet deep, Hank and John donned thick work gloves and dragged the dismembered remains of their prey into the hole. It took many trips for them to complete this task.

Lastly, I saw Hank Kreel pour the can of gasoline into the hole, stand back, then lit a rag and tossed it into the hole. There was a loud *foomp* and for the second time, I saw a column of flame up from the ground, up towards the sky. Hour after hour, it burned and when it finally died, the two men replaced the dirt, covering the remains.

"I guess it's over," Scott said, as my mind returned to the present. We stood by the grave amidst pungent gasoline fumes seeping up from the earth.

My eyes were watering. I hate the thought of any living thing suffering and the anguish that I had seen the thing endure, even in my own imaginings, wrought tears. Yes, I'd researched all the terrible things that it had done to people and animals throughout its near three centuries of existence, but I couldn't help myself. I had called it, and it had come. I saw it, touched it, and in those moments we stood facing each other, it had been nothing but gentle with me.

Scott put his hand on my shoulder. I shook it off.

No way I was going to let him touch me. Not after I overheard him speaking to "Jess" during a phone call outside my motel room. They were talking business, but it wasn't *I. On New Jersey* business.

*****

There isn't much more to tell.

My gig with *I. On New Jersey* ended and Jessica wrote me a generous check.

There have been no further sightings or attacks since then.

I broke it off with Scott, but he may be hearing from me again soon.

That's because I'm pregnant. If it's Scott's, he *will* step up.

Of course, it might not be Scott's.

If that turns out to be the case, I won't be pulling a Deborah Leeds number. I will not curse, but rather welcome my son. I will cherish, love, and nurture him. When the time comes, I will let him go, to seek out the hidden places his father knew. When the urge takes him, he will take his place in a world where the true monsters are the cruel, the faithless, the bigoted Henry Kreel types who treat you like dirt because of your heritage.

Scott was wrong. It is not over.

THE CROSSROADS

by Crawdeloch

I remember an interesting encounter from my youth, back when I was still living in a small farmstead not far from White's End. I was planning a travel to Tammerfors to take part in the traditional autumn's festivities, having acquired a sizeable sum of money from a recently deceased relative. Due to my aforepoor status however, I owned not a car yet, such vehicles being quite a luxury in those times. The house's horse was needed in the fields, and so, lacking means of transport, I decided to take off on foot. The city was a nigh hundred kilometers away, but I worried not, for it was summer, the weather pleasant, and I had gotten accustomed to long hikes during my hunting trips.

Thus, I started my journey at six o'clock in the morning, waving goodbyes for the family. As the sun greeted me warmly at the farmstead's stony steps, I smiled and adjusted my bag, then began walking the sandy road with pockets full of coins, a feathery spark in my step. Little did I predict of the peculiar traveler I was about to meet the next day.

The first day of journeying went by in a pleasant summer sun, though I observed a hint of autumnal redness to its orange glow. The winds had not yet started their north-bound travels, and so, in the still, seemingly timeless summer I had no trouble traversing the winding road. Various birds from the surrounding pine and spruce forests aided my mind to stay veering into the troublesome thoughts concerning the recent death of my grandfather, who'd been quite close to me.

So went an hour, went another, and yet another, until the sun deepened its glare to that of deep crimson, and my body grew weary. I recalled a crossroads tavern not long from where I was at that point, and so I wasn't worried, for I had pre-planned to spend the night there. Not long after thinking of a soft, feather-filled bed, I could see the building's smoking chimney peeking behind the pines. After one last hill, and there, resting in the summer eve, I saw the tavern - quite a welcome sight.

The crossroads tavern was situated - unlike the name would suggest - not directly at the crossroads of Whitend and Tammerfors roads, but a few kilometers to the east of it, in the direction I was arriving from. From there it'd still be many dozens of kilometers to the city, but I felt pleased at myself, having walked the distance faster than planned.

I noticed the courtyard empty (which was somewhat unusual), with just a lone well standing at the center of the dusty open area. Shrugging, I made my way to the door, and promptly stepped in.

The main hall smelled faintly of old whiskey and ale, as I entered, a faint reminder of past revelries. Again, no people were in sight. The emptiness of the tables seemed somewhat out-of-place in an usually lively location. Fire was dancing happily in the central fireplace though, and soon enough the tavern master - a bald, overweight man wearing a dirty apron - emerged from the backroom with a broom in his hand. He seemed strangely absent-minded, approaching me with a questioning look.

"Greetings," I said to the man, releasing the bag from my shoulder, "The place seems silent tonight?"

The tavern master merely tightened his grip at his broom as he stood behind the counter, staring at me for a few questionable moments. He then uttered out slowly, again with an absent mind, as if something more important was occupying his thoughts.

"Yes... I guess it's the coming festival..." He stood still for a moment, then glanced at the door.

"Also... there's been speak of a plague. Have you heard?"

I lifted an eyebrow. "No, I haven't. Where? How serious?"

The man kept glancing at me and the door for some reason - I felt the urge to turn myself as well, to see if there was anything out of place there but withheld my impulse.

"South. They say it originated from the coast. Maybe Helsingfors. Some say it came with the ships." He sniffed and coughed, then added; "Heading north, they say, perhaps reached Tammerfors already."

A worrisome thought visited my mind. I asked,

"Have you heard word of the festival? Has it been canceled?"

The man sighed and turned his head from the door to face me.

"I don't know mister, and I care not know." He put the broom down, leaning against the counter, "Now, is there something you want?"

Feeling somewhat unnerved, I couldn't think of anything further to ask. I requested a bed, and I quickly made my way to my designated room, where I spent the night with restless thoughts thinking of the strange plague and the Tammerfors' upcoming festival. Should I continue my journey or not? I had walked this far already, so I might as well continue just to see the state of things in town. And so, feeling a sudden surge of determination, I decided to press on. With that thought I finally fell asleep, the time already well-past midnight.

I woke up the next day with renewed vigor, the last night's events and the tavern master's worrisome words vanished from my mind. I quickly got up and gathered my things, then stepped out the room in order to enter the main hall. It was as quiet as yesterday, the fire now extinguished in its iron dome, just a pile of ashes resting on the cold stone.

The tavern master was nowhere in sight. I spent a few moments yelling for him, even visiting the storage room. Only empty shelves greeted me. The man had vanished, taking the task of maintaining the tavern with him. Shrugging, thinking of it being none of my business ultimately, I exited the place, though with an uncanny feeling in my stomach.

I exhaled when stepping out the door and letting it swing shut behind me, eager to continue the journey. Fortunately, the weather was as pleasant as the day prior, sun already rising with a bright orange glow. After filling my leather pouch with water from the yard's well, I continued my walk with haste.

*****

I was glad to be out of the eerie tavern, and soon as I got to my regular pace of walking and observing the surrounding nature with its plentiful birds and other creatures of life (even appreciating the occasional insect buzzing by my ear), I again felt at ease. I paused for a moment to eat a can of salted meat and get a few swigs from the leather pouch.

My surprise was a substantial one when I tasted the water. It was slightly off. I poured some of the contents on the ground, only to notice the liquid filled with black spots. Fearing the plague somehow already reaching this far north, I discarded the whole thing. At this point I seriously considered turning back, but, fool as I was, I packed my things and continued on, hoping I'd encounter a house where I could get fresh water.

Just a few kilometers ahead, I came to the crossroads, the juncture which I'd almost forgotten about. It was a welcome change from the constant woods, and I hoped that perhaps a fellow journeyman or travelling merchant had set up camp there (something that was a custom at the time).

The forests gave away to a large clearing as I neared the crossroads which was located on a level meadow and so I could see in all directions with ease. To my disappointment the surroundings were desolate, not a singular soul in sight. I sighed, adjusted my bag, and proceeded, thinking of resting for a moment beside the roadsign before continuing towards Tammerfors.

*****

I was sitting on the pleasant meadow, leaning against the crossroads sign and shuffling the surrounding vegetation with an absent mind when suddenly, I felt a shadow befall on me. Quite surprised, I lifted head to see what was blocking the sun. It was an old, bearded man in ragged clothes with a large hemp sack over his shoulder. But the first thing I noticed were a pair of... horns... or antlers, growing out of his forehead. They started like goat's horns, but then, as they proceeded upwards, turned into twisting, many-layered antlers of a reindeer. It was quite a sight, and even though this "man" didn't seem hostile, even smiling as he looked down upon me, I let out a little yell.

I quickly got up, thinking how he'd simply appeared there, perfectly silent in his approach. The large sack on his shoulder which he had a tight grip on seemed to contain something living, for it was twitching and ever slightly moving about, as if something, or multiple somethings, were trying to get out.

Still bewildered about the whole situation, I couldn't get a word out. He looked me in the eye and greeted in plain, lukewarm-pleasant, salesman's tone, "Greetings, friend. Travelling to Tammerfors?"

He extended his left hand, still smiling. I hesitated, but then grasped it. It was a solid grip, that of a seemingly honest man, though strangely chilly. My hand felt itchy upon release.

"Yes, uh." I still struggled for words, glancing at his sack and antlers, "I was just resting here. Who-who are you?" I wanted to ask about his antlers, but it somehow felt rude. He answered, still smiling, "Merely a fellow traveler, or to be precise, a travelling salesman. Although I'm of the unusual kind, for my products are completely free of charge."

I felt the situation quite off, but as he showed no signs of hostility, I decided to humour him. "Oh... I see. And what do you sell, if I may ask?"

He cocked his head a bit to the side, then gave an elusive smirk that of a seasoned salesman. The horn-antlers on his head cocked with the motion, producing quite a peculiar sight. "But my friend, nothing less than peace and tranquility!"

I observed his writhing, squirming sack. Despite his strong grip (and the sack's robust design), it seemed like at any moment the forces within could tear the sack asunder, breaking free the contents, opening up like Pandora's box. "That's... that's," I thought what to say to his strange claim, "That's an interesting thing to be offering."

His smiling didn't cease for a moment as he continued,

"Indeed, and one of its kind." He pondered on something, caressing one of the 'branches' of his antlers with his left hand, "Perhaps... perhaps, your grandfather would still be alive if I'd made here in time." He mused, "He was quite the worrier-type, always stressed, straining himself with troubling thoughts."

I opened my mouth to ask how he knew of my grandfather's recent death, but then decided to stay silent. He continued, looking into distance. "But alas, one can only travel as fast as his feet allow him - such is the state of any lonely travelling salesman."

He turned his eyes to me with a new-found spark, "Perhaps you'd like to receive peace and tranquility? Here," he lifted his sack from his shoulder and laid it on the ground. There was a robust quick-release knot around the throat. I heard animalistic, muffled moans of distress emanating from within as the sack quivered violently. "Just pick one for yourself, it's completely free, as I said."

I eyed the smiling man, then his sack. The situation was getting beyond unnerving by this point. I felt like asking about his sack, his horn-antlers, about the thousand things that circled my mind at that moment but found no words. I kept staring at the writhing sack on the ground, the unknown forces within it, only wanting him to take hold of it once more as to secure it to his grip. It seemed like the sack's mouth could at any moment burst open, releasing its unnatural abominations onto the world.

Struggling to get words out, the only thing that came to mind, was to ask, "Pardon me, uh, good Sir, but what's with the horns?"

His smile vanished in an instant, and he frowned, seemingly insulted, though I cannot say if his emotion was real or feigned.

"Ah, that's quite unfortunate," he said as he picked the sack back up, "You only needed to open the knot and choose one for yourself, and everlasting peace and tranquility would've been yours. Never would've needed to worry about a thing." He shrugged as he threw the sack over his shoulder. The muffled, high-pitched screams amplified for a brief moment.

"Such a shame," he sighed.

I watched as he took off, walking without saying a goodbye. He picked the road leading north, towards White's End. His horn-antlers waved and his sack struggled as he paced onwards along the dusty road, and soon he was already well on his way.

Dumbfounded of the whole thing, I foolishly wanted to have the last word and so I yelled after him, "Where are you heading?"

At first, I thought he would not answer, but to my surprise he stopped, though unturning. His back and squirming sack towards me, he shouted, voice steady, though now lacking his salesman's pitch, "North, I'm always heading north."

I still felt unsatisfied, so I continued, without thinking, "If that is so, what happens when you reach the north pole?"

There was this... silence. I felt like I'd done something profane. If my inquiry about his antlers was insulting enough, this question, *this question* seemed a whole other category. I cannot tell what, but something in his stature changed, a silent suggestion of something beyond the horizon of reason subtly shifting, moving just a little, like the whole world turning just a bit more towards the strange. A change that, if allowed to ferment to its fruition, would unleash forces no man could foresee.

A sudden feel of profound dread came over me, even though no immediate physical change had taken place in this mysterious man-animal-salesman. He stayed perfectly still; even the beings in his sack ceased their movements. I was frozen for a moment, holding my breath, then turned and ran, ran east, towards home, until exhaustion took over me, and I collapsed onto the road.

I'm quite sure that if I'd hesitated just a second longer, staying there waiting for his answer, I wouldn't be here today.

~

EMILY'S BRIDGE

by William Presley

"Not only do you know you died, they say your brain is supposed to be hyperactive for the first few seconds afterward. Weird, right? What if there is an afterlife, but it's actually just one of those dreams that feels like it lasts forever, even though it's only been a minute?"

"Eternity in a minute," I mumbled. "Guess that's better than going straight to the void. Still a pretty depressing thought, though, even for someone in his twent- fuck!" A sudden lurch forced me to slam on the breaks, my front wheels stopping directly on the threshold of the Gold Brook Bridge. Tristan and I both hopped out to assess the damage.

"Seriously? A flat? Here?"

My friend pushed his blonde hair off his forehead and slipped into his best Chris Hansen. "You see how this looks."

"Why don't you take a seat," I laughed. "I've got a spare; it'll only be a second."

A gust of crisp, Vermont wind caught me just as I reached the trunk, blowing sheets of snow from the surrounding treetops like shrouds in the moonlight. I looked back at the covered bridge – somehow less of a relic in the context of this wooded mountain road – with a shudder. No amount of joking could sap the sinister feeling out of the air for two people who'd grown up listening to the stories about this place. 'Emily's Bridge,' as it was known to anyone outside of Stowe, was supposed to be haunted the spirit of a jilted lover who'd hung herself from the rafters, and I'd long heard that nothing here was a coincidence. My tire certainly wasn't.

"What the hell! Look - someone made a spike board. Wh-" I cut myself off for the second time that night, following my friend's gaze to the other side of the bridge. There, glowing in the beam from the headlights, was a dark-haired young woman with her arms clasped behind a black nightgown. Her head was tilted, and though the corners of her mouth were twisted into a grin, the muscles around her deep-set eyes remained relaxed.

"Mike, we need to get in the car. Now."

"What? No! This stupid TikTok prank cost me a new tire. I'm not leaving without two hundred bucks… at least."

"Mike…"

"Oh, come on. You don't really think that's a ghost?"

"Obviously not," he hissed. "Dead people don't have shadows. But I know that look on her face. Every nurse knows that look. I see it all the time when I fill in on the psych floor. There is something wrong with this woman. Get. In. The car."

It was too late; she was rushing toward us. "Isaac? Isaac, Isaac, Isaac? Which one of you is my Isaac?"

Tristan's hospital training finally kicked in, his posture growing firm even as his voice softened. "Actually, ma'am, neither of us are named Isaac. But maybe there's something I can help you with?"

"You can help by telling me the truth. Which one of you is Isaac?"

"Well, like I said, neither of us are Isaac. Is-"

"Liar!" She whipped a long, double-sided noose out from behind her back and draped one end over her neck. "Don't you know who I am? Don't you recognize me? Emily! It's Emily. I used to be two people. When my soul came back, my body belonged to somebody else, and she tried to fight me. Tried to get rid of me. But I won. Now I can be free. Free with Isaac. His soul is inside one of you, and I'm taking him with me. I will not leave here alone again!" Her last syllable morphed into a hysterical shriek as tears poured down her cheeks.

Tristan remained calm. "Ma'am, there is no Emily. There never was. It's just a story. She's not a real person. But maybe there is an Isaac. Is that who you live with? Let's give him a call."

Another shriek. The woman lunged at my friend, somehow managing to wrap both legs around his waist during her desperate attempt to shove his head through the empty side of the noose. "It's you. He's in you!"

Fighting through the pain as ragged nails dug into my flesh again and again, I grabbed her by the shoulders and tried with everything in me to yank her back. "No, stop," Tristan screamed. "She's biting me! You're gonna pull out a chunk of my neck!

"Then quit flailing and grab ahold of her," I shouted before pushing the pair to ground. She finally let go when I kicked her in the ribs, giving me the chance to pry her off Tristan. We both made a mad dash for the car.

"Lock the door. Lock the door!" he yelled.

"We're good. I got it, we're good," I sighed, my heart still racing. "I'm calling the police."

Thwack.

Warm blood drizzling down our faces, Tristan and I turned to each other in a panic.

Thwack. Thwack.

The deranged woman was throwing herself against the driver's side window, squealing all the while. "I'm not leaving alone, Isaac! I'm not. Leaving. Alone."

"Mike, drive."

"The tire is flat."

"It doesn't matter – fucking drive!"

"9-1-1… what's your emergency?"

Thwack.

"We can't wait for the police; she's got schizo strength! If she gets in here, we're screwed!"

Glass shattered all over my lap as a hand reached for my face. That was all the prompting I needed to start the car and floor it with the deranged woman still clinging to the doorframe. And then it happened – my back wheel hit the spike board. The car went into a violent swerve on the other end of the bridge, flinging our assailant over the guard rail and down the roadside ravine.

"Tristan, I think…"

"Yeah. It's all rock down there. She has to be."

Yet, upon exiting the vehicle this time, we were greeted with a site even more horrific than we expected. The woman's head hung limply to one side, her body suspended over the edge of the brook. The free end of the noose had caught on a guard post.

"Well," Tristan whispered, "if there wasn't an Emily before, there is now."

THE WOMEN WITH DETACHED HEADS

by Jennifer Jeanne McArdle

2018

Delata didn't know why the childless Massachusetts couple who hired her thought they needed a live-in housekeeper. But, how could she complain about all the free time she had, the day trips she went on, and the money she sent back to her family?

She felt nauseous while following, her boss, Mrs. Griffin, with their picnic basket as they climbed up and down the rocky coast.

"It's a nice lighthouse, isn't?" Mrs. Griffin asked the young woman. The structure was white and not very tall, sitting in front of a red-roofed building. "We could come back here for your twenty-first birthday next month? I guess beach isn't as nice as those back in the Philippines, huh?"

Later that night, she stared at the white stick she'd just peed on. If she were to have this baby here, her family couldn't help her, and how could she tell Mrs. Griffin what had happened?

*****

While in graduate school in her mid-twenties, Dolores, or Dolly, met her now husband, Jake; he had been so wild, so tanned, while working as a lifeguard at a local beach. His father had just bought him a shiny silver BMW. Dolly taught yoga. Everything felt right then.

Dolly was in her mid-thirties now and writing articles on nutrition for a women's magazine. She made Jake breakfast every morning before he left for work.

Dolly hugged her extra-soft bathrobe tighter around her body and watched her husband, waiting for her kiss goodbye. She offered her cheek. He kissed her and purred, "You smell good."

He reached towards her shoulder, but she turned, and instead, his hand brushed the back of her neck.

She winced.

"Oh, sorry," he whispered.

She gave him a hard look. He finally turned to leave.

Sometimes when Jake worked late, Dolly would watch YouTube videos on psychology. A few years ago, she had tried to determine if her often inscrutable husband had Asperger's; she took online assessments pretending to be him. Eventually her pop-psychology research led her to Narcissistic Personality Disorder.

"Delata, do you think Jake might have NPD?" Dolly asked the housekeeper one evening. "Both his parents are rich, and he grew up so spoiled. They didn't want Jake to marry me because my parents aren't rich and I'm only half white; my mom is Korean. His grandma once said I looked 'white' enough. Can you believe that? His family made him a monster."

Delata could believe it. People back in Ligao had always complimented her own pale skin.

"Mr. Griffin seems kind to me."

"Ha! Tell that to his coworkers. They call him 'Adolf' behind his back. He's nice when it suits him. When they have something he wants."

"I'm no one important. He doesn't have to be nice to me."

2010

Two years after Jake and Dolly married, Jake had just been promoted. Dolly had been bouncing from job to job.

"I want a career first," Dolly kept insisting when Jake brought up trying for kids.

"I've always wanted to be a dad. You don't seem to like working."

Dolly wondered often if she could risk the vengeance from his family if she divorced him, especially if it proved their racist and classist ideas about her true.

"Let's go on an adventure," he interrupted her one Sunday night when she was reading on the deck. She put her book down slowly.

"What do you mean?"

"We should travel somewhere for a few weeks."

"I'm not eligible for vacation yet." She gripped her chair. She had just started working as a paralegal at a personal injury firm a month ago.

"Who cares? Just quit. You've quit plenty of jobs."

Dolly sat up and pulled her legs to her chest.

"I just think a nice adventure might pull you out of your slump."

Dolly felt angry, briefly, but then her heart fluttered in her chest. She felt bad about doubting Jake. "We could do that Italian food tour I always talk about!" She giggled.

"I was thinking somewhere more exotic, a real adventure. We're going to Borneo." Jake placed his hands on her shoulders.

"Borneo? That place on those reality shows where people live in the jungle?"

Jake had already booked the tickets. They flew from Boston to Dubai and then Jakarta.

"My grandfather visited Borneo when he was a young man. He had gone to Indonesia to explore selling Darber Cigarettes on the islands, and he was exploring buying up some land for plantations. He had heard rumors of headhunters living on Borneo, so he went into the jungle to meet them," Jake told her.

Dolly felt a little less resentful hearing this. Jake's maternal grandpa had been kind to him. He used to spend his childhood summers at his grandpa's home in Tennessee and he'd been a mess at his grandfather's funeral the year prior.

"I found his old notebook from when he was in Borneo in his attic."

Dolly tried to be happy. At the hotel in Jakarta, she enjoyed a fruity drink at the rooftop bar and watched the sun go down over the large-leafed trees jutting out from the mix of modern skyscrapers, wide highways, narrow streets, and dilapidated housing conglomerates. The air was humid and choking. Below her, dozens of motorcycles rumbled, and people shouted, hawking street food.

"I've booked a ferry from Jakarta to Pontianak, the port in Borneo," Jake informed her. "I feel like it's more authentic that way. God, how long ago did we order? People here take so long to do things."

Dolly wanted to ask him why they were going to someplace more remote if he was already frustrated with Jakarta's schedules. A few days later, a taxi driver, who asked Dolly when she was going to have a baby, drove them to the harbor. The locals on the ferry were staring at Jake and Dolly.

The wind whipped around them. Dolly felt seasick after a few hours of bouncing on rough water. She found a shady bench near a window on which she leaned her head and tried to stop feeling nauseous.

"Where do you come from?" Dolly opened her eyes to see a middle-aged man with a doughy, red face and a buzz-cut.

"My husband and I are from America— Boston."

"Ah, Boston. My nephew goes to Harvard. I'm from Singapore. Why didn't you just fly? You can afford it."

Good question, Dolly thought to herself.

He introduced himself as Andy before she could answer. "Pontianak," he continued. "It's a pretty modern city nowadays."

"Oh?" Jake folded his arms. "We were hoping to see some real jungle."

"Oh, yeah. You'll find that in Borneo, too. Just not in Pontianak. Lots of tourists come to see the orangutans. There's an interesting story about Pontianak. Pontianak are women cannibalistic ghosts. They say all of Pontianak was filled with monsters until a Muslim sultan came with his army and chased them away with canons sometime in the 1700s."

"That's a cute story." Jake yawned.

Andy looked at them carefully. "The Europeans, the Javanese, the Chinese, and other islanders keep moving to Borneo cities while the native Dayak people are pushed deeper into the jungle. The Dayaks are pagans and some of them were headhunters."

Dolly wrapped her arms over her own chest. Why did her husband want to go to Borneo?

2018

Delata had nightmares since she moved to Massachusetts. One night, she thought she heard an infant wailing outside her window, but when she looked, no one was there. As a little girl, she had dreamed about becoming a mother, even though her own mother had left her to work overseas as a housekeeper.

"You don't have money to go to university, but you could work in America for a few years, see the world, save some money," the woman who had recruited her into the housekeeping agency had told her.

But now, she didn't want to be like her parents, having children young and struggling to find ways to care for them. She needed money and education first. She screamed into her pillow. There were ways of getting rid of an unwanted child. She weighed her options as she stepped outside for a few moments, though it was cold. Tiny yellow droplets of water danced under the streetlamps. Cape Cod was so quiet at night, but even during the day, even in the towns, there always seemed to be fog creeping over everything. The Griffins' house with its controlled temperature, lack of insects, wide spaces, and clean, soft furniture, should have been more comfortable than her home in the Philippines, she kept reminding herself.

2010

When Dolly and Jake arrived in Pontianak, the sun had already gone down. Dolly had wanted to relax, maybe visit the spa, but Jake insisted they wander the streets bustling with food carts.

When Dolly's stomach finally settled, they bought some goat satay with peanut sauce and followed that with sweet, green avocado juice.

"I could use a nice beach day."

"We'll have time for the beach on the way back. I'm in contact with a man who lives in the Dayak village my grandfather visited. He's offered to let us stay at his house because there's no hotels there."

Dolly sighed but licked the last bit of sauce from the wooden satay pick. There was no point in arguing.

The ride from Pontianak to the village near a place called Meliau on the map began on the highway, then moved to narrow, tree-lined roads, yellow and crisp under the cloudless skies. They passed towns with concrete buildings painted bright colors. Banners, some even advertising Jake's family's Darber Cigarettes, hung from the metal roofs. Children in red and white uniforms marched along the side of the road and motorcycles carrying too many things and people passed them. As they kept driving, the paved roads became riddled with potholes; Dolly gripped the door hard while feeling her teeth rattle in her head.

They reached dirt roads. A family of wild boar ran across their path, and the towns appeared less often. The driver's leathery face with his high cheek bones and thin lips reminded Dolly of a mummy, and she couldn't work up the courage to talk to him.

They finally arrived at a town on a shallow river. The people there lived in connected gray wooden long houses on stilts over the water. Canoes with men in pointy hats navigated through the little islands of green river plants. Some people came out from their houses to look at them.

They didn't look like headhunters. The men were wearing plain shirts or soccer jerseys and shorts with sandals, while the women had patterned skirts wrapped up to their waists and tank tops. A man approached them.

"Are you Mr. Griffin?" the man said in accented but clear English.

"You can call me Jake." Dolly's husband put his hand forward. The man shook his hand and then touched it to his own chest.

"I'm Gusti. We are happy to have you visit. My grandma talks about your grandfather's visit." He smiled. Dolly swatted an insect away from her ear.

"This is my wife, Dolly."

Dolly smiled and Gusti bowed slightly to her.

"I hope you like staying in my home."

People stared as Gusti led Jake and Dolly up the stairs and into his home where curtains blocked most sunlight. An old rug had been placed on the wooden floor. Gusti's family included his grandmother, who had tattoos and elongated ear lobes, a quiet wife, two children around the age of ten, and his sister.

Gusti's wife served them sugary tea and some soup with white rice, vegetables, and pieces of chicken still on the bone.

"If you'd like, the men could take you fishing tomorrow. There are a lot of large fish in the river. If we catch something good, we'll have ikan bakar. There's an orangutan sanctuary not far from here. Lots of foreigners like to see them."

"Oh, I'd like to see that," Dolly said as she tried to adjust her crossed legs on her floor cushion so they were comfortable. Jake was too absorbed with reading his grandfather's notebook to continue conversing with the family.

"I am Noelle," Gusti's sister spoke in a hushed voice. "What's America like?"

"Much colder than here. You speak English really well," Dolly forced a smile. Gusti's sister giggled and pushed some of her long black hair behind her ears.

"Yes, I want to study English at university, but we can't pay it now."

Dolly nodded and sipped more of her tea, not really sure what she was supposed to say to any of these people. Jake suddenly looked up from his book and pulled out a hand drawn map.

"The fishing and orangutans sound nice, but I'd really like to go where I mentioned when I first contacted you. My grandfather described a waterfall north of here. I'd like to visit there."

Gusti's eyes widened and he scratched the back of his neck.

"There isn't much to see there, just some old houses. I can take you to a nicer waterfall. That one is dangerous. Many people have slipped and fallen there."

"But I contacted you specifically to take me to this place. If you don't want to take me, I'll find someone else here who will."

Gusti breathed out and put his cup of tea down noisily. He pulled a cigarette from a box next to him and lit it, watching Jake the whole time.

"Mr. Griffin," smoke billowed from his nostrils, "you will not find anyone in this village who will take you to that waterfall."

"I'm sure we can come to some kind of agreement. I have money."

"I have some things to take care of." Gusti suddenly stood up. "Tomorrow, you can let me know what you would like to do, or we will arrange for someone to take you back to Pontianak."

Gusti left abruptly. The rest of the family, except his sister, followed him.

"I am sorry," Noelle said to the American couple. "My brother just wants everyone to stay safe. Why don't you sit outside? There is a nice view of the river."

Noelle led them outside to a balcony. She gave them her cell phone number but apologized and said she had to take care of some errands. Jake lit a cigarette, although he rarely smoked, and paced a few times, back and forth, before Dolly finally spoke up.

"I know you like fishing back home. Why do you care so much about that waterfall? If it bothers them so much, shouldn't we just drop it? I don't wanna be on the bad side of headhunters." Dolly shuddered and looked to the river. She stretched her arms and legs out, feeling like sweat was collecting in her armpits and behind her knees. She brushed a few tiny ants off of her hand. Why did they have to come here?

"I'm not coming all this way just to be turned around. Gusti told me he would help me. He lied to me."

"I know you want to follow your grandfather's footsteps, but what if that place is dangerous? These people are nice enough to let us stay in their—"

"I am paying Gusti, you know."

"If you have a map, do we even need Gusti?"

"Not a good one. We risk getting very lost without a guide. My grandfather wrote about hiking there with a wealthy couple from Java. The wife was nearly on her deathbed due to lung cancer."

Jake took another drag of his cigarette and continued: "The wife had to be carried for most of the way. The couple claimed the witchdoctor who lived at the waterfall was an expert in magic. The witchdoctor brought the dying woman to his shack. In the morning, she was completely healthy. If there are descendants of this witchdoctor still living there, I want to see them. I want to know if the magic is real."

"Sometimes miracles happen. How do we really know this witchdoctor actually did anything to help this woman? If this man had a magical cure for cancer, wouldn't more people have noticed?"

"We don't know that for sure. What if people ignored or demonized him? Remember Andy's story about Pontianak? The Muslims and Europeans compared the Dayak to monsters."

"You're speculating a lot."

"We can't know until we see for ourselves, right?"

Dolly wanted to tell Jake he was an idiot, but then she noticed Jake was crying, which she'd only ever seen him do at his grandfather's funeral.

"If it's that important to you," Dolly realized that Jake not seeing the waterfall would mean she suffered through this "vacation" for nothing. "Maybe Gusti can't be convinced, but I think someone else here may respond to a financial incentive."

2018

"I heard Boston has plenty of Catholics. You won't miss church," Delata's mother had told her before she left for America.

Delata was glad the Griffins didn't expect her to go to church with them. Back home, abortions were illegal, but she still knew women who had gotten them, sometimes from shady doctors who used special massages or other crude methods. Surely, America had better options.

Delata was sitting across from Mrs. Griffin at the dining room table.

"Mrs. Griffin, I need to tell you something. I am…"

"Whatever you have to say, Delata, don't worry. If you want to work somewhere else, we can talk to your agency about placing you elsewhere. I wouldn't want your visa to be revoked—"

"No, Mrs. Griffin." She breathed in deeply. "I'm pregnant."

"Oh." Mrs. Griffin put down her teacup.

"I was wondering if you would help me…take care…"

"You want our help taking care of the baby?"

"No. I want your help ending the..."

Mrs. Griffin tapped her fingers on the table. "Is the father your boyfriend?"

"No," Delata told the truth.

"Is he around?"

"No," Delata lied.

"When I was your age," Mrs. Griffin placed her forehead in her hands. "I had an abortion. I regret it. It's one of the reasons it's been so hard for me to get pregnant now."

Delata felt dizzy. Something about Mrs. Griffin's tone seemed strange.

"Let me help you, Delata. I don't want you to make the same mistakes I did."

"But I'm not...should tell you…"

"Delata, don't cry. We're your family now." Mrs. Griffin walked around the table and wrapped Delata in her arms. Delata so rarely received any kind of physical affection since moving to the US.

Some of the women she knew who had gotten abortions became very ill afterwards. Maybe Mrs. Griffin was protecting her because it was risky. Riskier than having a baby she didn't want?

"You'd be a good mother. I sensed how strong you were when we first met." Delata knew Mrs. Griffin's compliment was genuine, but still, she didn't feel good.

2010

When Noelle returned from her errands, Jake went for a walk around the village, leaving Dolly alone with her.

"Do you know how to get the waterfall my husband wants to visit?"

"Yes." Noelle looked towards the door and then back at Dolly. "But no one from my village goes there. The place is evil and people disappear there. The man your husband's grandfather met is dead, but some new men live there now." Noelle swatted away a mosquito.

"Please, my husband will find a way to go with our without help. I'm afraid he's going to start trekking into the jungle by himself."

"My brother is not a bad man or a liar."

"Of course he's a good man. But what if your brother is wrong about this? Jake's grandfather saw someone get cured from cancer by the man who lived at that waterfall. Sometimes because of rumors, we believe untrue things about people. What if that man understood traditional things that your people, the Dayaks, have lost?"

"No, it's not that. My grandmother is also a traditional Dayak. She is Kaharingan, the religion

Dayaks practiced before the Muslims and Christians came here. But the people there are not practicing our normal traditions; they abuse the dead and attract bad spirits."

"We just want to see the waterfall and then we'll leave quickly. What if we paid for you to go to university? Wherever you want to go in Indonesia?" Dolly assumed that university tuition in a developing nation wouldn't be very expensive.

"You will do that? How do I believe you?"

"We have five million rupiah in cash that we could give you immediately. You guide us to the waterfall as far as you're comfortable. Once we can see the waterfall, you can wait at a distance until we're done looking. We'll set up a way to fund your tuition when we return to the village."

Noelle bit her lower lip.

"You don't have to tell anyone where you're taking us. We won't tell anyone."

Noelle finally agreed to take the couple early the next morning. She met them outside when the sky was still pink and the grass and all of their things were still covered in dew. Noelle wore black clothing, and she had long black and white feathers attached to her wrists.

"Hornbill feathers," she told them. "The animal might project us."

She implored the couple to wash their hands multiple times before they departed.

2018

When Delata was alone at night after she finished her work for the day, her mind raced. She still couldn't believe this was happening. She hadn't slept with anyone since she arrived in America.

Except for Mr. Griffin.

Her memory of the encounter was fuzzy. Delata had been off that Saturday. Some of the other ladies who worked for the same housekeeping agency had arranged a group trip to go sightseeing in Boston.

The other Filipino ladies from the agency were older and already bonded, and the other women in her cohort were from South American or Eastern European countries. They were friendly enough but had their own cliques, which left Delata alone. Still, it was pleasant, walking together through the indoor markets at Faneuil Hall. Some sparkly Christmas decorations were already for sale, although it was October. Maria, from Ecuador, rubbed a soft scarf on Delata's ever-cold cheeks.

When the mini-bus dropped Delata off in front of her home, she noticed extra cars out front. She unlocked the door to her apartment and went to the bathroom to wash her face.

"Delata?" She heard a knock at the door that connected her apartment to the rest of the house. "Do you want to come have a drink with us?"

Delata wiped her face and went to the door.

"Hello, Mrs. Griffin."

"We have plenty of wine and food. Why don't you join us upstairs?"

Delata didn't really want to join them, but most of the other housekeepers didn't have bosses as nice as Mrs. Griffin. She agreed to come upstairs, and Mrs. Griffin squeezed her shoulder a little too hard.

Mrs. Griffin poured her a drink, and Delata sipped as the Griffins talked to their friends. Delata didn't know what to say to any of them. Her cup kept getting refilled. The guests trickled out until there were just two or three left. Delata felt drunk. Mr. Griffin was loud and smiling and probably also drunk.

She didn't remember going back to her couch in her apartment, but somehow Mr. Griffin was also on her couch. She was too drunk to panic. She got up and knelt next to the sleeping man. Even though drool

dripped from the side of his mouth, his graying hair
and reddish beard framed a handsome face.

"Mr. Griffin," she shook his shoulders, "please
wake up."

"Where am I?"

"You fell asleep on my couch. You should go
back up to your bedroom."

He sat up and blinked at her.

"Delata, I think Dolly hates me. What should I
do? She wants me...There's this woman at work...I
shouldn't do this. I know I'm not the best husband, but
I loved...love...Dolly. I wish things could be normal
again."

Delata felt sorry for him and rubbed his back.
He grabbed her and pressed his face into her chest.

"It's okay, right, Delata?"

She nearly squealed, but she was very lonely,
and he was so warm. Delata thought she heard the door
to her apartment creak.

A few hours later, she woke up covered in a
blanket, and Mr. Griffin was gone. She took a shower
and tried to remember how far they had gone. Her
body was clean, she thought. Surely, she would have
stopped herself?

The only thing out of the ordinary were some strange new scratch marks on her door handle. Perhaps she had struggled to open her door while drunk.

When she saw the Griffins later that day, they acted normally, although her heart would stop every time she saw Mr. Griffin. After a couple of weeks of no consequences, Delata thought maybe her encounter with Mr. Griffin had just been a dream. Until she got morning sickness.

The day after Delata had admitted she was pregnant, Mrs. Griffin promised to take her to the obstetrician.

"I think we've become friends, haven't we Delata? We won't tell anyone yet, especially not the housekeeping agency." How could she tell Mrs. Griffin the child was likely her husband's, especially knowing the woman was having trouble conceiving? But what if Mrs. Griffin was right and she would regret an abortion?

"Have you thought about any names yet?" Mrs. Griffin asked her while they drank tea in the living room.

"Does Mr. Griffin know?" Delata thought her guilt might eat her from the inside out.

Mrs. Griffin sighed.

"I plan on telling Mr. Griffin. But you have to understand, Mr. Griffin's family is pretty conservative. He might judge you. What if we say you were engaged, and the guy had an affair and left you after he found out you were pregnant? I think that will make him feel sorry for you."

"Wouldn't he have noticed if I had a fiancé?"

"It takes Jake two weeks to notice if I've cut off six inches of my hair. What makes you think he pays any attention to what you're doing?"

"It's all so complicated. Mrs. Griffin, I'm not sure." Delata breathed in deeply. She thought of the money she sent back to her family. Mrs. Griffin really wanted her to have this baby. If she did get an abortion, would Mrs. Griffin fire her? Would the agency send her back home? What would she tell her family?"

2010

The journey through the jungle was not as bad as Dolly imagined it would be. Jake attracted more insects than she did and was the itchy, miserable one. Dolly actually felt refreshed, listening to the noises of the animals in the distance and the sound of water plopping on leaves. Perhaps they might end up doing something nice for the poor girl, even if they likely wouldn't find a magical cure for cancer or whatever Jake imagined.

After about two hours of walking, they heard running water.

Noelle stopped and sat on a large stone and pointed.

"If you keep walking that way, you'll see the waterfall. People call this place Air Terjun Hantu. Ghost Waterfall." She poured water over her hands to clean them. "You must be careful. People live here. But I don't know if they will be happy to meet guests. There is a Guru here. He teaches people how to use bad spirits. The birds know not to come here. The Guru was the student of the man your grandfather met."

Dolly shivered.

Noelle stayed on the rock while the couple slowly approached the area near the waterfall. Dolly's noticed a couple of shacks in the distance, and the sound of water rushing near them grew louder. As they approached, a short man wearing a white tank-top and a red skirt that ended at his mid-thighs came out from the building.

"Who are you?" he called out in English.

"We've come to see the Guru," Jake answered.

"Wait." He responded.

Suddenly they heard a woman's scream.

"Noelle!" Dolly shouted. They both dashed back to where they had left the young woman. She was holding her ankle, her face scrunched in agony.

"Snake!" she screamed.

"Help!" Dolly yelled. "Help! Someone was bitten by a snake!" Jake grabbed Noelle and lifted her up, bridal style.

"Bring me back to my village!" She slapped his chest.

"There's no time! We have to bring you to the Guru."

"No! I'd rather die!"

She tried shaking free, but he held her still.

"Jake!" Dolly shouted after her husband as he ran towards the waterfall and the shack, Noelle still screaming in his arms.

The man in white and red came back out from the house and was followed by an older man with long white hair and white paint decorating his face. He calmly raised his dirt-covered right palm.

"She was bitten by a snake," Jake shouted in-between Noelle's screams. "Can you help her?" His body heaved, soaked in sweat.

The older man nodded. The younger man walked to Jake and pulled the struggling Noelle from Jake's arms. She resisted, pushing weakly at him, but he held her fast and carried her inside. Dolly breathed deeply. Why was Noelle so afraid of these people?

"My student will be able to treat her." The door of the shack slammed closed. Suddenly Noelle's screaming stopped.

"Jake?" Dolly was behind him now. She grabbed his arm.

The Guru was approaching them, the bones and wood and beads of his jewelry clicking. He was not a big man, but the muscles of his chest, arms, and legs looked incredibly toned.

"She helped guide us here. We wanted to see you. My Grandfather was John Griffin. He met your Guru over fifty years ago."

The Guru crossed his arms over his chest and cocked his head slightly.

"Jake," Dolly whispered. "Maybe we should leave. Let's just run."

"I remember Mr. John Griffin. I am happy to meet his grandson. The woman needs to stay the night to heal. You and your wife can stay here."

Jake burst into smile and turned to Dolly. She offered a small smile back.

"Are you sure about this?" she whispered, but he ignored her. The Guru led them to a different wooden house on stilts. The Guru noticed Dolly looking at the wooden spikes under the house. "It keeps the monsters away," he said with a smile.

2018-9

Mrs. Griffin woke up early did and did many of Delata's chores. She took Delata to buy baby clothes and supplies. She told Delata to rest, more and more, as Delata's belly grew. Mrs. Griffin even bought Delata's favorite snacks from the store and took her out to eat, always to new restaurants they'd never been to before. Delata barely thought about Mr. Griffin because he worked late and rarely spoke to her, and she felt no affection or anger towards him.

As the child in Delata's womb grew, she thought maybe it would be nice to not be alone. And no one had ever spoiled her like she was being spoiled now. Sometimes she felt like Mrs. Griffin would do anything for her.

Except leave her alone.

"Do you think I should tell the other girls the story about the fiancé?" Delata asked Mrs. Griffin. "The other girls from Schreiber's?" Delata was starting to show now; the other girls would surely know she was pregnant if they saw her.

"I don't think that's a good idea. I haven't told the agency about your pregnancy. We don't know how they might react. It's very important you only go to the doctor with me, so I can pay for everything. I'm setting you up with a midwife. You won't even have to go to the hospital again. She can do everything from home, even the birth. Doesn't that sound nice?"

"Are you sure?" Wasn't healthcare supposed to be expensive here? But the Griffins were rich; maybe the cost was nothing to them? How much would Mrs. Griffin hate her if she knew the truth? Would it ruin the Griffins' marriage?

"Delata, it's fine. I'm here for you."

They went to uncrowded places, like the beach or the forest. If Delata left her apartment, Mrs. Griffin was always there, waiting by the car.

"Do you need anything, dear?" she'd say with a smile. "The midwife says to take it easy."

Delata sometimes dreamed of blood dripping down the walls and of snakes crawling around her body. She woke up often to the smell of flowers but none were in her room. She called her mother weekly but couldn't muster the courage to tell her mom about her pregnancy. Late into her pregnancy, all she seemed to do was dream and sleep. Mrs. Griffin sat next to her bed and held her hand on mornings she felt too sick to get up. Sweat had soaked her long hair and her sheets. Through half opened eyes, she saw Mrs. Griffin, who looked healthy and pink, practically glowing.

"Mrs. Griffin, you're so beautiful. Are you sure you aren't the pregnant one?" She mumbled and then hoped she wasn't insulting her boss.

"Shh. Delata, you need to protect your health, for you and the baby."

2010

"I am not Dayak. I was raised Christian in Central Java." The Guru told the couple while they ate. "I grew up thinking traditional pagan practices were evil. But then I met my teacher, the Guru who met your grandfather. He taught me there are spirits in everything around us. The forest and these spirits can be used by man for many things. But these uses have been lost, due to fear of the power they bring. The Dayaks are no better than the Muslims and Christians. They curse me, avoid me, and they cursed my master, too." The old man shook his head.

"That's awful," Jake said, completely entranced by the man's calm, smooth voice.

"But you Americans are curious, aren't you? You have a spirit just like your grandfather."

"I would love to learn from you." Jake seemed to blush, which shocked Dolly. He was never embarrassed.

"And how long would you learn from him? We can't stay here forever," Dolly interrupted.

"That's up to Jake. Sam, my student, and I will host Jake as long as he wants to stay."

Later in the day, the Guru offered to show Jake plants that he claimed would bring him to altered states of consciousness.

Dolly declined to join and instead went for a walk near the waterfall. Although the water in the pool was clear, she could not see the ground below, just darkness. Like Noelle had said, no birds were calling here. She wanted to jump in. What if a water-snake found her? But it was tempting. She stripped her clothing and dipped herself into the cool water. The liquid tasted sweet, and though they had hiked all morning, she did not feel tired. Perhaps she could spend weeks here. Not like she had a great career to go home to.

Hours passed, and the sun went down. As the moon rose higher, Dolly wondered where Jake was. She hadn't seen him, or the Guru, or Sam, or Noelle. Fireflies blinked in the bushes and crickets sang. Flashlight in hand, she made her way to the main shack, stepping carefully. As she approached the door, she heard humming coming from inside. She knocked on the door.

From her left, she heard banging, like something had hit the wall of the shack. Suddenly, the smell of metal and rot filled her nose. She held her breath and threw the door open. Before her were dozens of lit candles and the rising smoke of hanging incense. The Guru sat cross-legged on a pillow, his dirty palms open. Sam turned to her, the candlelight reflecting from his eyes. Jake was lying asleep, naked. In his arms was the body of a tan young woman.

Dolly screamed. The Guru smiled.

"What is this?" she yelled. The metallic smell grew stronger. "Jake?" Tears formed in her eyes. "Jake," she screeched. He moved and sat up. He looked at her through squinted eyes. Dolly approached her husband, rage boiling up in her stomach.

She stopped. She looked at the body of the woman. From the small feet to her round hips, to the small breasts and narrow shoulders. There was no neck and head.

"Oh my God," she choked.

Now Jake turned to look at the headless body he was intertwined with. He immediately scooted backwards, hitting his head on a wooden pole. Dolly felt something tickling her toes. That smell from before, *blood*--was bubbling up from the wooden floorboards. She froze. The blood quickly began to pile on itself, expanding and stretching until it formed a distinct human face and solidified into skin and bright white eyes. The rest of the blood transformed into long, gray tendrils. The tendrils lifted the head up, so it was as tall as Dolly's waist.

It looked up at her, and she recognized its features. It resembled the girl. Noelle.

The mouth opened, revealing pointed, sharp teeth. Dolly backed up to the wall behind her.

"In the morning, she'll be fine," the Guru laughed. "The head will reattach to the body. But at night, she hungers for the blood of other women."

2019

"Oh, he's so beautiful," Mrs. Griffin said as Delata held her newborn. Now Delata's son was here, so big and healthy. Everything Delata had gone through in the past few months was worth it. She was so elated; she barely noticed any lingering pain from the birth and could worry about her problems later. "Look at that big nose. He looks a bit like Jake, doesn't he?" Mrs. Griffin whispered in Delata's ear.

Delata nearly choked. Did she know?

"His daddy must have been an Irish Boston boy, too."

Delata could breathe again.

"May, I?" Mrs. Griffin reached for the child. Delata nodded. Mrs. Griffin started humming.

2010

"Jake," Dolly screamed.

"This isn't real!" Jake grabbed his hair and jumped to his feet. "I need water." He ran out the door of the shack.

"Jake!" Dolly screamed. The vampire head lunged towards her. She grabbed the candle next to her and slammed into to the creature's face. It shrieked.

"Please, help me," Dolly looked towards the Guru.

"You should have gone to the other house; it was protected."

A tendril wrapped around Dolly's ankle, causing her to fall on her back, a shock of pain traveled from her head down her spine. Another tendril grabbed her wrist and squeezed. The head lurched for her abdomen and bit down, hard. Dolly groaned, the pain nearly causing her to blackout. Dolly heard slurping. The head was drinking her. Her breathing got faster and faster.

"Help me," she cried. Out of the corner of her eye, she saw a foot and the glint of something kicked towards her. A knife. She grabbed at it with her free hand, her lower body feeling totally numb, her middle as though it were on fire. She wrapped her fingers around the hilt, gripped it as hard as she could and stabbed the blade into the back of the creature's neck.

Again. Again. Again.

The slurping stopped. The pressure on her wrist and ankles released, and the head flopped to the ground, motionless. Dolly looked at her stomach. Her whole shirt was completely soaked with blood, and it was continuing to pool on the floor.

"Help me," she repeated through shallow breaths. Suddenly the Guru's face was eye level with hers.

2019

Delata's son, Joseph, slept in a crib beside her bed. Now that he was here, she needed to talk to Mrs. Griffin. She couldn't keep doing this, hiding and lying. She had to be brave. Even if she lost her job or if Mrs. Griffin would hate her. She hugged a pillow close to her chest.

Delata heard something near the door of her bedroom.

It was probably just the old house creaking.

She heard someone humming, first softly, then louder.

Joseph started screaming.

Something tickled her right forearm lightly, then it pierced her skin. She gasped, her heart pounding in her chest. A woman's face, white as snow and glowing, stared down at her. The creature raised its right hand; each finger possessed a long claw as sharp as a surgeon's scalpel.

2010

"I can stop you from dying," the Guru told Dolly while holding a long, sharp nail. "You won't be like the village girl; her envy and ambition for a better life made her a penanggalan with help from my magic. But you're different; your vices are pride, wrath, and cruelty, and they're so much deeper than hers were. You'll be a pontianak and stronger than her. You'll resemble a normal woman whenever this nail is buried in your neck, but if you remove it, you'll be the monster. You won't be able to have children, but you will live and be strong."

In the morning, Jake was convinced everything that had happened was just a bad trip.

"Noelle died of her snakebite," she told him.

"How are we going back to that village without Noelle? They'll definitely have questions."

"Don't worry about them," the Guru told him. "Sam and I have connections. We'll get you back to Pontianak whenever you want to leave. The girl is no one important from a poor village. The police won't bother looking, and the villagers are scared to come here."

"They're scared of your magic power?" Jake asked him with wide eyes.

"They're scared of his friends who are government officials," Sam answered and laughed.

2019

Dolly swallowed the last piece of Delata's liver after she'd eaten most of her other vital organs. She felt a little bad; Delata had been a sweet girl, both in character and taste. Joseph was crying, so Dolly picked up little Joseph in her arms and sang to him. Dolly had hid Delata's pregnancy from her friends and family and had been faking her own pregnancy around them.

Dolly had revealed to Jake a few years prior that she had become a pontianak. He had tried to kill her, but she was stronger than him.

"You wanted to go to Borneo. You left me in the shack with those people. You did this to me. But we'll still have the 'normal' life you want."

Dolly found a shady housekeeping agency with a reputation for ignoring or punishing housekeepers who complained of abuse. The first Filipina they hired was too outgoing and had already been the US for a few years. There was no way they could have hidden her for nine months.

After she fired that girl, Dolly had been lucky enough to find pale, friendless Delata. If Joseph resembled his Asian mother, they could always point to his Korean grandma on Dolly's side.

"Why does it matter if you have sex with the girl?" Dolly asked her husband when he had doubts about Dolly's plan. "You've had affairs. Delata won't even remember with this drug. Since when do you care what happens to young girls from Asia? We didn't even tell that Borneo girl's family she was dead. You can't make up your mind about a surrogate and an egg donor because your family is too conservative for it. I can't smell an egg donor, but Delata smells amazing; she has great genes for a strong son."

"She'll go to the police." Jake had told his wife after he had gotten Delata pregnant.

"You think police help foreign housekeepers? She doesn't know about women's shelters or workers' rights in America. I've been in her dreams, ruining her sleep. She's too tired to fight us. I'm the only person who cares about her here. You want your child. She wants to go home to her family with money. We'll pay her off after the birth and send her home. Everyone wins."

Dolly looked at the remaining pieces of Delata's corpse. She'd tell Jake that the girl ran off in the middle of the night. They'd even report her to ICE. She touched the poor girl's face. Dolly really had been planning to send the woman away with money for her family,

"I guess I was hungry." Dolly shrugged.

PROTECT US

by Julia C. Lewis

A crying girl stumbles down the riverbank into the shadows of the night. Her feet are cut from lack of shoes, and her filthy clothing torn. She winces as she steps onto a sharp pebble and fresh blood flows.

She's been running for a while, but the man is still hot on her heels. In her desperation, she thinks of jumping into the Rhine, knowing she would surely drown. Her parents never taught her how to swim. She wonders if they miss her, if they even know she's gone.

The night is quiet, with no one in sight but the girl and her pursuer. The sharp knife of her frantic breathing cuts through the silence. Moonlight reflects off the water, the air fresh and crisp. The river water gently laps the shore, and soon a great steep rock comes into sight.

Faintly, the girl remembers the story of *The Lorelei*, a woman that threw herself into these very waters over a faithless lover. Instead of dying, she turned into a vengeful siren.

Oh, how the girl wishes she could meet the same fate. She would rip the man apart and make him pay for all he's done to her. All the agony. All the torment.

In her haste, she barely notices the statue on top of the rock. It's enveloped in a glinting mist, and from it a faint song emits. The statue depicts a longhaired maiden gazing down onto the Rhine River.

Running at greater speed, the man has almost caught up with his prey. He's not wounded, he's the one that wounds. He's so close. He can almost feel the girl's skin in his hands, and her taste on his tongue. They always taste better when they're terrified.

Angry with himself for letting her get away, he's desperate to catch up to her. He's had great plans for her, and she's ruined them with her pathetic will to live. How tedious this work of being a villain can be.

As he reaches out his fingers to grab her long black hair, he catches a note of a curious song in the air.

The song envelops him and he's all but forgotten about the girl in his sights.

On hands and knees, he crawls up the steep incline of the rock, blooding his fingers, breaking his nails, all the while creeping closer and closer to the top. He must find the source of the haunting melody.

Finally at the top, he stands before a beautiful maiden, her outline shimmering in the dark. She smiles at him, as he stands tall.

Her silken blonde hair falls over her shoulders to cover her naked breasts, her smooth skin the color of ivory. The man can feel himself being pulled towards this mysterious woman, entranced by her beauty. She's unlike any woman he's ever seen before. Even the girl seems unimportant now.

"Come," she whispers as she takes his hand.

He follows her in a deep trance. *Needing* her. *Wanting* her.

"Who are you?" He asks the apparition.

"I'm your wildest dreams..," she smiles at him, "and your biggest nightmare." The woman's face contorts in anger and flashes great sharp teeth. She hisses at the man and lunges at him.

Her teeth sink into his exposed throat, gnawing and gnashing at his flesh. Blood flows freely down his shirt, and he screams in agony. Relentless, the woman continues to feed upon him.

Suddenly, her hands release his shoulders, and she shoves him with great force.

The man stumbles backwards, rocks and gravel skitting down the incline. Unable to catch himself, he falls.. and falls...

The girl at the riverbank has stopped running. Her pursuer is no longer there. His screams echo in the dark.

She glances up at the top of the rock and sees him standing there next to a ghostly figure. The incline is over four hundred feet tall, so she is unable to make out the details.

Frozen in place, she watches as the figure shoves the man, and he tumbles down the precipice. His limbs flail, his head hits sharp edges, his teeth fly from a broken jaw, and his skin tears.

At last, he comes to a stop next to the girl. His face a bloody mess, contorted in fear. His throat ripped out, a gnarly mess seeping out onto the riverbank.

The girl smiles at his broken form and looks back up the incline. The shimmering form waves at her, and then vanishes back into the darkness.

*****

A group of local teenage girls find the man's battered corpse the next day. They prod him with a stick, not completely surprised by their find. As the World grows more crowded, and the men turn more viscous towards their female counterparts, they reckon this will be a common sight in times to come.

They grab him by his ankles and drag him into the river. As his corpse floats away with the current, the girls make their track up to the statue at the top of the rock.

At the peak, they form a semi-circle around the statue of *The Lorelei* and thank her for her service. They express their gratitude for her watch over the poor girl and defending her when no one else would.

At the foot of the statue, they lay fresh picked flowers they'd gathered along the banks of the Rhine. An offering for their protectress, their fair goddess.

With their hands linked, they chant, "*Protect us, Lorelei. Protect us from the men who want to do us harm. Protect our future daughters from their hands. Protect us from their wrong doings.*"

They stand up and walk back down the rock, just as they do each morning. A task they will continue to carry out until they grow old, just like their mothers before them. And one day, their own daughters will take their place.

UNDER KIPAPA BRIDGE

by Sarah Cannavo

He was zipping his camera back into its case when his phone buzzed in his pocket. Michael Iokepa fished it free, the strap of his bag slung across his broad chest, and smiled when he saw the name on the screen, pressing the phone to his ear. "Nala." Booted foot resting on a moss-furred rock, he pushed a handful of his long dark hair back from his face, a few droplets of sweat trickling down his amber skin. "I promise, I'll be home soon."

"Mm-hm," his wife replied, and picturing Nalani's expression made his smile grow. "I've heard that one before. I hope you got some good stuff out there, at least."

His free hand rested on his brown leather gear bag the way it would on the back of a beloved pet. "Don't worry, I did," Michael assured her, surveying the stretch of Kipapa Gulch he'd spent most of the July day exploring, photographing and sketching and soaking up the lush landscape. Growing up on Oʻahu, he and his friends had often taken their dirt bikes here on the afternoons they weren't down at the beach with their surfboards, and even now, a couple decades past his teen years, Michael found himself returning every so often and usually managing to come away with some inspiration whenever he did. He also tended to lose track of time on little ventures like these, whether to Kipapa Gulch or somewhere else on the island, which was why he was so grateful for his very loving, very patient wife. "I'll show you when I get back. Which, as previously stated, will be soon." He left his perch and started winding back the way he'd come, minding his footing on the rocky, root-roughened terrain. "How were things at the gallery today?"

Nalani's family owned an art gallery on the Big Island, and when she'd moved out to O'ahu after college she'd opened one of her own, where she showcased the work of other Hawaiian artists along with her own paintings and jewelry. It was how she and Michael had met, when she'd shown the photography of a friend of his and Pert had suggested she take a look at Michael's work; she'd wound up displaying several of his sculptures and photos, and on the last night of the exhibition, he'd finally worked up the courage to ask her out. Six years married, seven together, and one of the sculptures from the original show, a driftwood rendering of Pele and Lohiahu, still sat in their living room, a reminder of how it'd all begun.

"They were pretty good—I sold one of your photos, actually, the one of the thunderheads on Waikiki. I was hoping we could celebrate when we went out to dinner tonight, but my date is dangerously close to standing me up." Nalani's voice wavered, not through any play at emotion but the reception beginning to flake out—considering his location, Michael was surprised it'd lasted this long, gulches not exactly cellular hotspots even in this wired-up day and age.

"He sounds like a real idiot."

"He is," Nalani agreed readily, "but I love the lug anyway."

"He loves you, too," Michael said. "I'm on the way back to my car now; from there it's a straight shot across the bridge, and then I'll pick you up, okay? Just like I promised."

"All right. *Lolo.*" A mischievous note crept into her voice; he could picture her full lips curling in a teasing grin, dark eyes gleaming in amusement. "The Kipapa Bridge, right? Better make sure Kaupe doesn't get you. It *is* getting dark, after all."

Michael grinned, rolling his eyes fondly. "Now you sound like my Tutu, trying to scare the shit out of me with boogeyman stories so I'd get home in time for dinner."

"I can guess how well that wor—" The last of Nalani's sentence was swallowed by a swell of static. Michael stopped walking.

"Nala? You still there?"

A moment later she resurfaced. "Yeah, but I'll let you go now. Just be careful getting here, okay? Kaupe or no Kaupe."

"Always am. I'll see you back at the gallery, babe."

"I'll be waiting." With a kiss Nalani hung up, and Michael slid the phone back into the pocket of his jeans and glanced up at the sky. There was some light left in the day, but it was rapidly fading; by the time he got back to the secluded spot where his car was parked, near the bridge and the stream it crossed, it'd probably be full dark.

"Better make sure Kaupe doesn't get you." His wife's joking warning echoed in his mind as he went on, and he shook his head, a faint grin ghosting across his face. The spirit *was* one of the spook stories, along with the Night Marchers, his grandmother had used to

try and get him to keep curfew, just as she'd done for
his father when David Iokepa was growing up, just as
plenty of parents and grandparents on the island had
done for generations. As the legend went, Kaupe had
been a *kupua,* a demigod, with the power of the wind
and a form that could go between human and canine,
who'd ruled Nu'uanu Valley on O'ahu. He'd also been
something of a cannibal, and though he'd never gone
after any of the kin of the king of O'ahu he'd eaten his
fill through O'ahu and Maui, then gone to Hawaii and
stolen the son of a high chief, intending to sacrifice
him when they returned to Nu'uanu. With a kahuna's
help the high chief had rescued his son and killed
Kaupe when the dog-man followed them home to
Hawaii, but the cannibal's spirit was supposed to haunt
O'ahu, hunting fresh victims in Nu'uanu Valley but
more often where Kipapa Bridge now stood, beneath
the bridge itself.

Michael had never encountered Kaupe, for all
the time he'd spent in the area over the years; the
closest he'd come had been when he was fourteen and
he and a few other friends had pranked Pert's cousin
James, Pert jumping out from behind some boulders in
a dog mask when they were dirt-biking down a trail in
the gulch and scaring the shit out of James. He
couldn't say it *wasn't* real; his philosophy was there

were some things it was better never to completely discount, and his people's legends lay in that category. But he wasn't exactly looking over his shoulder for the ghostly cannibal as he walked through the spreading evening, either.

From his bag he pulled his black flashlight to help him navigate the way back, its white-blue beam skating over rocks and trees and slicing through the shadows that were reaching out for him, their fingers curling around him so they seemed part of the tattoos on the arms bared by his dark T-shirt. His height, his muscled build, his tattoos—all conspired to paint a picture of someone who made a hobby of cracking skulls, not painting landscapes. And it wasn't that he didn't appreciate the benefits of projecting such an image; he'd diffused more than a few bar fights simply by standing up and looking like he might get involved. But he was always amused by the look people got on their faces when they realized there were depths below the surface—it was like finding out a Hell's Angel was the Easter Bunny, as Nalani had once put it.

Maybe that's why Kaupe's never hassled me. He's too intimidated, Michael thought with a wry grin. The Kipapa Stream, a few yards to his right, chuckled and gurgled as if sharing his amusement, water rushing over the stones in the streambed.

The bridge that crossed the water was somewhat narrow, edged with open arches of concrete, and carried the Kamehameha Highway across the gulch in Mililani. As he neared it the faint sound of traffic wafted to Michael, but an instant later a louder, closer set of sounds drowned it out and hooked his attention: cries hoarse with pain, agonized moans and sobs, gut-knotting groans and screams. It sounded like somebody was hurt or dying—a hell of a lot of somebodies, a vivid chorus of suffering, and Michael stopped walking, startled, as its jagged tune cut through him.

Some kind of accident, maybe? Weird that I didn't hear anything before, though—it can't have been too long ago....

"Hello?" he called, his light sketching the area but finding no source for the sound. "Hey, is somebody out there? You need help?"

His voice echoed like a sounding call in the ocean's depths, but while the screams and sobs went on nobody broke off long enough to answer. He couldn't just *leave,* though, and he listened hard, trying to pick out a direction, at least. The voices were jumbled, overlapping each other, but as a collective they were distinct and seemed to be coming from the east, and Michael started that way without hesitation; if there was anything he could do to help, he was going to do it. "Whoever's hurt," he called, pulling his phone from his pocket as he wove, a bit unsteadily, off the thin dirt trail, uluhe ferns slapping at his legs and low-hanging vines and branches brushing his hair, his skin, "can you hear me? I'm calling for help, okay?"

"—one-one, ...hat's your emer...ency?" the dispatcher's voice crackled in his ear, the connection worse than it'd been with Nalani.

"I'm down in Kipapa Gulch, near the bridge," Michael said. The wounded voices were growing louder, clearer; he was going the right way, anyway, even if he still couldn't see shit. "It sounds like there's a bunch of people down here who're hurt pretty bad—I don't know if there's been an accident or what, but—" He paused again as static squealed in his ear. "Hello? Can *you* hear me?"

The dispatcher's reply was unintelligible, and then the call cut out completely. "Dammit," Michael muttered, and again when he tried to call back and couldn't even connect this time: *"Dammit."*

A horrendous scream knifed through the damp, vegetation-scented air, and something inside Michael told him whoever'd loosed it didn't have much time left. As it died down to thick, choking sobs, and as the other groaning voices swelled and fell around it, Michael rushed deeper into the undergrowth, the flashlight beam bouncing wildly off the darkness, his gear bag thudding against his right hip, his heart pounding against his ribs.

Not too late, please don't let me be too late, please, God, don't...

"Anybody out there, can you tell me where you are?"

They didn't, but the sounds did, growing ever louder and closer until he was convinced he was about to stumble over somebody.

What the hell...?

Up ahead. The light picked out a small clearing—that *had* to be where the wounded people were. Bracing himself for what he might see, Michael pushed through the rest of the bracken into the clearing.

The empty clearing.

He'd been moving so fast he rocked on his feet as he stumbled to a stop, head swimming as he tried to reconcile what he saw with what he heard. He shone the flashlight this way and that, scanning the area, but it proved as empty as it'd been at first glance even though, going by ear, whoever was sobbing should've been doing it right at his feet.

Not only was he alone in the clearing, he realized after a moment as the fact of this settled in, but it was colder here than in the rest of the gulch; even earlier, in the shade of the fan palms, Michael hadn't felt anything like this. This was a chill that sank in past the skin, spread through the nerves and wrapped itself around the bones, and the hair on the back of his neck prickled. "What the hell?" he repeated aloud, lowly, rubbing at the gooseflesh cropping up on his arms.

"Better make sure Kaupe doesn't get you." Nalani's teasing popped into his head again, but he was less inclined to laugh this time, because this was how it happened in the stories. He hadn't thought about it when he'd first heard the voices because he hadn't stopped to think, but—how had his grandmother put it? "Kaupe's spirit waits, and when a victim strays into his hunting ground he calls out to lure them in—not calling their name, mind you, or anything like that; no, Kaupe makes horrible noises that make the victim think people are terribly hurt nearby, but when they go to help, the scene is empty and cold. And that's when Kaupe, with his dog head and his long, sharp claws, comes out of the shadows

352

and *gets you.* " She'd hooked her thin, wrinkled fingers into claws of her own and bared her teeth to complete the effect.

"But why does he lure people in that way?" Michael had asked, not terribly thrown by his Tutu's mock-ferocity.

She'd waved him off. "I don't know. Maybe Good Samaritans taste better than the rest of us. More tender. Anyway, that's how he does it."

And now Michael was standing alone in a clearing in Kaupe's hunting ground after following the cries of the wounded and dying, a clearing that was freezing in comparison to the balmy night air elsewhere near the bridge. Any second now the cannibal's spirit would reveal itself; he'd come out from wherever he hid among the trees and lunge for Michael, ready to rend with tooth and claw.

"Stop it," Michael snapped at himself, disgusted. The odd cold he couldn't readily explain, but he wasn't a scientist; it was highly possible a Google search could make sense of it, once he had access to the internet again. As for the voices, it didn't have to be a dog-man's lure, just a trick of acoustics; they hadn't actually been coming from this spot, maybe even this direction, only sounded like they were. He needed to keep searching, keep following the sounds until he found whoever was hurt and did whatever he could to help. But when he listened again, trying to reorient himself, he realized the sounds were gone.

His stomach clenched and another chill skittered down his spine, and he didn't, couldn't, stop it. It didn't make sense, all the voices cut off so abruptly—

—just as the cold, refusing to abate, didn't make any sense, just as none of this was making any sense—

—at least, not any sense he was eager to consider.

"Just figure out where you are now and go from there," Michael told himself, his head clearing somewhat as he drew a deep breath. "And no more charging blindly off like that. If you get yourself killed out here, Nala'll be pissed."

It was sudden, soundless. As Michael turned, sweeping the clearing with the flashlight beam, the figure slipped out of the darkness on the clearing's edge, just a few feet away from him, and he froze again as the chill in the air grew even greater, as though his companion was gathering it to himself as he

cast off the shadows he'd been cloaked in. Michael
didn't speak to him, couldn't; in the first instant he'd
thought it was a member of the wounded party who'd
gone for help, or maybe someone who, like him, had
heard the moans and sobs and gone searching. But
somehow the figure was visible even without the
flashlight's aid, not luminescent but still limned in a
way that let Michael see him in detail he shouldn't've
been able to: a man, taller even than Michael and with
a body corded with muscle and etched with tattoos,
ancient *kākau uhi* designs, family totems and symbols
that spoke of high rank inked onto his copper-colored
skin; he was barefoot and dressed only in a malo, a
loincloth made of kapa barkcloth. He carried no
weapon and didn't need one; the dark claws that
curved from his thick hands seemed like they would
serve him well, and if they failed there were always the
sharp teeth in his leathery muzzle, part of the dark-
furred canine head set so seamlessly atop his broad
shoulders it couldn't have been a mask, no psychotic
prankster's trick. This was real; he was here.

Kaupe.

The demigod's ghost smiled, a cruel, jagged
baring of teeth, and something deep inside Michael
shattered at the sight of it, all rationalization and
skepticism stripped away, leaving him in the raw state

of prey before a predator, a mortal before a monster, a living thing before a legend. His whole world had been knocked off its axis, and he did the only thing he could do in the wake of such a blow.

He ran.

Kaupe howled behind him, the gleeful cry of a hound lusting for the hunt, for blood in its mouth and the tearing of flesh from bone, and the echoes of it set after the fleeing Michael a few moments before the spirit did. A cold wind swelled, shaking the fan palms and uhule as Michael crashed through, and the whipping leaves sounded like mocking laughter as the stars looked coldly down through the churning verdant sea. He couldn't hear Kaupe's steps, but when he chanced a glance back he saw the ghost was chasing him with long, powerful strides and sped up his own pace, sparks of pain erupting in his right hip every time his gear bag threw itself against it.

Get to the car, he thought, picturing the spot, tucked away near the bridge, where he'd parked his Mustang. It wasn't too far a trip as the crow flew; in daylight, with the way clear before him, it probably would've taken just a few minutes. But now, skidding down inclines and half-guessing when to turn, with a murderous dog-man on his trail, he wasn't sure he could get there as fast as he had to.

He also wasn't sure a car would offer any real protection from nor deter a ghost. But he *did* know he could drive a hell of a lot faster than he could run, and he hoped if he got far enough away Kaupe wouldn't be able to follow. After all, in none of the stories he'd heard had Kaupe ever actually crossed the bridge, just attacked beneath and near it. As flimsy a theory as it was it was his best bet, because the lore itself offered little help. The kahuna who'd aided the Hawaiian chief against Kaupe, skilled in *kilokilo*, reading signs in the sky, sea, and earth, had given the chief a prayer to use, and after he'd rescued his son from the heiau, or temple, in Lihue he'd recited it; the pair had run faster, keeping ahead of Kaupe for a time, and when the cannibal had begun closing in again the chief had repeated the prayer, leading them to find a boulder to hide behind. Apparently that'd done the trick, because afterward the chief and his son had made it back to Hawaii, and although Kaupe had ridden the wind and followed them there, the legend ended with the chief killing Kaupe once and for all. The method for that had been left out, though, and even if it hadn't been it wouldn't have mattered for Michael; he'd hardly be able to kill Kaupe again.

The prayer, though…

That *was* given in the legend, and as Michael scrambled down another short but steep incline, stones and clots of earth dislodged by his passage tumbling alongside him, his mind raced to call it up. *O Ku, O… O what?* Maybe it wouldn't matter, either; maybe the prayer was meant only for a living Kaupe and trying it against his ghost would be as effective as flinging a handful of sand in his dog face. But this was an all-hands-on-deck sort of situation, so he tried frantically to remember the kahuna's prayer as his grandmother had recited it, clinging to each word he could remember like a lifeline helping him inch closer to safe shores.

O Ku, O… Laka? No, that's not i—

The root caught his foot and he pitched forward, breath fleeing his body as he slammed hard into the ground. Pain exploded in his hands, his chest, his legs and a heart-stopping crack accompanied the collision, but when the initial shock receded and he gingerly tested his limbs he found everything sore but intact, except for some stinging, blood-beaded scrapes on his palms. The camera, he realized as he pushed himself upright and his battered, dirt-stained bag nudged him; that was what he'd heard. Maybe it was dead, maybe just wounded, but something had definitely happened to it.

Michael had no time to triage the Nikon, though. In the brush behind him came the sound of a dog sniffing for a scent and he got hurriedly to his feet, ducking into a grove of paperbark trees and pressing himself hard behind one, heart pounding, his short and shallow breath cutting into his lungs like bits of broken glass. Kaupe stalked into view a moment later, a few yards to Michael's right, and though the wind had died down the trees began to shudder again at his presence, the silver-white light of the nearly-full moon flowing over him. He looked for all the world to be solid, a beastly creature of flesh and muscle, but his silent steps gave away that he was at once less and more than that; no living creature's tread had ever been so quiet, no matter how deliberately they were moving, and Michael's ears ached for the snap of branches and rustle of grass underfoot as though the noise would somehow make this more palatable.

Kaupe hadn't picked up on his hiding place yet, but the way he was scenting the air said he would soon, his clawed fingers flexing and muscles rippling in anticipation.

"Maybe Good Samaritans taste better than the rest of us. More tender."

There was a rock beside Michael's left foot, a fist-sized gray stone that looked to have some heft to it; slowly, never taking his gaze off the prowling spirit, he bent, grasped the rock, and straightened again. In high school he'd played on the baseball team at Mililani High, where his arm had saved a fair few games for them, though since then his throws had mostly been limited to tossing beers to Nala or their friends, Frisbee on the beach, and the occasional handful of clay or paint. He wound up and aimed, and as Kaupe moved a little further forward Michael let the rock fly behind the ghost with a silent prayer.

It landed in the brush several yards distant, with enough of a racket that the dog-man whipped around and sped after it, a growl ripping from his throat. Relief mingled with Michael's adrenaline, and as Kaupe vanished from the grove Michael slipped away himself in the opposite direction, moving more carefully now than in his initial flight but as quick as he could to take advantage of however much time he'd bought himself.

Not much, as it turned out. He made it out of the grove and found the stream again, but he'd been moving along it for only a minute or so when the trees began to stir in their unnatural dance and his racing heart shot back into his throat. He looked behind him and saw Kaupe crowning a rocky rise, starkly outlined against the rising moon, and despite the distance their eyes locked for a moment that stretched out molten and vivid, Kaupe's lips drawing back in a snarl, ears flattening against his skull. Then Kaupe bounded forward, and as the moment shattered it was if a dam had given way in Michael's skull, allowing the rest of the kahuna's prayer to flood free. His deep voice drummed across the open air, blood surging hotly through his body as he flung the ancient words into the night.

"O Ku! O Lono! O Ka-ne! O Kanaloa!

By the power of the gods,

By the strength of this prayer,

Save me, save me!"

The original closing line had been "Save us two, save us two!", but it didn't quite apply here. *Call it artistic license,* Michael thought as he began to run again, and maybe it was just adrenaline, or maybe Someone up there really was listening, but every stride seemed to take less effort than the last, the burn of exertion flowing from his muscles; the stitch that'd been developing in his side vanished, and if the burgeoning bruises from his fall were still throbbing, he couldn't feel them. He hadn't run like this since high school, at best, speeding with ease over terrain that just moments before had been determined to take him down by any means necessary, and as he whipped along the streambed he head Kaupe's howl of frustration, the echoes farther and farther behind, and couldn't hold back a breathless smile.

Sorry, man. Not my fault if you can't keep up.

The sound of traffic on Kipapa Bridge was the sweetest thing he'd ever heard, and at the sight of it looming over the stream in the distance he charged harder ahead, the wind whipping around him now that of speed and motion instead of the spirit's making. The car wasn't far, he realized, recognizing his surroundings from his initial descent into the gulch, though he'd come out on the wrong side of the stream. He paused for a precious moment, seeking a spot where the water was shallow enough for him to cross, and just as he found it he felt the slash of claws across his right calf, jeans and flesh rent in the same swift savage blow, and a cold weight slammed into him from behind and threw him again to the ground. He landed half in the water and half on the bank, and whatever had been keeping him from feeling pain was well and truly gone; his wounded leg was screaming at him, mud and blood painting his skin, and every other ache he'd accumulated over the course of the chase roared back full-force.

God dammit!

Michael's wet hair striped his face, clinging like a second skin, but through it he saw just enough— a flash of blazing eyes, a dark bulky form—to roll out of the way of Kaupe's next strike, agony knifing through his wounded leg and wrenching a guttural cry from his throat. Flicking his hair back, clearing his vision, he discovered the spirit had shifted its shape and wore a fully canine form now, a hulking monster no less muscled than it'd been as a humanoid, its heavy paws nearly as large as Michael's hands. Michael scrambled back as it stalked toward him, its claws already streaked with his blood, and made the bank, but the mud and his leg kept him off-balance, a jerky progress that Kaupe seemed to be savoring as if he knew he could afford to, his prey wouldn't be outrunning him again, supplication to the gods or no.

"No," Michael said, the word hoarse but not lacking any conviction for that. "You don't get me, you understand? *A 'ole!*"

Kaupe laughed, and the sound of such sadistic, human amusement issuing from an animal's visage roiled in Michael's skull, crawled down his spine, and coiled in his gut. As he pushed forward, the laughter shadowing him, he wondered briefly if this was how it'd been for that long-ago chief and his son on their desperate flight to safety, if they'd begun to think, kahuna's prayers or not, they'd never see their island again, just as he thought of Nala now, waiting back at the gallery long enough for mock-impatience to have given way to the real thing, or maybe worry at this point. He pictured her pacing, calling and texting his no-doubt-ruined phone and getting more anxious with every non-answer, never knowing what had happened to him, of his last limping flight beneath Kipapa Bridge and how the cannibal's spirit had finally brought him down laughing in the moonlight…

Why the fuck *couldn't I just go home on time?*

"Why the fuck did you decide to be an artist?" he corrected, huffing the words as he maneuvered up another incline, his cuts throbbing in time with his racing pulse. "Dad wanted you to play baseball and you could've; you were good enough. That scout even came up to see you in college." A small rock slipped loose under his left hand and he scrabbled for a new hold, his breath stilling in his lungs until he found it.

Gritting his jaw, he pushed on, "But *nooo,* you *had* to pursue your goddamn art. Had to take inspiration from nature. If you were a fucking baseball player you wouldn't be scrabbling around in a gulch about to become dinner for Cujo the cannibal king, no sir. You'd be stealing second, looking up to see a bunch of people in the stands wearing Iokepa jerseys cheering you on. And what would've been so bad about that that you couldn't—"

He stopped berating himself as he reclaimed terra firma, leg stiff with dried mud and blood even as fresh streams of scarlet flowed from his wounds, and was greeted by the sight of his car sixty feet or so ahead of him, the moon through the branches of the trees glinting off the Mustang's aqua-blue surface.

Thank you God gods whoever thank you—

Limping quick as he could for the car, out of the corner of his eye he caught sight of a figure darting through the trees to his left: Kaupe, bipedal once again. The distance between Michael and the car, which had been shortened by relief, was stretched by dismay; he might as well try to hobble across a football field with the ghost so close, ready to spring at a moment's notice. Fear, anger, adrenaline had all been surging electric through him like a tidal wave, sweeping everything else away. The pain in his wounds ran deeper, the ache in his muscles and bones clung tighter and hung heavier on his limbs, and he was going to die within eyeshot of his car, of Kipapa Bridge, of safety and the normal world.

"O Ku. O Lono," he whispered, eyelids sagging shut and every ounce of energy he had left weaving itself into this reprise. "O Kane. O Kanaloa.

By the power of the gods,

By the strength of this prayer,

Save me, save me."

There were rocks nearby, scattered indiscriminately through the clearing and the growth that lined it. He knew that, remembered it from his arrival in the area this morning. But the rock he saw when he drew a deep breath and opened his eyes hadn't been; he was sure of that, too. Yet there it sat now, a rough-edged gray one humped like a sleeping beast halfway between Michael and the car, and though the rational part of his mind halfheartedly tried to convince him it *had* been there all along and he'd just forgotten or overlooked it, it was quickly shouted down by the part of him that'd accepted what was happening here tonight was completely impossible yet no less real for it, the part that replied to rationality's protests *No, that rock* wasn't *there before, but it is now. Just like the legend.*

Legend or no, as Michael managed to hobble to the rock—flickers of movement from among the trees haunting the corners of his eyes all the while—and crouch behind it, he felt foolish, like a child curling up behind a heap of clothes on the closet floor to hide from the monster beneath the bed. As if Kaupe wouldn't just sniff him out, or think *Hm, maybe the human is behind the large rock that wasn't there thirty seconds ago.* And as Kaupe flowed into the clearing, scenting the air with hungry sniffs, black nose twitching after his trail, Michael braced himself, wishing there was a better way to fight than this—*any* way to fight.

The ghost passed close enough on the other side of the stone that Michael felt the chill emanating from it, the same that had pervaded that first clearing, and again it bored into him body and soul, setting his teeth on edge and his nerves to screaming. He could make out the bristling dark hairs of Kaupe's dog-head as they cloaked his thick muscled neck and spread down his shoulders like a swarm of ants on the march before growing sparser, thinning eventually to leave his ink-laden skin clear, so near was the spirit and so bright was the moonlight above them both. Had it been a man, Michael could've struck it now in a surprise attack, if not killing him then at least wounding him grievously enough to get him down for the mortal blow; instead Michael tensed as Kaupe loomed over him, already feeling those cold merciless claws sinking again into his flesh as the dog-man arched his back, drawing in a long deep breath that couldn't just be perfumed with fragrant night blossoms, no, it *had* to carry Michael's scent, betraying him—how could it not?

Yet Kaupe only loosed a low, deep growl when he'd considered the scents the night air brought to him, no victorious snarls, no lunging down behind the rock to snatch his dinner at last. It was a frustrated sound, that of hunger unfulfilled, and even as confusion threaded itself through Michael's anticipatory fear Kaupe moved off again, disappearing into the brush on the opposite side of the clearing from his quarry.

For the first few moments once he'd gone Michael couldn't move, disbelief overwhelming relief, overwhelming all else. How had the spirit not sensed him, seen him, smelled him?

Then it hit him: the rock. Maybe it'd hidden him in more ways than one; maybe the same force that had summoned it, created it, stuck it right in Michael's path for shelter had also kept Kaupe from picking up on his presence. Maybe he hadn't been aware of the rock at all—after all, if he was, surely after what had happened with the chief and his son, it'd be the first place he'd look for Michael, especially when Michael had outrun him with the help of the kahuna's prayer just a short time earlier.

Even when his fear-frozen muscles unlocked, for another moment or two Michael couldn't, didn't move, a rabbit-like part of his mind wanting to stay curled up here, where he was evidently safe. But there was no telling how long the enchantment would last, nor how long Kaupe would stay away, and Michael forced himself to rise, gritting his teeth against the pain that swelled in his leg and the fresh blood that trickled down from his calf from the ragged edges of his flesh. The car gleamed tantalizingly, a beacon of escape, and he made his unsteady but determined way toward it, alert for any sign of Kaupe's return.

The seconds it took to pull his keys from his pocket and unlock the driver's door were some of the longest of his life, second only to the ones between fitting the key into the ignition and the engine springing to life, the sound a roar in the silence of the clearing. Hands shaking, he reversed and, when he reached a spot wide enough, whipped the car around toward the main road, jostled in his seat as the tires spun over the uneven earth.

Come on, come on...

The car rocked as if struck, strong enough to throw Michael to the left and give his head a solid whack against the window. His mind swam and for a moment he thought he'd driven into some rut in the trail, struck some rock or root in the earth, but as he blinked and his stunned senses cleared a branch broken from a nearby fan palm slammed into the windshield, its green leaves flapping and writhing before the whole thing ripped itself away again and revealed the full scene to him. Debris was swirling, spinning, twisting through the air, branches and uprooted uhule, severed tree limbs and stripped leaves, and what hadn't been uprooted was whipping and tossing in the rising wind, bowing before the force as if beaten. It reminded Michael of a storm he'd weathered with his father as a child, watching as the driving rain and lashing wind had ripped his grandmother's garden to shreds, sent a neighbor's deck chair flying into the tree in their front yard, seemed ready to wrench the roof off their own house, no matter how much his father had assured him it wouldn't.

But for all its ferocity that had been a natural event, kin to the pull of the tides, a volcanic eruption, the light of the sun and the moon. This, though, was supernatural in every sense of the term, and as Michael pushed the car onward, projectiles battering its body, he could see closer to the main road the trees were still, untouched, serene; this was a localized attack, meant just for him—Kaupe's last gasp.

The car jolted and a hulking form filled his view: The dog-man had leapt onto the hood of the car, crouched there and raked his claws down it, ripping jagged furrows deep into the metal. Michael's leg throbbed in sympathy; he cut the wheel sharply to the right and wove as best he could through the sea of flying debris, straining for the road, for the bridge. A back window burst in a cloud of shattered glass and ravaged leaves as a branch hurled itself through; Kaupe's muscles coiled and he sprang for the last time, moving in a perfect arc toward the windshield, and Michael had just enough time to wonder if Kaupe would crash through too or simply melt through the glass—

—and then the way was clear and the air was calm, and Michael had to jerk the car to the left to keep from crashing into the back bumper of a dark green Corolla ambling across Kipapa Bridge, and for several moments his mind and heart were still racing a bit ahead of reality and couldn't comprehend what'd happened. His time in the gulch hadn't been too long, all told, but had impressed itself so deeply on him that to be free of it, to be so suddenly delivered, was almost incomprehensible, like being tossed by a raging sea onto a sunny shore. Other cars moved along the highway unperturbed, drivers heading to work or home from it, out with their families or over to friends' houses, none with any idea what the man in the clawed-up, busted-up Mustang they gaped at as they passed had just escaped. Not that all would believe it even if they *did* know, and not that Michael would blame them for it.

Nalani was waiting; life was waiting, and he drew in a deep breath, unaware of how badly he was shaking or the burning pain in his leg, knowing only how good it felt to still be breathing, and merged into the rest of the sparse traffic flowing across the bridge toward home.

He looked back only once, when he was halfway across; he saw no dog-headed figure in pursuit, no trees thrashing in a conjured wind, and knew in his heart that he *had* escaped, completely and truly, out of Kaupe's hunting grounds and his ghostly reach. But—perhaps it was his imagination, not quite free yet, or perhaps it wasn't—he thought he heard, rising into the night, a faint but lingering howl, the keening cry of a thwarted hunter.

*****

The gallery was dark but for the front lights and Nalani was sitting on the front step, her right hand fidgeting with her white-shell necklace and her left holding her phone to her ear as she bit her lip and tapped her sandaled feet on the ground. As the headlights swept the gallery she jumped up, her long navy-blue-and-white skirt sweeping the walk, her black hair rippling down her back, and ran to the car, reaching it just as Michael with some effort worked the door open and climbed out, gripping the frame to help keep himself upright as a great weariness descended on him all at once.

"What happened to you?" Nalani gasped, gaze flying between the car and her husband. "Michael, Jesus, are you all right?"

"Yeah, Nala, I'm okay." He tried to smile and wave her off; neither attempt went well, and she darted forward and snaked his right arm around her slender shoulders to support him as he took a step forward. "Sorry I ruined date night."

"Come inside—come into the bathroom, we'll get you cleaned up." As they headed toward the gallery Nalani repeated, "What *happened?*"

"Kaupe," Michael said simply, and she stopped short.

"Kaupe? As in the cannibal ghost of Oʻahu, *that* Kaupe?"

Michael nodded. "The one and only."

Nalani blinked. "But… But how… what...?"

"I stayed out in the gulch a little too long," Michael said as they started moving again. "But don't worry. I think I'm gonna stick to beach scenes for a while now."

FARSIGHTED

by Robert Allen Lupton

Krista Gray gently brushed the dirt and gravel from the Grecian pottery shards in the square foot she was slowly excavated at the archeological dig just south of the ancient city of Marathon. She sat upright, pushed back her large hat, and wiped the sweat-caked dust from her forehead.

The broken edges of a single pot with faded paintings were barely visible within the string delineated boundary of her designated area for today. The strings divided the current dig area into exactly eight hundred separate sections.

Krista removed the first shard, photographed it, wrapped it, and placed it in a container. She repeated the process twice more. A smooth piece of marble peeked through the dirt, exposed when she'd removed the third piece of pottery. She considered calling the dig manager, Spiros Kolovos, but for some reason couldn't make herself. She decided not to call him until after she'd inspected the marble.

With brushes and soft plastic tools she slowly uncovered the marble artifact. It was round and about the size of a golf ball. Krista looked around quickly to see if any of the other workers were watching her. Everyone was busying working their individual squares. Spiros was busy on his laptop inside the control tent. She picked up the heavy artifact but kept it below ground level.

She held her breath and turned it in her hand. It was almost a perfect sphere. A human eye was carved on one side. The eye stared at her and she stared back. She should put the orb down, photograph it, and call Spiros. She sighed and reached for her camera.

A rivulet of stinging sweat ran down her dusty forehead and into her eyes. She flinched and closed her eyes at the sharp burn. She rubbed her face on her sleeve. She blinked a few times, but it burned too much, and she held her eyes closed.

Something wasn't right. Her eyes were closed, but she could still see. And it was like she'd moved, her point of view was different. She was looking upward from inside the hole she'd dug. The taut strings formed a square above her. Krista saw a sweaty twenty-year-old woman overhead. The woman's face was caked with dirt and her eyes were clenched closed. Her lips were cracked.

Krista opened her eyes. Had the marble eyeball in her right hand stared at her? She closed her eyes and her point of view shifted. The sweaty twenty-year-old with her eyes closed and the sun at her back knelt above her. She blinked again. What the hell was going on?

Eyes open and she looked at the marble eye. Eyes closed and she looked upward from the position of the marble eye at herself. I've been in the damn sun too long, she thought.

She opened her mouth to call Spiros, but she couldn't articulate the words. She changed the croak into a cough, covering her mouth with her left hand. She looked down at the marble eye. Whenever she blinked, she saw herself in a quick, almost subliminal flash.

She turned the eye in her hand. It was heavy, smooth, and warm. The longer she held it, the more it felt part of her. Giving the eye to Spiros was unthinkable. She'd rather cut out one of her own eyes. She had to have it. She'd found it, it was hers.

Her head hurt. She blinked her eyes, like everyone, at least four times a minute and those flashes of changing perception were annoying at best, disorientating at worst. She pulled her bright red bandana from her pocket, and casually wrapped the orb.

Her vision quit shifting points of view. She slipped one finger inside the bandana, touched the warm marble, and closed her eyes. Her world turned red, the sunlight shining through the cloth. She moved her finger and her vision returned to normal. Krista stuffed the bandana into her pocket.

She finished her shift, excavating, photographing, and cataloging the broken pieces of pottery. She'd turn in her work to Spiros at the end of her shift. He'd invited her to share a bottle of Ouzo that evening. She'd been trying to catch his attention and had planned to accept, but things had changed.

All Krista could think about was the eye. She couldn't keep her hands off the marble orb. She touched it every few minutes. A quick reach into her pocket, a glimpse of red bandana and a hint of khaki, and she was reassured enough to work for another two or three minutes. Spiros could be a problem. If he learned about the eye, he'd want it. She knew she'd kill him if he touched it.

Spiros repeated his Invitation. Krista smiled, "Thank you, but I've a horrible headache. Must be the sun. Dehydrated too! Another time, please. I just want to go to my room and rest. I hope you'll ask again."

Spiros winked. "Absolutely, sometime soon then. See you at sunrise. I hope you feel better."

Krista thought, *See me at sunrise. He doesn't want me, he wants the eye. He can sense it. I know he can.*

She walked the two miles to the ramshackle hotel and locked herself in her room. She touched the eye for reassurance every minute or so while she cleaned up and kept it within reach while she bathed.

She sat on her bed with the orb in her lap. She'd refused to allow herself any prolonged contact with it, like a lover delaying the final act in order to enjoy the anticipation. She held her breath, picked up the orb, and closed her eyes.

Her point of view shifted. The room became clearer, colors more pronounced, previously invisible dust motes danced in the air, and the fading sunlight brightened. She turned the orb in her hand. She watched a fly crawl on the opposite wall near a cheap and faded reproduction of a landscape painting.

Krista felt compelled to lift the orb and place it against her forehead. She gasped when it touched her skin. The walls became transparent. She could see into the next room. It was empty. She turned and looked out through her door. She thought about the dig site and her vision raced along the road to Spiros's tent. She watched him finish his daily report.

"I wonder what he's writing," she said to herself and suddenly she stood over his shoulder. She moved closer. She looked at the side of his face, a day's growth of black stubble and a little sunburn, but nothing a fresh shave and lotion wouldn't handle. She looked harder and her vision moved inside his mind. His thoughts were her thoughts.

She saw herself as Spiros saw her. She'd never considered herself that attractive and certainly not that desirable. Spiros considered her something of a tease. He imagined touching her face. He shoved her against the wall and forcibly kissed her. His stubble scratched her cheek.

She screamed and dropped the orb. It was pitch dark in her room. The sun had set and she hadn't turned on the lights. She floundered around in the dark room, found the orb and picked it up. She could see through the marble eye the instant she closed her eyes.

She turned on the lights and put the orb on the bureau. She opened her eyes, but she couldn't see. She touched the eye and her vision returned.

She was blind without the orb. She sat on the edge of the bed and cried. Twenty minutes later her regular vision returned. She experimented and finally realized the cost to use the eye was a direct tradeoff. For every minute she used the eye to see, it cost her a minute of blindness. She could live with that. She'd just time things to sleep through the blind bits. There was no reason to worry.

She stayed awake until midnight and used the eye in ten minute intervals. Krista waited out the blind periods in silent impatience. The ten minutes of blindness seemed to last forever.

Krista didn't go to the site the next day. She thought of being separated from the orb made her want to puke. If she took the eye to work, she'd have to keep it hidden. Sooner or later Spiros or one of the others would catch her touching it. Given the opportunity, he'd take the eye and she couldn't stand that.

She believed that she couldn't be the first person to find the eye. Maybe it was the mythical Eye of Horus or the one that belonged to those old Greek witches. She searched the internet and reread the myth about three old crones who guarded the gorgons, magical creatures with snakes for hair. Medusa was the most famous. The old women were called the Graeme and they shared a single eye amongst them. Deino, Enyo, and Pemphredo. Dread, Horror, and Alarm were their names.

The three women were blind except for whichever crone held the shared eye. Personal experience had taught Krista that the orb holder could see anywhere she wanted. She could see places, thoughts, dreams, and memories. No wonder the old women were blind. They'd used the orb so often that the blindness tradeoff was more time than they could serve. *Careful*, thought Krista. She promised herself moderation, but she knew she was lying. She turned off her computer, wrapped the red handkerchief around her face so she wouldn't be tempted to peek, and picked up the orb.

She held it against her forehead and her vision went outside to explore. She was drawn to the dig site. The moon glistened on the evening dew. The area seemed abandoned at first, but the generator chugged away, belching smoke, and providing power to Spiro's tent. She looked inside. Spiros typed away at his computer, recording the day's activities, detailing payroll, and updating the work schedule.

He logged out of the site and opened a communication app. He messaged one of Krista's friends and coworkers, Betty from Ontario. 'hey bett, whatsup with krista she left early?'

The reply came in about a minute. 'no idea, weird yesterday'

'maybe took something'

'nope, she's a white hat just like the heroes in western films.'

'I'll go by her place tonight'

Betty texted a thumbs up emoji. 'take a bottle of ouzo with you, she's sweet on you.'

Spiros sent back a smiley face, closed the app, and grinned to himself.

Krista winced the almost violent pornographic images that flashed through Spiros's mind. Did he plan to hurt her? She focused her thoughts and eye let her see deeper into his mind. She felt some slight relief. He was one of those men who didn't know that no means no, but he wasn't actively planning a violent rape. She was amused to learn he was addicted to bodice ripper romance novels, especially ones that featured a lord of the manor and a beautiful serving girl.

She followed his thoughts while he opened an encrypted list of items that weren't on the official inventory. The man was a thief. He carefully selected choice artifacts and hid them in his room. He liked small items like coins, jewelry, and statuettes. *Spiros, you rat bastard*, she thought.

Spiros sensed her. He couldn't imagine that she was inside his mind, so he believed that she must be in the tent. Spiros jumped upright, picked up a hand shovel, and glanced around. "Who's there? Krista, is that you?"

He grabbed an electric torch and threw back the tent flap. He waved the torch around outside the tent. "Krista, I know you're here. I won't hurt you. Let's talk." After a minute, he growled, "Fine, don't answer me. I'll find you later."

He packed his computer and added a trowel and a sharp scraper to the case. He wondered how had Krista figured out what he was doing and how had she been quiet enough to sneak up behind him, and then get away before he caught her?

Spiros was angry. He didn't understand how she'd spied on him and he didn't care. He'd never killed anyone, but he was ready to try. She deserved a lesson, if nothing else, and he was going to teach it to her. He started his van and drove toward town.

Krista's vision quest was over. She abandoned Spiros as soon as she saw his deadly intentions. The bastard was coming for her and if she put down the eye, she'd be blind for at least an hour. Protecting herself while holding a marble eye in one hand was a recipe for disaster. She couldn't let him see it. Spiros was strong, he'd would overpower her and take the marble eye. She had to hide.

Her room had a bed, two chairs, a bureau, and a table. The small doorless alcove that served as a closet was only two feet deep. The bathroom was a toilet, a sink, and a handheld shower. No place to hide. She remembered the old movie about the blind girl, "Wait Until Dark?" She considered turning out the lights so Spiros couldn't see her! That won't work, she told herself, the bastard has a torch.

She heard his van and picked up her trowel. Eye in the left hand, trowel in the right. Lights out. *I'll knock the torch away from him and run. Sucky plan, but any plan's better than no plan.* She pressed herself against the wall near the door and held her breath.

The knob turned, first one way and then the other. The door was locked. Spiros called her name and knocked. She didn't answer.

"Krista, It's Spiros. Hope you're feeling better. I brought *Avgolemono*, lemon chicken soup, homemade. Ouzo if you feel like it."

She stayed silent.

"I know you're there and I know you were in my tent. We should talk. Open the door."

He waited a moment. "You stupid girl, open the damn door or I'll kick it down. Counting to three! One, two…" On two he kicked the door and Krista's sucky plan went to crap.

The door blasted open and smashed Krista against the wall. She was stunned. Her face hurt and she rubbed her nose. Her empty hand came away dripping blood. *Shit,* she thought, *where's my trowel?* Then she realized that both hands were empty. She'd dropped the eye and the trowel. *Stupid, blind, and unarmed. Gonna be bad.*

She dropped to her knees and groped the floor blindly. The door slammed shut behind her. Spiros put one foot on her back and pushed her flat. He laughed and picked up the trowel. "Looking for this? Good luck for me you hid on the wrong side of the door. Bad luck for you. Oh, dear, dripping blood on the floor. Won't get your damage deposit back."

Krista sneezed and then spit out a mouthful of blood. She gasped for air like a half-drowned rat. "Leave me alone."

"It's your own damn fault. Spying on me. I liked you, but that doesn't matter now." He grabbed the back of her shirt collar, jerked her upright, and shoved her against a wall. Her foot kicked the marble eye and it rolled across the floor and bumped against the brass bed frame. The sound was distinct.

Spiros's breath tasted foul. "God, Krista, you're a mess. Blood, tears, and yesterday's dirt from the dig site. Don't you ever shower? Look at me when I talk to you."

Krista turned her face to one side and kept her eyes closed. She sobbed, "Wasn't at your tent. Please don't hurt me again."

He clutched her chin and forced her to face him. "Open your eyes. Look at me."

She shook her head. He said, "Have it your own way. I'll open them for you."

He pinched her broken nose and squeezed. She screamed and her eyes snapped open.

"That's better. I don't want to hurt you, but you've learned things that you shouldn't have. Can't have you telling on me. Best for us both if you leave Greece. Let's clean you up and I'll take you to the airport in the morning."

"What happens tonight?"

"We'll see. Go clean yourself up. I'll help with your nose."

Spiros stepped to the side and pulled Krista away from the wall. She took two steps and stumbled. She moaned when she fell.

Spiros pulled her back up and shook his finger in her face. She didn't flinch. Spiros thought a moment and then waved his hand in front of her face.

"You can't see, can you? How many fingers am I holding up? Don't even want to guess? Never mind. Guess I'll have to undress you and clean you up myself. Morning's a long way off. One of us is going to enjoy the next few hours, but it won't be you."

Her mind recalled the violent images she'd seen in Spiros's mind.

"I'll clean myself. I won't fight you."

"Damn right you won't. I'll be watching." He guided her to the bathroom.

Her skin crawled. Her embarrassment quickly gave way to anger. Pretending to be oblivious to her audience, she drew out the shower to give herself time to think. She'd heard the eye hit one of the bed posts. It had to be one of the two posts nearest the door. If it rolled all the way under the bed, she couldn't reach it anyway. *I'll leave my clothes off. He'll look at me, not at anything else. I'll pretend to trip again. Once I get the eye and can see, I'll figure something out.*

"I'm tired of waiting. Dry off and come to bed."

"Promise you'll take me to the airport tomorrow."

"Promise."

"Fortune favors the brave," whispered Krista and she felt her way toward the open bathroom door. Spiros took her arm and pulled her close. He was naked, at least from the waist up. She gasped.

"Don't want you bleeding on my clothes," Spiros shoved her toward the bed.

She exaggerated the momentum, staggered two steps, and fell forward. Her face hit the brass bedpost and she heard her nose break again. She fought the pain and patted the floor repeatedly. She brushed the marble eye and had a brief flash of vision, but her frantic fumbling pushed it away. She couldn't find it and screamed in frustration.

Spiros used his bare foot to push her to her belly. She crawled a little forward under the bed. Her right hand touched the eye. She stretched and grasped the orb, but all she could see was her hand. She turned the orb and saw Spiros standing over her prone body. She rotated the eye again. His clothes were piled on the floor.

Spiros grabbed her feet and pulled. "Come out, come out, wherever you are," he laughed.

Krista screamed and flailed with her free hand. She touched his clothes and searched hoping to find something to use as a weapon. She clutched a sock. She moaned in frustration. A sock wasn't much of a weapon.

She kicked her feet, but Spiros just laughed. Then another bad plan came to her. Even though it meant blinding herself, she put the marble eye into the sock and pushed it all the way to the toe.

Spiros rolled her onto her back, and she rolled with him swinging the sock like a blackjack. She heard a crunch.

"You bitch, that's my knee."

Krista swung the sock backhanded at the voice and hit him in the face. He let her legs go and tried to stand, but his damaged knee wouldn't hold his weight and he rolled onto his side.

Krista lifted herself onto her knees. She could hear the harsh rasps of his breath and targeted them. She missed and missed again, but the third time she hit him. He groaned and she swung again. He grasped her right wrist. She switched the sock to her other hand and used his arm to guide her. She kept hitting him until the harsh breaths stopped and he released her arm.

She sat back and rested. Krista slid the orb from the sock. It was covered with blood. She wiped it on the bedspread. She considered checking to see if Spiros was breathing, but instead she held the orb to her forehead and used it to see inside of Spiros's mind. Nothing was there.

Time to go home, just like he said, she thought. *How long will I be blind? Three hours, maybe four, to be safe. I probably can't sleep, but I'll be able to see without the orb by daylight. I gotta get him out of here. I'll put him in his van tonight and dump it somewhere tomorrow.*

She used tape and a bandana to make a headpiece to hold the orb against her forehead like a headlamp. She wrapped Spiros in the bedspread, dragged him outside, and levered the body into his van. She found the truck keys in his pants. She threw his clothes in after him, spent an hour cleaning the room, and another hour cleaning herself before she took the eye off and waited out the night in total darkness. Her last thoughts before she finally went to sleep was about how much her nose hurt.

Her regular vision returned just before sunrise. She kept her eyes open and put the marble eye in the kangaroo pocket of an oversized sweatshirt and loaded two suitcases into Spiros's van. She parked the van at the small airport after making sure there were no cameras. Krista took one final look at the body and spit at it. "You were right about one thing. It turns out that only one of us had a good time last night"

She tossed the keys in a trash can at the terminal entrance, went inside, and checked the schedule. An hour and ten minutes before flight time. The marble eye looked like a golf ball to the security scans and the plane was on time. After takeoff, she went to the restroom and briefly held the eye against her forehead. She returned it to her purse and waited until her regular vision returned before she returned to her aisle seat.

The woman seated in the window seat nodded politely. Krista pointed to the woman's unfastened seatbelt. "I'd fasten that if I were you. It's going to be bumpy flight."

"You sure? The captain hasn't said anything."

Krista tightened her own belt. "Trust me. I'm positive."

.

BLACK VOLGA

by Emilian Wojnowski

The clock struck three in the afternoon. That day, Stefan was to leave his office earlier than usual to, although it was a weekday, celebrate his birthday with his loved ones.

Besides, he hoped to play a game of chess with his son Ksawery before the guests came. "If you lose, it will be the best present for you, Dad," the boy had said.

Excluding the period of his studies completed in 1966, Stefan had been occupying himself with hydrology for more than ten years, and for more than five years he'd been working in Warsaw Water Filters.

His interest in this field of study hadn't waned since then. Each time he cleaned his workplace with the same reluctance, and recently he'd started working on something new.

Stefan stood in front of a mirror and fixed his hair that overlapped his ears, and then he... then a button fell off his collar. Fine, he'd sew it later on, but now something he'd been hiding from his family and friends, something only his wife Danuta knew about, could be seen on his chest now.

"All right," he whispered to himself and put on his coat. "I'll do up my coat at least."

He entered the main laboratory where his colleagues worked amidst colorful vials and said goodbye. They knew he was to leave earlier that day, yet they raised their brows.

Having left the building, he ran down the stairs to his Fiat 126p, a blue one with a chrome bumper and rims called lemons. He immediately hit the streets, drove down Nowogrodzka Street toward Novotel Warszawa Centrum, from where he could see the Palace of Culture and Science, and soon after pulled up before the school Ksawery attended.

Ksawery was supposed to be waiting at the bus stop, under a tree, on a shabby stone on which kids sat if the nearby bench was full.

He was supposed to be waiting there. But he wasn't.

Stefan thought, *He's waiting at school so as not to stand alone. Or he's buying something in a kiosk.*

Stef parked illegally, got out without turning the engine off, and looked around.

"Crap." He noticed the janitor, slammed his car's door, and ran onto the school grounds. "Excuse me…"

The janitor was sweeping the leaves before the entrance. He was wrinkled like an orange that a pleasure-delayer had got for Christmas and then forgotten, and his grey hair was uncombed. Gale—that was how they called the janitor. He leaned against the broom and frowned.

"Excuse me," Stefan repeated.

"Hmm?"

"My son, red hair, short, with a pageboy haircut, wearing a claret jacket. Have you seen him?"

"I prolly have, I'm sure I have. I work here. I saw him, yes, but I dunno, it don't ring a bell," he said and kept on sweeping.

"Wasn't he waiting at the stop, there, a moment ago, there, under the tree?"

The janitor shrugged his shoulders.

"Please think about it. I'll be right back. And if anything happens, I have a car there. A Maluch."

When Stef came back onto the street, he started running along and across it, then sat down at the bus stop and tried to analyze where Ksawery could have gone. He ran up to the kiosk where a guy, leaning, was buying a newspaper.

"Excuse me," said Stefan, trying to squeeze into the little window of the kiosk.

"Wait a sec, man, I'm buying a newspaper."

"Nah, you aren't, you're talking rubbish here. Think about others."

"Ah shit, too late to teach you manners now. The school won't let you come back unless you wanna work in this position."

When he pointed at the janitor, Stefan pushed him with his shoulder, asked the newsagent about his son, and heard:

"I see hundreds of such kids every day." The woman took off her glasses chain. "Hundreds, literally."

Stefan began to pluck his temple hair, which made him only more nervous since they fell out so easily. The man, who had just been served, was reading the newspaper next to him and in a hurry, as if to return it because of its insipid content.

"You're reading this nonsense?" Stefan asked. The headline read about the Black Volga, a black limousine made boogeyman with which parents scared their children. "I don't think you have children. Thought it had already gone out of fashion, the Black Volga scaring and all, but no, as we can see… no." He hid his head in the window of the kiosk and asked: "Can I get a bus timetable? Or anything like that?"

"Sure, but what do you need it for?" She took off her chain glasses again. "There's the schedule, at the stop. Look."

"Oh, thank you," he said and thought: Maybe his friends were going to spend time by the Vistula River and dragged him into the bus, or he didn't want to wait for me and took the bus home.

Reading the timetable, Stefan was moving his index finger up and down the tables divided into hours, working days, and holidays.

"God, there is no bus, no bus at that time Ksawery could've taken," he whispered to himself and ran to the other end of the street, to a green glass-paned telephone booth.

Thank God that there was no queue. Only a kid inside was wondering what number to dial.

"Excuse me, can I call first? I'm worried about my son," Stefan said and described who he was looking for, but the boy hunched and ran away.

"Seven, five," Stef was whispering while dialing the number home.

"Hello?" said a female voice.

"Danka? Listen, honey…"

"Stef?"

"Yes. Look, I…"

"Where are you calling from? Will you be late?" Danka was walking around the room with the receiver, the cable stretching from wall to wall. "They'll come any moment, remember? Want me to change the water in the aq…"

"No, no, listen…"

"The doorbell's ringing. Probably my brother. Too early, as usual."

"Has Ksawery…"

"Well, have you picked him up?"

"We'll be there soon." Stefan hung up the phone, realizing Ksawery wasn't at home, and ran back to the school. The janitor was sweeping leaves and sand onto a shovel.

"Hmm?" Gale asked, having straightened out.

"Have you not seen him? My son?"

"Already told you, I may've seen him, but…"

"But think about it." He grabbed Gale by the sleeve.

"Don't touch me, or I'll call the MO." The janitor, while picking up the shovel, hit Stefan's elbow with the shaft. It hurt.

"What are you, crazy? To hit me with a shovel? And you work with children on a daily basis? The principal's at school?"

"No one's here, not now. Never gone to school, or what? I haven't, that's why I go to school now, but you?"

"He's a weirdo!" shouted the newspaper man above the school's fence.

Stefan squinted his eyes. "You'd better go and read about the Black Volga!" he yelled back, turned around to enter the school, and inadvertently ran into the janitor. Both of them fell onto the pile of sand and leaves.

Gale lost his nerve and started struggling with Stefan. The newspaper guy ran up to them and tugged the hydrologist away. The men gave in to their primitive instincts and started using their fists.

"He's a crazy, told you," said the newspaper man to Gale who grabbed the spade and hit Stefan in the back.

Stefan took a deeper breath, looked around, and noticed that some shadows were moving inside a classroom on the first floor.

"What's going on there?" Stef asked.

"It's for brains, not for you."

"What kind of father are you?" the newspaper guy asked. "May the Black Volga kidnap your children!"

Stef was about to clench his fists even harder when somebody shouted: "Hey, hey! Wait a minute, gentlemen! What's going on out there?" A militiaman entered the school grounds.

"He's some kind of a…"

"We fought over a torn newspaper!" Stef outshouted the newspaper guy, picking up *Życie Warszawy* from the lawn. "It's nothing!"

"Whose car is this? The one with the engine on, can't be parked here."

"I'm coming, I'm coming!"

The militiaman let things go hang and drove away, apparently having sensed that Stefan had a bad day.

Stefan stood before his Fiat. A scratch on the hood, the wipers moving up and down. He thought:

What the hell does that mean? He got in the *Maluch* and tried to calm down.

"All because of work," he whispered to himself, looking at the vials on the rubber mat, "and I remember Dad say: 'Don't think about work after work. And never take work home.' And he was right!" Stefan picked up one of the vials and wiped it with the newspaper's page that said about the Black Volga. Yellowish drops were moving up and down the vial. He could drink it with pleasure now.

Stef rolled up his sleeve and, out of habit, looked at his watch. It was three o'clock in the afternoon.

*****

Danuta opened the front door. "Hi, come in, come in."

"No parents yet?" asked her brother, who didn't have a good relationship with the hydrologist.

"Should be here any minute." Danuta heard steps on the staircase. "Oh, maybe they're even coming now."

Their parents appeared at the door with a bottle of cognac.

"Put it in the freezer," her dad said, taking off his corduroy jacket.

"Nah, c'mon, Dad," his son said, "you don't put cognac in the freezer."

"You do if it's Armenian!" When taking off his shoes, he leaned against the wall and the paneling creaked. "And where's, where's your offspring... and Stefan?"

*****

Stefan stood at the bus stop again. Hands in pockets, he neared the shabby stone, on which kids sat while waiting, and thought: He should be sitting on it, why isn't he?

He leaned over and found a bag pumped with water. Two orange fish were swimming inside.

"What the hell? Can't leave you here," he said and pushed the fish transport bag into his inside coat pocket.

Going to the phone booth again, he turned back to his car, changed his mind, and then headed towards the booth. At first, he did it thoughtlessly, and then deliberately, to see if anyone was watching him. He was afraid that someone would whack him on the back of his head at any moment.

The sky was cloudy, and the wind was sweeping the leaves down the street.

Stefan dialed the number to Warsaw Transport Authority and asked for the numbers of the buses that left his son's elementary school. He was gasping so badly that the walls around him were already steamy.

"All right, I'll give you the number, but the schedule is at the bus stop unless it was demolished by those brats."

"Just tell me the numbers, please."

The lady from WTA said what Stefan asked for and wrote it all down with a pencil on the jagged page about the Black Volga. Of course, the schedule differed from the one at the stop. He also asked her to make sure she wasn't mistaken, but the woman assured that she wasn't.

Panicked, Stefan was turning around in the booth whose walls were getting more and more steamy. He could feel the fish moving as if stressed under his coat.

Knowing he was being watched, he thought, *Wipers don't turn on by themselves, a scratch on the Fiat's hood doesn't appear for no reason. They kidnapped Ksawery and are now following me so that they can play with me. Probably it will be best to wait for their sign, for a ransom note. If I report the kidnapping to the Citizens' Militia, the kidnapper will only be more reluctant to give Ksawery back.*

Stefan dialed the number, picked up the receiver, and heard his wife's voice:

"Hello?"

"I'll... we'll be late. Ksawery got lost somewhere. I just wanted you to know that we'll be late. Don't worry."

"Uh," she sighed, as if letting him know that she'd be worried now.

"See you later, bye."

Stefan ran to his Fiat. The fish were moving under his coat. He regretted having told his wife about... Ksawery having been kidnapped?... about this situation... but Stefan had once promised to tell her everything, especially the truth. The worst would be the guests finding out about Ksawery and his irresponsible father. They'd call the police, making it only worse.

Stefan got into his Fiat, put his hands on the steering wheel, and took a deeper breath, tilting his head back. He could feel something. Something between his fingers. Ink. The ink from the newspaper *Życie Warszawy*.

"Crap," he said, as if having come up with a sinful but fun idea. "The newspaper guy was there for a reason and showed me the article about the Black Volga for a reason, and he ran up to me and the janitor for a reason. And didn't want money for the torn newspaper." A drowning man will clutch at a straw and will believe in the kidnapping by the Black Volga.

The greatest proof of the existence of the Black Volga was the absence of his son.

"Where can I find a car that doesn't exist, that kidnaps children to drain their blood for a cure for rich Germans dying of leukemia? God, where am I?"

Stefan started the engine, looked in the rearview mirror, and backed up. He turned into Emilia Plater Street, stopped before the nearest intersection, and waited for the right moment.

"We'll find the Black Volga, yes, we will, Maluch." Stefan stroke the steering wheel. "They can't be far away if they're watching us."

Stefan throttled up and soon after hit the brakes. The cars started honking when he'd stopped in the middle of the intersection. One streetcar stopped on one side of the Maluch, and one on the other side. More cars, buses, and streetcars joined the row, blocking one another. After a while, everyone was blocking someone. The traffic jam was growing and resembled a faulty jigsaw puzzle.

Drivers, if not honking, were getting out of cars. Some supported each other, uniting to find the violator of the whole confusion, while others shouted that a walk on the street wouldn't improve the traffic flow. Screams and curses were flying over the intersection.

Stefan, stuck in between cars, went out the window onto the Fiat's roof. With a penknife, which he used to pick up mushrooms, he punctured his tires and finally broke the windshield with the metal handle of the penknife.

One of the cars nearby, Syrenka, tried to back up, but the hydrologist punctured its tires as well, happy with the thought that the Black Volga would soon be stuck in the traffic jam too.

Careful not to slip, Stefan jumped from roof to roof, so desperate to find the Black Volga, but he hadn't thought he'd expose himself to those who weren't amused by the whole situation.

Clenching his teeth, Stefan thought each of them has problems, but not everyone's just had their son kidnapped.

There were a few daredevils who noticed Stefan and were chasing him now. One of them jumped from hood to hood, and two more were running along the endless column of Fiats, Mikruses, and Nyskas.

Stefan was looking around for the Black Volga, but there wasn't a trace of it. Careful not to touch the live line, he climbed a streetcar, popularly known as "sausage," and looked around again. He saw no black limousines.

A stone hit him in the back. He slipped and fell between cars, getting stuck. He could feel his clothes shrink.

"Grab him harder, by the collar," said a man, helping the other.

"Help me, you hear me?"

They pulled him by his collar and legs and threw him onto the street, in a puddle. Stefan got up on his knees and then on his feet, knowing that fists would land on his jaw any moment. Instead, he felt a muddy shoe on his cheek.

"Hey, what are you doing?" Stefan's teeth had red rims.

"Felt like blocking the street, like destroying cars? Have you escaped a nut-factory?"

"Black Volga," said Stefan.

"What? Black Volga? May it kidnap your kids, you psycho. You'd better get back to your Fiat."

Another man, a little more determined to show Stefan what he thought of all the confusion, joined the two strangers. He threw his fists out and Stefan, imagining having face made of metal, stood up to him. And soon they were swinging their fists. A huge mouse popped on the hydrologist's face, but he sprang to attention, clenched his fists even harder, thinking, *It's probably someone from the kidnappers. He wants to kick my ass so bad.*

A car ran into Stefan's back.

"What's that mean?!" shouted a driver of a Żuk. "Wanna kill that man? Resuscitate him! The ambulance won't get here now. For God's sake!"

Stefan was choking. When they unbuttoned his coat and ripped his shirt, the buttons fell off onto the street.

And they learned his secret.

The one which he'd been hiding even from his loved ones.

The tattoo on his chest said: DO NOT PUSH.

*****

410

Danuta's father ate so much that he didn't dare to pour himself a drink after drink.

"So, where are they?" he asked.

Chewing the dumplings as carefully as possible, Danuta gave herself time to think.

Her brother, still laughing at the joke his father had spontaneously invented, finally took a deeper breath.

"What did you ask for, Dad?" He stuck his fork in a dumpling.

"Dad's asked where they are," repeated his mother.

"Oh, and where are they?"

Danuta poured herself a glass of cognac, drank it, and said:

"Ksawery... Ksawery's disappeared." A tear came down her cheek.

"Dear God, call the MO."

*****

Bruised, scratched, and in torn clothes, Stefan was sitting by a building from where he could hear songs, which probably were coming from Operetka Warszawska. He lowered his head and extended his legs, though his knees could barely bend.

411

"Thank God you're alive," said a driver who was a priest. "You should love your neighbor as yourselves." Turned away from the men who'd beaten Stefan, the priest poured more water from the bottle onto Stefan's face and then put the cold lid onto his forehead. "Whole's district blocked. No way the ambulance will come any time soon."

"Ambulance?"

"Yes. Don't move, because you don't know if your back's not broken. Do you understand? Can you breathe? How are your lungs?"

A lot of drivers got out of vehicles and lined up in front of the victim.

"What's this tattoo?" the priest asked. "Don't push? Do you have a defect in your chest?"

"Yes. In my breastbone. It is funnel-shaped and fragile." Thinking that if the ambulance arrives, they'll ask what's wrong with me and will call the MO, and I'll have to tell them what happened to Ksawery, and there will be little chance that I'll ever see him again.

"Feeling better already? You better not get up. Rest."

Stefan grimaced. An ambulance can drive on the sidewalk. Maybe the kidnapper's people took care of me, making sure I was alive so that they could demand the ransom. Otherwise, they would have to let Ksawery go. Unless they kidnapped him only to drain blood for rich Germans dying of leukemia.

The Black Volga.

Stefan saw the Black Volga.

The driver, as if he wanted to eye the kidnapped child's father, was driving very slowly into an alley, one of the few unobstructed. The limousine had white wheel rims and white curtains.

"I'm sorry," said Stefan, getting up from the sidewalk, "but I have to go. Thank you for your help. And I'm sorry for the trouble."

Stefan's legs were moving faster and faster; the faster he ran, the more painful his bruised ribs and jaw. The fish were still swimming under his coat. Strange the bag hadn't popped.

From time to time, he held his breath, tightening his neck and gritting his teeth. When he got used to the pricking here and there— or had rather forgotten about it— he started running.

The Black Volga, slowing down, tempted him but sped up when he was at a stone's throw distance.

The limousine turned into one of the narrower streets, and then into another alley where, even if half the district wasn't jammed, no one would turn. It smelled of rotten fruit, moss covered the brick walls, and a huge game board was drawn with chalk by children.

Stefan's lungs were burning. He promised himself to smoke his last cigarette after catching the Black Volga. And to encourage all parents he knew to do so. Hoping to make it easier for him to run, he took off his hat and threw it into an ajar dumpster. The cold air stabbed him in the forehead like icicles. The fish were still moving under his coat.

Stefan thought, *Yes, finally, yes!*

The Black Volga stopped in a blind alley. Stefan stood, rubbing his chest, and spread his legs wide. He sensed that the limousine was going to back up but too late, it knocked him to the ground.

The Volga's rear door opened by itself, as if by springs, and Stefan's breath got heavier. A belt—a very long one—sprang out of the car. The hydrologist did nothing. He neither bent down nor covered his face. The belt wrapped around his neck and tightened like a snake. Stef could feel the cold metal tongue on his neck. He couldn't breathe; he was coughing and snorting, trying to push his fingers under the belt. But it only squeezed more forcefully.

"Dad? Dad, can you hear me?"

Stefan heard his son's voice. Or he didn't. It might've been pure imagination.

Being dragged over the remains of glass and stones, Stefan doubled up with pain. The wheels with white rims began to spin backward. The hydrologist tried to stay put, his face and chest to the ground. The limousine ran over his foot, but at least didn't rip his head off.

Stef turned red, fighting for air. Then the car, while backing up, pulled him all the way up to the street. And then back again to the end of the blind alley. Stefan hit his head against the dumpster and then against some steps. He thought only the fish would survive.

Stefan begged for mercy, but the driver heard nothing. Nobody heard Stefan. A second belt sprang out of the Black Volga and wrapped around his legs. The belts pulled him towards the door. The limousine was to devour him like a monster from the worst nightmares.

"Stop it! Stop it!"

Stefan wasn't only stripped of his clothes and skin but also of his dignity.

"D'you hear me? Tell me how much you want! How much?!"

The back door was flapping, as if threatening to smash his head in case he continued to scream.

Stefan's head was in the limousine already. Now he was wondering whether to prop his feet against the car or let himself be pulled in. But Ksawery, probably also wrapped with seatbelts, wouldn't free himself.

A passenger was sitting next to the driver. Ksawery! The boy's head was swinging inertly, as if he was a puppet.

*****

"Take it easy, easy." Danuta quieted the guests and got up from the table. "Have a drink, Daddy. Mommy, you, too. Calm down, calm down. They should be here any minute."

Danuta had been trying to get the guests drunk for a long time. But to do so, she would've had to drink with them, which she could've done, but not when she should keep a sober mind, to be ready to help, to talk, in case she had to, for example, see the MO.

"No, I'm calling the MO now. Where's the phone?" Her mom got up. "And when Stefan comes back, I'll tell him what I think."

"The phone's out of order," Danuta said, swinging her arms so nervously that her buffy sleeves were like opened parachutes. Fortunately, she'd pulled the plug in advance. "Eat some more, have a drink, Mom, Dad. Mom, be careful, because you are pulling down the tablecloth."

Only Danuta's brother was sitting at the table, with his elbows on top of it, and with his head leaned over his empty plate with dumpling leftovers.

The doorbell rang. A wave of heat spread over Danuta, and the rest of the family was paralyzed.

"Oh, there they are." Danuta smiled and fixed her Afro-Look haircut. "Y'all sit here, try to smile."

Turning away from the table, she almost knocked her chair over. Danuta opened the door and shouted out loud: "Finally, oh, my child!"

*****

"Are you comfortable there?" asked the driver of the Black Volga. "You aren't too squeezed by the belts?"

Because of the curtains, Stefan didn't know where they were or where they were going. He was surprised that, after what he'd done, some roads were passable.

"It's not that bad," Stefan said. Not only the seatbelts but also great sorrow and sadness squeezed him tightly when he'd seen the side of Ksawery's head. The boy was exhausted, unable to fight against the kidnapper. "Who are you? An SB agent, a communist from the GDR, or the Russian mafia? Or maybe, as they say, a vampire? Or a Satanist?"

"See those mascots on the dashboard?"

"Yes," he said, blinking. "So what?"

"I leave them at a place of kidnapping. Different mascots are left after different children who have different parents."

"You're crazy! Man... that's not funny at all... you're a... a monster!" Kicking the front seat, Stefan tried to free himself. But the belts only tightened. "Let me out. Me and my son! D'you hear me?!"

"Scream all you want. No passer-by can hear or see you."

Stefan still couldn't see the driver's face. Neither in the rearview mirror nor as a reflection in any of the windows. Additionally, a grille, like in a confessional, protruded from the seat to protect the driver from the passengers at the back.

"Have you calmed down?"

Exhausted, Stefan calmed down, he could feel all his pains and bruises, and his head was pulsating sorely.

"Can we start a normal conversation now?"

"Sure."

"I asked if you saw these mascots."

"Said I did."

"Good. I have, for example, a bear." There was a teddy bear stuffed with sawdust that could be bought in Pewex. "I leave a teddy bear after children to whom no one was tender, who weren't hugged enough, you understand? But I have other things too. Footballs, board games. To leave them after children whom no one helped develop their passion. The worst is when I leave something and a parent can't associate it with their own child. Truly heartbreaking."

"What's that have to do with me?"

"I am looking for children who are neglected by their parents. Guess what, Stefan."

"And you left fish after Ksawery? Live fish in a transport plastic bag?"

"Yes."

"And what's that supposed to mean?" Twisting his wrist, he took out the fish from his jacket.

"They're dead, aren't they?"

Stefan looked at the orange fish. "They are."

"You see, you can't even take care of fish. You even ask your wife to change the water in your aquarium. Don't you think, Mr. Hydrologist, that you work too much? Soon you'll leave work and be surprised when you don't have to pick up your son from school. But not because someone else's picked him up, just because he'll be at the university. Or at work, living in an apartment given by the government. And then he'll forget to pick up his kids from school, you understand?"

"You're fucked up, man!"

"When you call your wife, doesn't she in the first place ask whether to change the water in the aquarium? Or to feed the fish? Don't you think that Ksawery should be her first thought?"

"He doesn't need to be changed. Neither fed with a spoon at a certain time, at least not anymore. What the hell do you expect?"

It got dark in the limousine, as if they had dived in a shadow or in an endless tunnel.

"Confess to me."

"What?"

"Confess to me all your sins. I am particularly interested in those committed against children."

"Are you—?" The belts tightened around his neck, squeezing his chest which seemed about to crack any moment.

"I am a priest. One of my brothers revived you by pouring water on your face."

"Everything happens for a reason."

"That's right. Okay, why don't we start, huh? God be in your heart to confess your sins. The last time you confessed was..."

"I don't remember. What do you care... Ykkkkh." Stefan turned all red, thoughts swimming through his head. *I'll confess, fine, at least I'll die with a pure heart if he strangles me.*

"You ready?"

The hydrologist dropped the bag with the fish, then stopped it with his foot so that it wouldn't roll under the front seat.

"Ksawery, help me! D'you hear me, Ksawery? What did you do to him?!" Stefan kicked the front seat with his knee. "Son, move, say something, anything!"

Ksawery's head was swinging inertly.

"I also like to sew cuddles," the priest said, grabbed Ksawery's head, and threw it behind his back. The plush head bounced off the back window and flew under the passenger's seat. "Did you think that I'd give such a ride to an already harmed kid? That'd be a good way to scar him for the rest of his life."

"You son of a bitch!"

"Add another sin to your list and..." he took a deeper breath "...and confess!"

*****

Danuta pulled her daughter into the entrance hall.

"Listen, honey," she whispered, crouching, "we'll prank your grandparents. Put on Ksawery's clothes. The boys aren't home yet," she added. "So put on his clothes, go to say hello, and we'll see how long it'll take for them to notice. How do you like it?"

"I don't wanna look boyish," she whispered, frowning.

"Grandpa loves pranks. He'll be surprised and will appreciate your sense of humor."

"Fine."

*****

Stefan leaned away from the grille, which was protruding from the front seat, and took a breath while closing his eyes.

"As I told you, if men don't repent and better themselves, the Father will inflict a terrible punishment on all humanity. God, the Father of Mercies, through the death and resurrection of His Son has reconciled the world to Himself and sent the Holy Spirit among us for the forgiveness of sins; through the ministry of the Church may God give you pardon and peace, and I absolve you from your sins in the name of the Father, and of the Son, and of the Holy Spirit."

"Amen."

The priest hit the brakes and said: "You can go now."

"That's all?"

"If you repent your sins and promise to do better, you may go."

"Fine," Stefan said.

The belts loosened and finally, Stefan could breathe freely. The curtains went sideways, letting the cloudy day into the Black Volga, and then the rear door, as if pushed, opened by itself.

Stefan put one leg outside the limousine, said, "God bless," and unnaturally jumped out of the car.

The door closed by itself, the curtains covered the windows, and the Black Volga left.

Stefan now resembled a homeless man, who fetched and carried for other homeless people. With his gaze fixed on the sidewalk, he approached a fence to hold onto it and gather his thoughts.

He looked around. He was before the elementary school. The kiosk was already closed and Gale had disappeared from the entrance to the building.

A few children walked out of the school including a short carroty boy in a claret jacket.

"Ksawery?" Stefan whispered. "Ksawery?! Where are you going?"

"Dad? Dad, what happened? Why do you look like that? Where am I going? To the bus stop, to sit on the stone, just like you told me to. Tell me what happened! Dad, should I call the ambulance? Where's your Maluch?

424

"Had to sell it for scrap." Stefan pulled out the article about the Black Volga from his pocket to see what time the bus departed. "What were you doing at school this late?"

"This late?"

Stefan raised his eyebrows.

"Logical Games Club. I was waiting for you, playing chess to warm up to beat you later on."

Stefan smiled. That's what Gale meant by saying that it's for brains, not for you.

"We're going home. Mom's worried."

"Going how?"

"I have the bus schedule here. Hurry up, the last one's about to arrive. Hard to say, though, because it's a bit trafficky on the other side of the district."

Looking at the paper in his father's hand, Ksawery giggled, "Dad, are you reading this rubbish about the Black Volga? Come on, even my friends' parents have stopped scaring them with some black limousine."

After about a quarter of an hour, they got on the bus but didn't go far before getting stuck in the traffic jam.

"It'd be good to inform Mom that we'd be late." Ksawery looked at a telephone booth. "You could hop out to make a call."

"Don't worry. I've already called Mom," said his dad and realized that two fish had been swimming in the bag.

"Son, what about your sister? Where is she?"

"I dunno."

After Stefan had heard someone's question, "Why are we standing?" he thought, *That's correct. The traffic's on the other side of the district.*

Soon after, the bus driver opened the door and a militiaman approached the bus.

"Unlucky day we have today. Over there was a Fiat crash and all's blocked, and here some Black Volga drove into a streetcar. So hard the streetcar left the tracks. The voltage lines are broken."

Instead of being nervous, Stefan sighed with relief and thought: He shouldn't have messed with a hydrologist that works overhours, with a man who takes work home.

The fish had died not because Stefan had taken bad care of them, but because he'd let that poisonous substance, which he'd been working on recently, inside the plastic bag and then popped it while getting out of the limousine. The first test had been carried out, the experiment had been successful.

"Probably drunk, just like that one in the Maluch," said the bus driver to the militiaman. "Hope you'll find out."

"Won't be that easy. There are no license plates, and the upholstery's burned with some acid."

Stefan sighed again, *No license plates? Scratches on the hood, moving wipers. It was probably the kid I'd kicked off the phone booth that had additionally stolen the plates. Or the brats the lady from WTA had mentioned.* Stefan fell asleep from exhaustion and woke up when they arrived home.

"Stefan?" Danuta stood before their block of flats. "Where have you been?"

"Easy, Danka, easy," said Stefan, seeing Danuta stopping her father from doing something. "I had to sell our Maluch for scrap. Did you put the cognac in the freezer?"

"In the freezer?" she asked. "Cognac?"

"Yes, you do put cognac in the freezer if it's Armenian."

Danuta's father smiled and turned back to their apartment to celebrate Stefan's birthday.

To my father,

who showed me the Warsaw of his childhood

BLACK VOLGA LEXICON

Maluch = In Poland the car became a cultural icon and earned the nickname Maluch, meaning "The Little One" or "Toddler", eventually becoming an official model name in 1997 when it started appearing on the rear of the car.

Milicja Obywatelska (commonly abbreviated to MO), in English written as Citizens' Militia, = was the national police organization of the Polish People's Republic. The Citizen's Militia would remain the predominant means of policing in Poland until 10 May 1990, when it was transformed back into Policja.

Syrena (or Syrenka) = was a Polish automobile. A Siren is a mermaid who, according to the legend, protects the river Wisła and the Polish capital city, Warsaw. She is featured on the city's coat of arms. Also ,a diminutive name Syrenka (little siren) is commonly used for the car in Poland.

Żuk (pl. beetle) = was a van and light truck produced in Lublin, Poland, between 1958 and 1998 by FSC.

<u>Życie Warszawy</u> = (meaning Life of Warsaw in English) is a Polish language newspaper published in Warsaw.

BEDS ON FIRE

by Vincent deDiego Metzo

Weaver headed uptown. It was gonna be a long walk, but he hadn't been sleeping well and maybe it would help. Plus, he'd been away for 6 years, he wanted to see how things had changed or how they'd stayed the same.

It was hard to think of himself as Weaver, just Weaver, not Second Lieutenant Weaver. He left the Lieutenant behind him, overseas, in the jungle. He left the squad and he left Sergeant Gordo behind. The same way he had left the neighborhood behind when he enlisted. It was the easiest way to get out, to get away from the drugs and the gangs and the limited possibilities the neighborhood offered.

Now he was going to Fordham University, heading uptown, GI bill, plus a stipend and free rent at the dorm as an RA. He didn't have to stay in the neighborhood, in the apartment he grew up in, the apartment he outgrew. He could visit his mom, but she wouldn't have to know about the bad dreams, the flashbacks, the battle neurosis.

It was out of the way, but he wanted to hit Times Square, the Deuce, see if it was still seedy. He walked through, head down, hands in the pockets of his jeans. He hadn't lost his street smarts, and he didn't survive the war to be mugged in his own hometown.

A man sat in an army jacket under the marquee of a porno theatre holding a sign – Veteran please help. Weaver put some bills in the crumpled blue and white paper coffee cup on the sidewalk in front of the man's crossed legs. The man snatched the bills from the cup and put them in his pocket. He acknowledged Weaver with a nod and a mumble. Weaver thought of Gordo seizing on the stretcher. His head jerking, foaming at the mouth, eyes rolling back as the corpsman jammed the morphine syrettes into his thigh.

A dead smell, rotten dead shit, pulled Weaver back to the Deuce just before he bumped into the homeless man standing on the corner. He stepped back, saying excuse me, and read the cardboard sign the man was holding. Written in thick black marker: Repent, He is coming. YOU WILL BURN IN HELL!

"You're a sinner, I can see it. You've killed, he knows what you've done. Make a donation to pay your penance."

Weaver stepped around the prophet, eyes watering from the man's smell. He was afraid he'd never get it out of his nostrils. He headed toward the park at a faster pace. He was already sweating and looking forward to a shower when he got back to the dorm.

*****

The park seemed like a good idea. At first the cut grass and smell of the dirt was welcome and relaxed him. As the path took him down into a valley covered with trees and the humid August air enveloped him, he saw something moving in the trees. Weaver bent his knees and felt the weight of his rifle hanging across his shoulder. He raised a hand to tell the unit to stop and looked for Gordo.

A boy in a blue and white t-shirt darted out of the trees three yards ahead of Weaver and ran across the path enjoying a game of hide and go seek with his mother. Weaver puzzled why the boy was in the jungle, then he realized he was home. The mother

433

looked at him with concern. Weaver touched his heart and shrugged his shoulders.

"Startled me," he said, to put her and himself at ease. He grabbed his dog tags. He wasn't aware that he did that from time to time. Feeling the metal in his hand somehow calmed him. He squeezed them, and they pressed into his palm.

There was only a slight breeze on the Willis Avenue Bridge. Weaver stopped in the middle to feel the warm air being pushed over his face, through his hair. He could smell the ocean buried in the breeze, mixed with car exhaust and oil water. He thought he might get a slice of pizza before getting back to the dorm. It felt too hot for pizza. He'd burnt the roof of his mouth too many times growing up. The inferno of the pizza oven didn't appeal to him either. He'd wait until fall for pizza. Maybe a nice Italian sub?

He walked on and found himself at the gates of the campus, having forgotten to stop for food. The campus was a ghost town. One maintenance man worked on the flowers that flanked the entrance. He ignored Weaver. The security guard nodded from his tiny glass-enclosed station with an oversized air conditioner sticking out of the side. Weaver wondered how long they'd let the guard keep his Rube Goldberg-looking AC set up. He nodded back with a smile.

*****

Weaver managed himself. He tried to make himself as tired as possible by keeping busy and trying to pretend he wasn't afraid to go to sleep. He took a shower and washed the smells of the city off. He blew water through his nose to clear out the "repent and burn in hell" smell. He walked the halls and explored the dorm, deciding which laundry and which showers were the cleanest and had the best pressure.

He sat in the common room and read *Man Against Himself*. After an hour he decided that was not a good book for him to be reading. He wasn't going to get into bed until his eyelids were heavy, so outside he went to smoke a joint.

The security guard was illuminated in his glass kiosk. Weaver walked over, staying in the lighted path, careful not to sneak up on or startle the guard. The guard smiled and put down his magazine as Weaver closed the last six feet.

"You look a bit old to be a freshman," the guard's scratchy brogue said as he pulled up one of the windows and leaned out. Weaver felt the air-conditioner blowing onto his arms and torso. It made him shiver. He grabbed his dog tags. Feeling the metal in his hand, he squeezed them, they pressed into his palm.

"You look a little young to be a security guard," Weaver said. The guard actually looked about 50, but his hair and the neatness of his uniform made Weaver think he'd appreciate the veiled compliment.

"Mahoney. Am I out of line to ask if you served?" The guard stuck his hand out to shake Weaver's.

"Hey Mahoney, I'm Second Lieu- Sorry. Well, I'm Weaver. I guess that answers your question though."

Mahoney nodded.

"Sergeant Mahoney, but you can just call me Mahoney. You're the RA?" He asked.

"Yes Sir. I grew up on the lower east side, but I don't want to commute every day and I don't want to be in the old neighborhood." Weaver figured in civilian life it'd be better to defer to the man's age rather than his rank. Mahoney seemed to appreciate it.

"You hear the stories about this dorm?"

Weaver shook his head no.

"Well, there's a movie they just come out with, The Exorcist. You heard of it?" Mahoney opened his thermos, poured some coffee into the top, and sipped.

"I think I saw it on the marquee when I walked through 42nd street."

"They filmed it here. You're living in a famous dorm. Or maybe infamous. Should be a bit of craic with the freshmen."

"I'll go check it out. I'm just gonna take a walk around before bed. Just wanted to let you know so you don't call the cops on me or have to come out of your refrigerated compartment there. It's still pretty steamy out here." Weaver was gonna ask him if he wanted to smoke a joint but he figured Mahoney for the whiskey generation. He could smell it faintly coming from the thermos cup on the counter.

"Keep in touch, kid," Mahoney said as Weaver headed out on the path.

Fordham had a good radio station and Weaver could see the red light flashing on the tower as he finished the joint and headed back inside.

He turned on the transistor radio in his room and sat in the chair by the window, leafing through the class catalogue. He started to feel his eyelids and got into bed.

*****

He was sitting upright in bed before he realized he was awake. It took a minute to orient himself, he remembered he was home but uptown at his new home in the dorm. No need to get tactical. Maybe Mahoney came in to use the bathroom. Maybe wind blew a door closed. Something woke him up, and it wasn't the radio.

Weaver turned the radio dial off and listened carefully. He heard something but he wasn't familiar enough with the building to know what it was. He slowly opened his door and peered into the hallway.

All the doors along the hall were open, and the lights drew yellow rectangular shapes on the floor. Weaver walked into the hall in his boxers and undershirt. As he passed each dorm room, he saw the

mattresses standing upright next to their bed frames.
Weaver went back to his room and leaned out the
window. Mahoney was still sitting at his station, the
light bathing him and making a cross pattern on the
path and surrounding bushes.

A chill went up Weaver's back as the cooler
night air and memory of Mahoney's air conditioning
hit him. He went down the hall to call the number
they'd given him for maintenance emergencies.

The phone rang seven times before a Father
Michael answered. Jesuits, Weaver figured, he had
expected the super, not a priest. Father Michael
sounded young, but it was hard to tell without seeing
him. He said he would come right over to check out
the situation and not to worry.

Weaver turned the radio back on and laid down
in bed. A knock on the door woke him up. Now that he
was finally able to sleep, he kept getting interrupted.
He opened the door, still in his boxers.

A gaunt priest with slicked back hair stood in
the hall.

"I'm Father Michael. Are you Weaver, the
RA?"

Weaver grabbed his dog tags. Feeling the metal in his hand, he squeezed them, they pressed into his palm.

"Hi, yeah, sorry I fell back asleep. What's up?" Weaver looked down the hall. The hall light was on and all the room lights off.

"Yes, sorry for the inconvenience. This usually doesn't happen this time of year. It's all taken care of. Sorry to wake you, I'll let you get back to sleep."

Weaver nodded thanks and slowly closed the door. Part of him wanted to ask the priest what time of year it does usually happen. Rush week? Most of him wanted to sleep.

*****

Weaver woke up around ten. He was pleased he slept that late and hoped he could keep it up. Typically, he was up at six. If he could reset his circadian rhythms and get on a schedule, this would be great. Maybe he'd turned a corner.

He took the catalogue and went to the admin building to register. He got most of the 101 classes he wanted. Another benefit of being an RA, early registration.

"Are there a lot of other people on campus yet?" Weaver asked the woman with the cat eyeglasses at the registrar's office. She pushed the glasses up her nose so she could focus on Weaver's face. The chain that held them around her neck twinkled as it bumped her cheeks.

"Just a few of the post-docs in Loschert." She half smiled, used her chin to vaguely indicate where that was, and went back to her work. Weaver nodded and half smiled back.

He spent the rest of the day exploring the campus and went and got that Italian Cold Cut Special sub he had thought of yesterday. All day he tried not to think too much on the hazing or whatever happened with the mattresses. He had to manage his focus or he could get out of control.

He stopped at the security kiosk on his way back to the dorm after spending the rest of the day exploring the Bronx.

"Hey Mahoney, how's it shaking?"

"Grand, grand boyo. What's the craic?"

"Do you know that Father Michael that came by last night? I think somebody was playing a prank on me."

"Father Michael?" Mahoney looked at a loose-leaf directory, running his finger down the list of names. "No boyo, no Father Michael here. We've got a Father Montgomery, Father Murphy, and a Father Matthew O'Shaughnessy, but no Michael."

"Nobody else with an M for a first name?" He grasped his dog tags. Feeling the metal in his hand, he squeezed them, they pressed into his palm.

Mahoney shook his head. "Something happen last night? I'll put it in the book."

"No, no, don't bother, just a prank. If it happens again, I'll let you know." Weaver headed back to the dorm.

*****

Weaver braced for the rotten dead shit smell, but it didn't come. The man yelled at him.

"You will burn in hell. He knows what you did. Repent. You will burn in hell."

The jungle was thick and hot but the man wore a black suit and tie, worn leather shoes and a hat. Weaver saw Gordo come out from the tree with his knife. No, don't. But the words wouldn't come out. People started to appear as the jungle turned into Time's Square. No, Gordo, there are witnesses, don't. But the words wouldn't come out. Gordo pulled the knife across the man's throat. Nobody noticed. The man slumped down against the lamp post. People went on about their business. Gordo was gone. The light changed and the cars zoomed down 8th avenue. Weaver read the sign – Second Lieutenant Weaver REPENT You will burn in Hell. REPENT! Second Lieutenant Weaver.

Weaver opened his eyes. The streetlamp shining through the window cast the shape of its panes over his legs. He was already sitting up. The sweat on his back made him chilly. He pulled on his pants, hopping on one leg, and opened the door.

The yellow lights from the dorm rooms illuminated rectangles on the hallway floor. All the doors on the corridor were open. Weaver stepped out to investigate. You mother fuckers don't know who you're dealing with. The mattresses were standing vertically at the foot of each bed. Weaver didn't run, he turned and walked purposefully down the hall to the large foyer, down the steps and to the security kiosk.

It wasn't Mahoney, it was a younger man with light hair and a clean shave.

"Mahoney off tonight?"

The guard furrowed his brow.

"Something I can help you with?"

"I think somebody's playing a prank. Mahoney didn't write it in the book last night, but I need you to come in and look at this."

The guard stared at Weaver, barefoot, shirtless, sweaty, and begrudgingly grabbed the large ring of 30 or 40 keys, locked the security kiosk behind him and followed Weaver into the residence hall.

"Same thing happened last night, and I called the maintenance number. They sent a priest over and he took care of it but he didn't check in with security, so I think it's important you see this." He grasped his dog tags, squeezed them, they pressed into his palm.

The hallway was dark. Weaver hit the light switch as they approached. All the doors were closed. He opened the first one and was actually relieved to see the mattress standing at the foot of the bed. He grabbed it and laid it on the frame.

"They did this last night, too." He continued along that side and the guard began to open the rooms and put the mattresses back along the other side. Weaver turned about two thirds of the mattresses and met up with the guard by the door to his room.

"Thanks for your help. I'm Weaver." He offered his hand. The guard took it and did that awkward thing Weaver hated. He hooked Weaver's thumb and brought their hands up to chest level. Weaver hated when white guys did that, but he didn't have many, have any civilian friends, so he let it go, figured the guard was trying to be nice, to be cool.

"I'm Dave. Nice to meet you Brother. What about this one?" The guard pointed to Weaver's door.

"That's mine. Open it up."

The guard opened the door and leaned in. The light and the radio were on. Half a joint lay on the side of the ashtray with Weaver's zippo on the nightstand.

"Must be some good stuff." He winked at Weaver and headed back to the kiosk.

"Hey you wanna get high?" He didn't want to be alone just yet, and he didn't have any civilian friends, yet.

Weaver followed the guard out to the security kiosk, understanding the guard couldn't abandon his post. They passed the joint back and forth through the kiosk window.

"Write that in the book, okay? Write about the mattresses," Weaver said, after silently staring at the shadows the flowers cast on the walkway.

"When's Mahoney in next?" He asked as the guard slowly tried to write in the logbook.

The guard shrugged his shoulders, cracked a smile and chortled. Weaver laughed back and saluted as he turned to head back to bed.

*****

Weaver propped his pillows up against the wall, leaned back against them in bed with his pants still on, took the course catalogue off his night table, squeezed his dog tags, they pressed into his palm. He hoped sleep would come but he tried not to scare it away by worrying about it. The idea of scaring sleep away amused him.

He took a step and started to fall into a pit with punji sticks at the bottom. He thought of the urine and feces and the infection… His body jerked and he woke up still sitting in bed.

"Fuck." He figured maybe a walk or a shower.

A few steps down the hall, the yellow rectangles stopped him in his tracks. Lifting his head, he confirmed all the doors were open and all the mattresses were upright.

His first instinct was to get help, tell the guard or somebody with power. Realizing how crazy it would sound, he walked the other way to the center of the building.

He followed a noise down the next hall and ended up at the center staircase. He was sure he heard the squeak of shoes on the stairs from below. Probably the priest, Father Michael. He followed. As he descended, he could hear a furnace running. Hot water he thought, way too hot for radiators. The burning sound pulsed, louder and softer. ROUSH – roush. ROUSH – roush.

The basement had a damp smell and was cool. Weaver wished he'd thrown a shirt on. He squeezed his dog tags, they pressed into his palm. He followed the ROUSH-ing sound. Old furniture, boxes, and maintenance supplies cluttered the passages. He entered the boiler room.

The glow and ROUSH-ing sound from the furnace drew him past the metal shelves with old paint supplies. He stared into the furnace door entranced by the yellow and red fire inside. The plumes of flame, the burning trees, his men running toward him as the napalm fell from the planes. He saw Gordo running toward him with his entire left side and back on fire. Weaver ran toward him calling for a corpsman.

Then seeing Gordo on the stretcher, screaming, incoherent. Then the seizure. Weaver nodded at the corpsman. The syrettes in Gordo's thigh and the haze over his eyes as his breathing slowed and stopped. But he still heard breathing – ROUSH – roush. ROUSH – roush. REPENT - repent. REPENT – repent.

Weaver saw his feet, the stains on the concrete floor. The streetlights coming through the high basement windows. He opened his hand, saw the blood on his palm where the dog tags cut him. He walked past the metal shelves and back up the stairs.

The hall was dark. The dorm rooms closed. Weaver searched the wall for the light switch and got the hallway lights on before panic overtook him. He opened the doors and cleared the rooms visually. All the mattresses were back on the beds.

Weaver went to the common phone and called the maintenance number. It rang seven times, and then nine, and fifteen. He hung up. He thought to call his mother, but he didn't want to wake her. He promised himself he'd go to the VA tomorrow and wait as long as it took to be seen.

Back in his room he took the padlock off his footlocker and reached down to the bottom where the towel was wrapped around the service weapon he reported lost. his service weapon. He often wondered if reporting it lost was worth the punishment. Now he was pretty sure it was. Wiping the drying blood off his palm with the towel, he hated that a weapon made him feel safe. How could something so dangerous make him feel safe? He leaned back against the pillows, holding the weapon across his lap.

Sleep did not come. He reached out with his senses. He squeezed his dog tags harder and harder with his free hand. They cut into his palm. He didn't hear anything in the hall. Nothing. No footsteps. No bed springs. No ROUSH – roush. His anxiety grew, filling him up like a balloon until he couldn't sit any longer, he knew there was something. Something his senses couldn't perceive.

Weaver held his weapon and got ready to enter the hallway fully prepared for combatants. He turned the knob quietly getting ready to pull the door open. Don't shoot the priest. Don't shoot the priest. He yanked the door open.

The yellow rectangles of light crisscrossed the hallway. He saw the vertical mattress in the room directly across. He put on a t-shirt, stuffed his gun in the back of his pants and headed down the hall toward the foyer, looking over his shoulder. He broke into a run down the steps and to the security kiosk.

The kiosk was empty. Maybe doing rounds Weaver convinced himself. He waited there as long as his anxiety would allow him. It wasn't very long. He felt like he had to pee. He bent and straightened his knees. He paced. He figured he looked unhinged. Barefoot, wrinkled t-shirt, blood shot eyes, bloody palms, hair a mess, and a gun stuck in the back of his pants.

ROUSH – roush. REPENT – repent. BURN IT
DOWN – burn it down. Weaver ran back inside.

*****

The yellow light rectangles on the hallway
floor moved like search lights or spinning emergency
beacons as Weaver ran to the basement. He looked
over the metal shelves and found large cans of paint
thinner and turpentine. Grabbing them like ammo cans
he wired his shit up tight and marched up stairs.

He went into the first room and doused the base
of the mattress with the accelerant. He left a trail of
fluid connecting the mattresses in each room and got
his zippo from the nightstand.

The orange flame flickered eagerly as he
touched it to the fluid fuse. He dropped the lighter as it
burned his thumb. He tried again holding it from the
base. The fluid wouldn't light.

He went into the adjacent room and applied the
flame right to the base of the mattress. It wouldn't
light. Weaver's body started to shake. He sat cross-
legged on the floor, holding the flame to the mattress,
blood dripping from his palms.

He thought of Gordo on fire, of his men on fire. He shook and tears flowed down his cheeks. Weaver couldn't feel his body. He floated to the common phone at the end of the hall and dialed his mother's number. The first phone number he ever learned. The same number she'd had his whole life. Nothing happened. He slammed the switch hook to get a dial tone but there was none. The line was dead. He left the receiver hanging and walked down the hall.

The lights from the dorm rooms mocked him as they moved on the floor. The vertical mattresses were like middle fingers flipping him off as he walked the gauntlet. The ROUSH – roush, REPENT – repent, pulled him down the stairs to the furnace.

Weaver stared at the flame showing through the furnace door. BURN IT DOWN – burn it down. He turned all the furnace valves up to full, toppled the metal shelves and spilled their flammable liquids on the floor.

The mattresses and lights mocked him, doors opened and closed as he walked back to his room. He could hear them laughing at him. Weaver locked his door behind him, pulled his weapon out of the back of his pants, and sat on the bed squeezing his dog tags into his palm. Sirens mixed with the laughter. He looked out the window. Mahoney and Father Michael waved goodbye from the security kiosk.

Lightning Source UK Ltd.
Milton Keynes UK
UKHW020830060223
416538UK00016B/1801